WYOMING BOLD

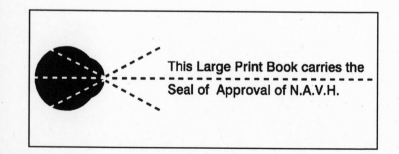

WYOMING BOLD

DIANA PALMER

THORNDIKE PRESS
A part of Gale, Cengage Learning

Detroit • New York • San Francisco • New Haven, Conn • Waterville, Maine • London

GALE
CENGAGE Learning®

LIBRARY OF CONGRESS CATALOGING-IN-PUBLICATION DATA

Palmer, Diana.
  Wyoming Bold / By Diana Palmer. — Large Print edition.
    pages cm. — (Bitter Heart Series ; #3.) (Thorndike Press Large Print Romance)
  ISBN 978-1-4104-6288-6 (hardcover) — ISBN 1-4104-6288-9 (hardcover)
  1. Homecoming—Fiction. 2. Ranch life—Fiction. 3. Wyoming—Fiction. 4. Large type books. I. Title.
PS3566.A513W93 2013
813'.54—dc23   2013033870

Published in 2013 by arrangement with Harlequin Books S.A.

Printed in Mexico
1 2 3 4 5 6 7 17 16 15 14 13

To Ellen Tapp,
my childhood friend,
with love

CHAPTER ONE

It was one of the worst blizzards in the history of the Rancho Real in Catelow, Wyoming. Dalton Kirk stared out the window and grimaced as the flakes seemed to grow in size by the minute. It was the middle of December. Usually weather like this came later.

He pulled out his cell phone and called Darby Hanes, his foreman. "Darby, how's it going out there?"

"Cattle are pretty deep in it," Darby replied, his voice breaking up with static, "but we're holding our own with feed so far. Getting hard to reach them, though."

"I hope this doesn't last long," he said heavily.

"Me, too, but we need the snow for the spring water supply so badly, I'm not complaining." Darby chuckled.

"Take care out there."

"Sure. Thanks, boss."

He hung up. He hated the storms but Darby was right about their desperate need for snow. The summer drought had made it hard on ranchers all over the West and Midwest. He just hoped they'd be able to get feed to the cattle. In an emergency, of course, federal and state agencies would help to airlift bales of hay to the animals.

He went into the living room and turned on the History channel. Might as well occupy himself instead of worrying so much, he thought amusedly.

Mavie, the housekeeper, frowned as she thought she heard something at the back door. She was clearing away dishes in the kitchen, nervous because the storm seemed to be getting worse.

Curious, though, she went and peered through the white curtains and gasped when she saw a pale, oval face with wide, green eyes staring back at her.

"Merissa?" she asked, shocked.

She opened the door. There, in a hooded, bloodred cape, almost covered with snow, stood a neighbor. Merissa Baker lived with her mother, Clara, way back in the woods in a cottage. They were what local people called "peculiar." Clara could talk out fire and talk off warts. She knew all sorts of herbal remedies for illness and they said she had the "second sight" as well, that she could see the future. Her daughter was rumored to have the same abilities, only magnified. She recalled that when Merissa had been in school, her classmates had shunned her and victimized her so badly that her mother pulled her out of the local high school because of her ongoing stomach problems. The school system had sent a homeschool worker with her classwork and oversaw her curriculum. She had graduated with her class, with grades that shamed most of them.

She'd tried to work locally, but her reputation was unsettling to some of the conservative businesses, so she went home and helped her mother, earning her living with a combination of fortune-telling and online website design, at which she was quite good. She had an older computer, and a cheap internet connection at first, but as her business grew, she'd started making money. She'd managed to afford better equipment and higher internet speed. Now, she was very successful. She designed websites for at least one quite famous author and several businesses.

"Come in out of the snow, child!" Mavie exclaimed. "You're soaked!"

"The car wouldn't start," Merissa said in her soft, delicate voice. She was almost as tall as Mavie, who was just above five feet seven inches. She had thick, short, wavy platinum hair and pale green eyes that were huge in her face. She had a rounded little chin and a pretty, naturally pink bow-shaped mouth, and tiny ears. And a smile that could have melted stone.

"What are you doing here in a storm?"

"I have to see Dalton Kirk," she said solemnly. "And it's urgent."

"Tank?" Mavie asked blankly, using the youngest Kirk brother's affectionate nickname.

"Yes."

"Can I ask what it's about?" Mavie asked, confused, because she didn't think the family had any business dealings with Merissa.

Merissa smiled gently. "I'm afraid not."

"Oh. Well, let me go get him, then."

"I'll wait here. I don't want to drip on the carpet," the young woman said with a laugh that sounded like silver bells.

Mavie went into the living room. There was, fortunately, a commercial. Dalton had turned the sound off.

"Damn things," he muttered. "One minute of program and five minutes of commercials, do they really think people are going to sit there and watch so many at once?" he huffed. He frowned at Mavie's expression. "What's wrong?"

"You know the Bakers, don't you? They live in that cottage down the road, in the cottonwood thicket."

"Yes."

"Merissa is here. She says she has to talk to you."

"Okay." He got up. "Bring her in here."

"She won't come. She got wet walking here."

"She walked? In this?" He gestured at the window where huge flakes of snow were falling. "There's almost a foot of snow on the ground already!"

"She said her car wouldn't start."

He sighed. He turned off the television and put down the remote control. He followed Mavie into the kitchen.

His eyes took in the slender figure of his guest. She was very pretty. Her lips were a natural red. Her eyes were big and soft and green. Her face was rather pointed, and her rounded chin made her seem vulnerable. She was wearing a hooded red cloak and it, and she, were soaked.

"Merissa, isn't it?" he asked gently.

She nodded. She was self-conscious around men. Afraid of them, too, really. She

11

hoped it didn't show. Dalton was very big, like all the Kirk boys. He had jet-black hair and dark eyes and a lean, angular face. He was wearing jeans and boots and a chambray shirt. He didn't look like a very wealthy man at all.

"What can I do for you?" he asked.

She glanced toward Mavie.

"Oh, I'll just go dust the living room for a bit," Mavie said with a grin. She left them alone, pulling the door closed behind her as she went into the hall.

"You're in terrible danger," Merissa said without preamble.

He blinked. "Excuse me?"

"I'm sorry. I just blurt these things out, I don't mean to." She bit her lip. "I have visions. My mother does, too. The neurologist says it's an aura from migraine, which I also have, but if that's all, why do the visions always come true?" She sighed. "I had a vision about you. I had to tell you about it right away so you wouldn't be hurt."

"Okay, I'm listening." Privately he thought she needed a good psychologist more than a neurologist, but he wasn't going to say that. She was very young; barely twenty-two if he remembered correctly. "Go ahead."

"You were attacked in Arizona by four men, just a few months ago," she said. Her eyes were closed. If they hadn't been, she'd have seen Dalton's suddenly still posture and taut features. "One of the men with you was wearing a paisley shirt . . ."

"Damn!"

She opened her eyes and grimaced as he glared at her.

"How did you know that?" he asked, moving forward so fast that she backed up too quickly and stumbled into a chair, almost falling. She caught the table just in time. "Who told you?" he demanded, although he stopped going toward her.

"Nobody . . . told me. I saw it," she tried to explain. Heavens, he was fast! She'd never seen a man move like that.

"Saw it, how?"

"In my head. It was a vision," she tried to explain. Her cheeks were flushed. He thought she was crazy. "Please, let me finish. The man in the paisley shirt, he was wearing a suit and you trusted him. There was another man, a man with dark skin wearing a lot of gold jewelry. In fact, his pistol had gold plating and pearls on it . . ."

"I only ever told my brothers that!" he said angrily. "Them, and my supervisor and, later, the DOJ guys!"

"The man in the paisley shirt," she continued. "He isn't who you think he is. He has

13

ties to a drug cartel." Her eyes closed again. "He's made some sort of bargain with a man high up in politics in this country. I don't know what, I can't see it. But I do know this. The other man is running for public office, some very high office with money and political superiority in the balance . . ." She swallowed and opened her eyes. "He wants to have you killed."

"Me?" he asked. "What for?"

"Because of the man in the paisley shirt," she explained. "He was with that man who shot you, who's now second-in-command to the leader of the drug cartel. But it isn't known. The cartel put up money so he could run for public office, high public office. Once he's elected, if he is, he'll make sure the drug convoys get across the border with no interference. I don't know how." She held up a hand when he looked as if he might question that. "They're going to try to have you killed so that you can't tell on him."

"Hell, I identified the shooter to the authorities. They have notes on my debriefing," he scoffed. "It's all in there, about the shooter with the gold-plated weapon, the gold jewelry, the lizard-skin boots, the gold tooth with a diamond that he wore for a front tooth — the works." He laughed

14

curtly. "It's too late for them to silence me."

"I'm just telling you what I saw," she stammered. "It isn't about the man with the gold-plated weapon — it's about the man wearing the paisley shirt. He's working for the politician. He's already tried to have a sheriff killed, a man who might have recognized him. The sheriff was shot . . ." She closed her eyes and squinted, as if her head hurt. In fact, it did. "He's afraid of both of you. If you recognize him, his ties to the politician will be made public and the politician will end up in prison. So will he. It isn't the first time he's killed to protect his boss."

Tank sat down. This was intense stuff. It brought back nightmarish memories from the shooting. The impact of the bullets, the smell of blood, the dark-skinned man's insane laughter while he fired the automatic pistol. There really had been another man there, a man in a paisley shirt, as she said, wearing a suit . . .

"Why didn't I remember that?" he mumbled out loud. He put his hand to his eyes. "There was a man in a paisley shirt. He asked for backup. He said a drug deal was going down, a big one. I drove out there with him. He said he was from the DEA —" He broke off and gaped at Merissa.

"You hadn't remembered that," she said slowly.

He nodded. His face was ashen. There were beads of sweat just above his chiseled mouth.

She knelt on the floor beside his chair and held his big hand, the one that wasn't rubbing his eyes. "It's all right," she said in a tone of voice that sounded like he imagined an angel of mercy would sound. "It's all right."

He didn't like being babied. He jerked his hand away, and then was sorry when she stood up and backed away, looking hunted.

She couldn't imagine the memories she'd kindled within him. He was trying to deal with them, and not very successfully. "People say you're a witch," he blurted out.

She didn't take offence. She only nodded. "I know."

He stared at her. There was something really otherworldly about her. She was almost fragile, despite her height; quiet, docile. She seemed so much at peace with herself and the world. The only turmoil was in her big, soft green eyes, which were looking at him with a mix of sympathy and fear.

"Why are you afraid of me?" he asked suddenly.

She shifted. "It's nothing personal."

"Why?"

"You're very . . . large," she faltered. She shivered.

He cocked his head, frowning.

She forced a smile. "I have to go," she said. "I just wanted you to know what I saw, so that you could keep your eyes open and be alert."

"We have a fortune invested in surveillance equipment here, mostly because of our prize-winning bulls."

She nodded. "It won't matter. They sent a professional assassin after the sheriff in Texas. He had surveillance equipment, too. Or at least I think he did."

He drew in a long breath. He stood up, calmer now. "I know some people in Texas. Where?"

She shifted uneasily. He towered over her. "South Texas. Somewhere south of San Antonio. I don't know anything else. Sorry."

That should be easy to track down. If there'd been a shooting of a law enforcement official, it would be public and he could search for it online. He wanted to do that, if only to prove her so-called vision false.

"Thanks anyway. For the warning." He smiled with pure sarcasm.

"You don't believe me. That's all right.

17

Just . . . watch where you're going. Please." She turned and pulled up her hood.

He recalled that she'd walked here.

"Just a sec," he said. He went to the hall closet, pulled out a shepherd's coat and threw it on. "I'll drive you home," he said, digging in his pocket for his car keys. Then he remembered that he'd put them on the hook beside the back door. With a grimace, he retrieved them.

"You shouldn't do that," she began uneasily.

"What? Drive you home? It's almost a blizzard. You can't even see where you're going in this!" he said, waving his hand toward the window.

"Hang your keys there," she faltered. There was a strange, opaque look to her eyes. "You shouldn't do that. He'll find them there and get access to the house."

"He, who?" he asked.

She looked up at him and blinked.

"Never mind," he muttered. "Come on."

They were going into the garage when Darby Hanes pulled up in one of the other ranch pickups. He got out, shaking snow off the shoulders of his wool jacket. He seemed surprised to see Merissa, but he tipped his hat to her and smiled.

"Hi, Merissa," he said.

She smiled back. "Hello, Mr. Hanes."

"Been riding fence," he said, sighing. "I came back to get the chain saw. We've got a tree across a fence." He shook his head. "Bad weather, and more forecast."

Merissa was staring at him without speaking. She moved a step closer. "Mr. Hanes, please don't take this the wrong way . . . but . . ." She bit her lip. "You need to take somebody with you when you cut the tree down."

He gave her a wide-eyed look. "Excuse me?"

She shifted, as if she was staggering under a burden. "Please?"

"Oh, no, not one of those premonitions?" Darby laughed. "No offense, Miss Baker, but you need to get out more!"

She flushed, embarrassed.

Tank narrowed his eyes as he studied her drawn features. He turned back to Darby. "Let's err on the side of caution. Take Tim with you."

Darby sighed and shook his head. "Waste of manpower, but if you say so, I'll do it, boss."

"I say so."

Darby just nodded. His expression was eloquent. Darby had a degree in physics and was a pragmatist. He didn't believe in that supernatural stuff. Tank didn't, either, but Merissa's worried face haunted him. He just grinned at Darby, who threw up his hands and went to find Tim.

Tank led the way to his big black ranch double-cabbed pickup truck and helped her up into the passenger seat.

She looked around with fascination when he climbed in under the wheel, and started the engine.

"What is it?" he asked.

"Can it cook and do laundry, too?" she wondered aloud, her eyes on all the displays and controls. "I mean, it looks as if it can do everything else. Even satellite radio . . ."

"It's a big ranch and we spend a lot of time far away from the house. We have GPS, cell phones, you name it. The trucks are loaded with electronics on purpose. Plus big, expensive V-8 engines," he added with a wicked glance of dark eyes. "If we weren't green fanatics who generated our own energy, we'd be singled out for our inexcusable use of gasoline."

"I drive a V-8, too," she said with a shy smile. "Of course, mine is twenty years old and it only starts when it wants to. It didn't today."

He shook his head. "Maybe Darby is

right. You do spend too much time alone. You should get a job."

"I have one," she said. "I do web design. It means I can work at home."

"You won't meet many people that way."

Her expression went stiff. "I can do without most people. And they can certainly do without me. You said it yourself. People think I'm a witch." She sighed. "Old Mr. Barnes's milk cow went dry and he blamed me. He said it was because I lived near him. 'Everybody knows that witches cause those things,' he said."

"Threaten him with a lawsuit. That will shut him up."

She blinked and turned her head toward him. "Excuse me?"

"Hate speech," he elaborated.

"Oh. I see." She sighed. "I'm afraid it would only make things worse. Instead of that witch woman, I'd be that witch woman who sues everybody."

He chuckled.

She drew in a breath and shivered. She could barely see through the blinding snow as he drove. "I'll bet you have problems in this sort of weather. They say the old trail drivers used to stay with the cattle herds during storms and sing to them, to calm them, so they were less likely to stampede.

The ones I read about were summer storms, though, with lightning."

He was pleasantly surprised. "Those old trail drivers did baby the cattle. In fact, we have a couple of singing cowboys who do night duty for us with the herds."

"Are their names Roy and Gene?"

That took him a minute. Then he burst out laughing. "No. Tim and Harry, actually."

She grinned. Her whole face lit up. She was very pretty, he thought.

"Good one," he told her with a nod.

They were nearing her cabin. It wasn't much to look at. It had belonged to a hermit before the Bakers bought it about the time Merissa was born. Her mother's husband had left suddenly when she was ten. People whispered about the reason. Most people locally thought it was her mother's eerie abilities that had sent him to the divorce court.

Tank stopped the truck.

"Thanks for the ride," she said, pulling up her hood. "But you didn't have to do this."

"I know. Thanks for the warning." He hesitated. "What did you see, about Darby?" he asked, hating himself for the question.

She swallowed, hard. "An accident. But if he takes someone with him, I think it will be all right." She held up a hand. "I know, you don't believe in all this hoodoo. I don't know why I was cursed with visions. I just tell what I know, when I think it will help." Her soft eyes met his dark ones. "You've been kind to us over the years, all of you. When we couldn't get out because of snow-drifts, you'd send groceries. When the car got stuck one time, you had a cowboy drive us home and get the car out." She smiled. "You're a kind person. I don't want anything bad to happen to you. So maybe I'm crazy. But please watch your back anyway."

He smiled gently. "Okay."

She smiled, shyly, and climbed out of the truck. She closed the door behind her and ran for the porch. Her red cape, against the fluffy white snow, reminded him of the heroine in a movie he'd seen about a were-wolf. The red was stark, like blood, in that background of pure white.

An older woman, with silver hair, was waiting. She looked past Merissa and waved a little awkwardly. Merissa waved, too. They both went inside quickly.

Tank sat with the engine idling, staring at the closed door for a minute before he put the truck in gear and drove off.

"What in the world are you laughing

about?" Mallory asked his brother as he came into the living room later. Mallory and his wife, Morie, had a baby boy just a few months old — Harrison Barlow Kirk. They were just now able to sleep at night, to the relief of everyone in the household. Of course, Cane, the middle brother, and his wife, Bodie, were expecting. So it would begin all over again in the spring. Nobody minded. The brothers were all gooey over the baby.

A huge Christmas tree sat in the corner, with presents already piled up to the first set of limbs. It was an artificial tree. Morie was allergic to the live ones.

Tank was chuckling. "You remember the Bakers?"

"The strange folk in the cabin?" Mallory said with a grin. "Merissa and her mother, Clara. Sure."

"Merissa came over to warn me about an assassination attempt."

Mallory did a double take. "A what?"

"She says a man is coming to kill me."

"Would you like to explain why?"

"She said it was related to the shooting in Arizona, when I was with the border patrol," he explained, still uneasy from the memory. "One of the shooters thinks I could recognize his companion and cause trouble for a politician who plans to run for federal office. Drug-related stuff."

"How did she know?"

Tank made a weird sound and waved his hands. "She had a vision!"

"I wouldn't laugh too hard at that," Mallory said strangely. "She warned a local woman about driving across a bridge. She said she had a vision of it collapsing. The woman went over it anyway a day later and the bridge fell out from under her. She barely survived."

Tank frowned. "Eerie."

"Some people have abilities that other people don't believe in," Mallory replied. "Every community has somebody who can talk out fire or talk off warts, dowse for water, even get glimpses of the future. It isn't logical . . . you can't prove it by scientific method. But I've seen it in action. You might recall that we have a well because I hired a dowser to come out here and find water for us."

"A water witch." Tank shivered. "Well, I don't believe in that stuff and I never will."

"I just hope Merissa was wrong." He clapped an affectionate arm across his brother's shoulders. "I'd hate to lose you."

Tank laughed. "You won't. I've survived a war and a handgun attack. I guess maybe

I'm indestructible."

"Nobody is that."

"I was lucky, then."

Mallory laughed. "Very."

Dalton sat down with his laptop, having recalled Merissa's statement about a sheriff in south Texas being shot.

He sipped coffee and laughed at himself for even believing such a wild tale. Until he looked through recent San Antonio news reports and discovered that a sheriff in Jacobs County, south of San Antonio, had been the victim of a recent assassination attempt by persons unknown, but believed to be involved with a notorious drug cartel across the border in Mexico.

Tank caught his breath and gaped at the screen. Sheriff Hayes Carson of Jacobs County, Texas, had been wounded by a would-be assassin in November, and later kidnapped, along with his fiancée, by members of a drug cartel from over the border. The sheriff and his fiancée, who was a local newspaper publisher, had given a brief interview about their ordeal. The leader of the drug cartel himself, whom his enemies called El Ladŕon — the thief — was killed by what was described as hand grenades tossed under his armored car near a town

26

called Cotillo, across the border in Mexico. The assassin hadn't been caught.

Tank leaned back in his chair with a rough sigh. He was disturbed by what Merissa had told him about his own ordeal, details that only his brothers and members of law enforcement had ever known. She couldn't have found out in any conventional way.

Unless . . . well, she had a computer. She did website design.

His brain was working overtime. She had enough expertise to be able to break into protected files. That had to be it. Somehow, she'd managed to access that information about him from some government website.

The difficulties with that theory didn't penetrate his confused brain. He wasn't willing to consider the idea that a young woman who barely knew him had some supernatural access to his mind. Everyone with any sense knew that psychics were swindlers who just told people what they wanted to hear and made a living at it. There was no such thing as precognition or any of those other things.

He was a smart man. He had a degree. He knew that it was impossible for Merissa to get that information except through physical, and probably illegal, means.

But how did she know that he'd forgotten

details of his ordeal, like the man in the suit, the DEA agent, who'd led him into the ambush and then disappeared?

He turned off the computer and got to his feet. There had to be a logical, rational explanation for all this. He just had to find it.

He'd left his car keys in the truck. He threw on his coat and trudged out through the snow to the garage to get them. The snow was getting really deep. If it didn't let up, they were going to have to implement some emergency procedures to get feed to the cattle stranded in the far pastures.

Wyoming in snowstorms could be a deadly place. He remembered reading about people who were stranded and froze to death in very little time. He thought about Merissa and her mother, Clara, all alone in that isolated cabin. He hoped they had plenty of firewood and provisions, just in case. He'd have to send Darby over.

He frowned as he noticed that Darby wasn't back yet. It had been several hours. He pulled out his cell phone and called Darby's number.

It was Tim who answered.

"Oh, hi, boss," Tim said. "I started to call you but I wanted to make sure first. Darby got hit with a limb when we brought the tree down."

"What?" Dalton exploded.

"He's going to be okay," Tim said quickly. "Bruised him a bit and broke a rib, so he'll be out of commission for a bit, but nothing too bad. He said if he'd been there alone, he'd probably be dead. Tree pinned him, you see. I was able to get it off. But if I hadn't gone with him . . . He says he owes his life to that little Baker girl."

Dalton let out the breath he'd been holding. "Yeah," he murmured unsteadily. "I believe he just might."

"Sorry I didn't call sooner," Tim added, "but it took us a while to get to town, to the doc. We'll head back in a few minutes. Have to go by the pharmacy to pick up some meds for Darby."

"Okay. Drive carefully," Tank said.

"You bet, boss."

Dalton hung up the cell phone. He was almost white. Mallory, coming into the room with a steaming cup of coffee, stopped short.

"What's wrong?" he asked.

"I just got cured of my skeptical attitude about psychic phenomena," Tank said, and laughed shortly.

CHAPTER TWO

Dalton couldn't find a cell phone number for Merissa, or he would have thanked her for the information that saved Darby's life.

He looked up her business on the internet, though, and sent her an email. She responded almost immediately.

"Glad Darby is okay. Take care of yourself," she wrote back.

After that experience, Tank took her advice a lot more to heart. And the first thing he did was to place a call to Jacobsville, Texas, to the office of Sheriff Hayes Carson.

"This is going to sound strange," Tank told Hayes. "But I think we have a connection."

"We're talking on the phone, so I'd call that a connection," Hayes said dryly.

"No, I mean about the drug cartel." Tank took a deep breath. He didn't like speaking of it. "I had an experience on the Arizona border not too long ago. I was with the border patrol. A man who identified himself as a DEA agent took me out to a suspected drug drop and into an ambush. I was pretty much shot to pieces. I recovered, although it's taking a long time."

Hayes was immediately interested. "Now that's really odd. We're looking for a rogue DEA agent down here in Texas. I arrested a drug dealer a couple of months ago in company with a DEA agent that nobody can find information about. Even his own guys don't know who he was, but we think he may be linked to the cartel over the border. Several of us, including the local FBI and DEA, have been trying to chase him down. Nobody can remember what he looks like. We even had our local police chief's secretary, who has a photographic memory, get a police artist to sketch him. But even then, none of us could remember having seen him."

"He blends."

"I'll say he blends," Hayes said thoughtfully. "How did you connect your case to mine?"

Tank laughed self-consciously. "Now, see, this is going to sound really strange. A local psychic came over to warn me that I was being targeted by a politician who has something to do with the drug cartel and a mysterious DEA agent."

"A psychic. Uh-huh."

"I know, you think I'm nuts, but . . ."

"Actually, our police chief's wife has the same ability," came the surprising reply. "She's saved Cash Grier's life a couple of times because she knew things she shouldn't. She calls it the 'second sight,' and says it's from her Celtic ancestry."

Tank wondered if Merissa's ancestry was Celtic. He laughed. "Well, I feel all better now."

"I wish you could fly down here and talk to me," Hayes said. "We've got a huge file on El Ladrón's operation, and the men who've taken over after his unexpected demise."

"I'd like to do that," Tank said. "But right now we're pretty much snowed in. And with Christmas coming, it's a bad time. But when the weather breaks, I'll give you a call and we'll set something up."

"Good idea. We could use the help."

"You're recovering okay from your kidnapping?"

"Yes, thanks. My fiancée and I had an interesting adventure. I wouldn't wish it on my worst enemy." He laughed. "She held one of our captors at gunpoint with an AK-

47, was really convincing. And then she confessed, when it was all over, that she didn't know if it was loaded or the safety was on. What a girl!"

Tank laughed. "What a lucky man, to be marrying a woman like that."

"Yes, I am. We're getting married tomorrow, in fact." Hayes chuckled. "And going on our honeymoon to Panama City for a few days. Next week is Christmas, so we have to be back by then. You married?"

"No woman in Wyoming crazy enough to take me on," Tank said dryly. "Both my brothers are married. I'm just waiting to be snapped up by some kind passerby."

"Good luck to you."

"Thanks. Keep safe."

"You do the same. Nice talking to you."

"Same here."

Tank hung up and went looking for his brother Mallory. He found him in the living room, by following the exquisite sound of a score from a popular movie. Mallory, like Tank himself, was a gifted pianist. Mallory's wife, Morie, was better than both of them.

Mallory noticed his brother standing in the doorway and stopped playing with a grin.

Tank held up a hand. "I'm not conceding that you're better than me. I was just thinking, however, that Morie puts us both in the shade."

"Indeed she does," Mallory replied with a smile. He got up. "Problems?"

"Remember I told you what Merissa said, about a sheriff in Texas whose case was connected to the shooting I was involved in?"

Mallory nodded, waiting.

Tank sighed. He perched himself on the arm of the sofa. "Well, it turns out that there actually is a sheriff in Texas who was kidnapped by a drug cartel — maybe the same cartel that shot me up."

"Son of a gun!" Mallory exclaimed.

"His name is Sheriff Hayes Carson. There was an assassination attempt against him by one of the drug lords he arrested, just before Thanksgiving. He and his fiancée were kidnapped by some of El Ladrón's men and held across the border in Mexico. They escaped. But Carson says he had a run-in with one of the drug cartel henchmen before that. There was a DEA agent in a suit who was at the scene. The local police chief's secretary saw the guy, and has a photographic memory, but even when the police artist drew him, neither Carson nor the feds could recall him."

"Curious," Mallory murmured.

"Yes. I remembered, after Merissa came

here, that it was a DEA agent, in a suit, who led me into the ambush on the border."

Mallory let out a long breath. "Good God."

"Merissa says the same guys are coming after me because they're afraid of what I'll remember. The damnedest thing is, I don't remember anything that would help convict someone. I only remember the pain and the certainty that I was going to die, there in the dust, covered in blood, all alone."

Mallory got up and laid a heavy, affectionate hand on his shoulder. "That didn't happen, though. A concerned citizen saw you and called the law."

He nodded. "I vaguely remember that. Mostly it was a voice, telling me that I'd be all right. Had a Spanish accent. He saved my life." He closed his eyes. "There was another man, arguing with him, telling him to do nothing. It was too late — he'd already made the call by then. I remember the other man's voice. He was cussing. He had a Massachusetts accent." He laughed. "Sounded like old history tapes of President John Kennedy, actually."

"What did he look like?"

Tank frowned. He closed his eyes again, trying to remember. "I just vaguely remember. He was wearing a suit. He was tall and very pale with red hair." He started. "I never thought of that." He opened his eyes and looked at Mallory. "I think he was a DEA agent." He frowned. "But why would he tell the other man not to get help for me if he was a fed?"

"Was he the same one who took you out there?"

Tank frowned. "No. No, it couldn't have been him. That guy, the DEA guy, had dark hair and a Southern drawl."

"Did you describe him to the sheriff?"

Tank got up. "No, but I'm about to."

He picked up his cell phone, found Hayes Carson's number in the stored files and autodialed the number.

It only took three rings before Hayes answered. "Carson."

"It's Dalton Kirk, in Wyoming. I've just remembered a man who called for help when I was shot. There was another man with him who tried to stop him from calling 911. The other man was tall, with red hair and a Massachusetts accent. Does that sound anything like the man you remember?"

Hayes actually laughed. "No. Our guy was tall and sandy-haired and had a slight Spanish accent."

"A Spanish guy with blond hair?" Tank

chuckled.

"Well, people from Northern Spain are often blond and blue-eyed. Some have red hair. And they say the Basque people of Spain settled in Scotland and Ireland."

"I didn't know that."

"Neither did I, but one of our federal agents is a history nut. He knows all about Scotland. He told me."

"This whole thing is really strange. The man who led me into the ambush was tall and dark-haired. The man who was with the guy who called 911 was a red-head. But I remember them both wearing the same suit." He shook his head. "Maybe the trauma unseated my memory."

"Or maybe the man uses disguises." Hayes was thinking, hard. "Listen, did you ever see that movie *The Saint* that starred Val Kilmer?"

Tank frowned. "Once, I think."

"Well, the guy was a real chameleon. He could change his appearance at the drop of a hat. He could put on a wig, change his accent, the whole deal."

"You think our guy might be someone like that?"

"It's possible. People who work in the covert world have to learn to disguise themselves to avoid detection. He may have a background in black ops."

"If I knew somebody in military intelligence, I might be able to find out something about that."

"We have a guy here, Rick Marquez. He's a police detective in San Antonio. His father-in-law is head of the CIA. I might be able to get him to check it out."

"Great idea. Thanks."

"I don't know if he can find out anything. Especially with the odd descriptions I'll have to give him."

"Listen," Tank said quietly, "it's worth a try. If he's ever used disguises in the past, there's a chance somebody will remember him."

"It's possible, I suppose. But in covert work, I don't imagine using disguises is exactly a rare thing," Hayes said. He hesitated. "There's another interesting connection, in my case."

"What?"

"My fiancée's father, her real father, is one of the biggest drug cartel leaders on the continent."

There was a very significant silence on the other end of the line.

"He helped us shut down El Ladrón," Hayes added quietly. "And he saved the man's family who helped rescue me and

Minette. For a bad man, he's something of a closet angel. They call him El Jefe."

"A sheriff with an outlaw for a future father-in-law," Tank said. "Well, it's unique."

"So is he. I can ask him to dig into his sources and see if he can come up with anything, like a budding politician with drug cartel ties."

"That would be a help. Thanks."

"I'm just as much involved as you are. Stay in touch."

"I'll do that. And we should both watch our backs in the meantime."

"Couldn't agree more."

Tank's next move was to drive over to Merissa's house through the blinding snow. What he wanted to talk to her about wasn't something he was comfortable discussing over the phone. If there was an assassin after him, he might monitor calls. Anyone in black ops would have that talent.

When he pulled up at the front door of the small cabin, Clara, Merissa's mother, was waiting there. She smiled as Tank got out of the truck and came up the steps.

"She said you'd come," Clara said with a sheepish smile. "She's lying down with a migraine headache," she added worriedly. "She woke up with it, so the medicine isn't working very well."

"Medicine from a doctor?" Tank asked softly, and with a smile.

Clara lowered her eyes. "Herbal medicine. My grandfather was a Comanche shaman," she said.

His eyebrows arched.

"I know, I'm blonde and so is Merissa, but it's true just the same. I had a little boy just after I had Merissa. He died —" she hesitated, still upset about it after all the years "— when he was just a week old. But he had black hair and dark brown eyes. It's recessive genes with Merissa and me, you see. Our coloring, I mean."

He moved a step closer. He noticed that Clara, like Merissa, immediately backed up, looking uneasy.

He stopped dead, frowning. "Recessive genes."

She nodded. She swallowed, relaxing when she saw that he wasn't coming closer.

"Clara, I don't really know you well enough to pry," he began softly, "but it's noticeable that you and Merissa start backing away from me if I come close."

Clara hesitated. Oddly, she trusted Tank, even though she barely knew him. "My . . . ex-husband . . . he was scary when he lost his temper." She managed a laugh. "It's an

40

old reflex. Sorry."

"No offense taken," he replied gently.

She looked back up at him with wide green eyes the same shade as Merissa's. "I divorced him, with help from our local sheriff — the one before this one. He was so kind. He got help for us, sheltered us through the divorce and made sure my ex-husband left not only the town, but the state." She managed a weak smile. She swallowed, not dealing with it well, even now. "We were always afraid of him, when . . . when he got mad. He was big, like you. Tall and big."

Tank looked into her eyes. "I'm a teddy bear," he told her with pursed lips. "But if you tell anybody on my ranch that, I'll send an email to Santa Claus and you'll get coal in your stocking."

Clara, shocked, burst out laughing. "Okay." She sobered. "Merissa says the man who led you into the ambush is coming."

His face hardened. "When?"

"It doesn't work like that," she said. "It's why you can't prove it scientifically, because experiments under scientific control very rarely work. It's sporadic. I know things, but they're usually nebulous in my mind and I have to interpret what I see. Merissa is much more gifted than I am. It's made her the subject of much cruelty, I'm afraid."

"I heard about that. May I see her?"

"She's not well . . ."

"My older brother Mallory is subject to migraine headaches. He has high-powered medications that can prevent them if they're taken in time. The ones he wakes up with, though, don't even respond to meds. He has to try to sleep them off."

"Merissa's are bad," she commented. "Come on in. I'm sorry I kept you out here talking in the freezing cold!"

"I'm wearing a very heavy jacket," he assured her, and smiled.

Merissa was not in bed. Terrible sounds of a meal returning were heard in the bathroom.

"Oh, dear . . ." Clara began.

Tank walked right into the bathroom, found a washcloth and wet it while Merissa, kneeling at the toilet, was still heaving.

"You shouldn't . . . be in here!" she protested weakly.

"Bull. You're sick." He waited until the last of the spasm was over, flushed the toilet and bathed her pale face. Her green eyes were enormous. "Is it over, you think?"

She swallowed, tasting bile. "I think so."

He pulled out mouthwash and poured a

little in a cup, smiling as she took it and ruefully washed her mouth out. He turned on the faucet to flush it away when she pushed it out into the sink.

He bathed her face again, as he would a child's, appreciating her delicate, elfin beauty. Her complexion was truly peaches and cream; exquisite, like that pretty bow-shaped mouth. "You are beautiful, you know that?" he murmured softly.

She stared at him blankly.

"Never mind." He put the washcloth in her hand, swung her up in his arms and carried her to bed. He tucked her in. "Just lie still. I have a friend who's a doctor. Do you mind if I call him to come out here?"

"Doctors don't make house calls," she protested weakly.

"Oh, this one does." He pulled out his cell phone, punched in a number, waited for a second until it was answered. "John. Hi. Tank here. Have you got a couple of minutes to take a look at a young woman with a massive migraine and no meds?"

He paused, grinned. "Yes, she's gorgeous," he said, eyeing Merissa.

There was obviously a question.

"Merissa Baker," Tank replied.

Merissa closed her eyes. He wouldn't come now. He'd know it was the witch woman, whom everyone in town avoided.

But Tank was laughing. "Yes, she is a phenomenon. I can attest to her skills. Yes, I know you would. We'll be expecting you. Want me to send one of the boys to drive you over?" He nodded. "No problem. I'll call Tim right now." He hung up, phoned Tim and gave him directions to get to the doctor.

He turned back to Merissa and sat down next to her on the bed. "His name is John Harrison. He's retired, but he's one of the best physicians I've ever known, and his medical license is kept current."

Merissa removed the comforting cold wet cloth from her eyes and winced at the light. Photophobia was one of the symptoms of the condition. "Dr. Harrison? He's fascinated with psychic phenomena," she pointed out. "They say he was friends with one of the researchers who used to work in the parapsychology department of a major college back East years ago."

"That's true. He thinks you're fascinating. He can't wait to meet you," he told her.

She sighed and put the cloth back over her eyes. "That's a new thing, all right. Most people never want to meet me. They're afraid I'll curdle the milk."

"You're no witch," Tank scoffed. "You just

44

have a gift that's outside the area of established science. In a couple of hundred years, scientists will research it just as they research other conditions. You know, two hundred years or more ago, there was no antibiotic, and doctors had no clue about exactly how disease processes worked."

"We've come a long way from that."

He nodded. "Indeed we have. Tummy feeling better?"

"A bit, yes. Thanks."

Clara was standing in the doorway, looking perplexed. "The herbs always worked before," she commented.

Tank looked up. "Can you make her a cup of strong black coffee?"

She blinked. "Excuse me?"

"Old home remedy for asthma attacks and headaches. You know, most of the over-the-counter medicines for headaches contain caffeine."

Clara laughed. "I've learned something. I know herbs, but I'd never thought about coffee as a drug. I'll make the coffee right now."

"I love coffee," Merissa whispered. "I couldn't face breakfast this morning, so I missed my first cup of the day."

"We'll get you better. Don't worry."

She swallowed. The pain was intense.

"This is really nice of you. The doctor, I mean."

"He's a good friend."

She peered at him from under the washcloth. "You're good with sick people."

He shrugged. "I thought about being a doctor myself, at one time. But I have a hard time sticking to things. Maybe a touch of adult ADD." He chuckled, alluding to Attention Deficit Disorder.

She smiled. "Well, thanks."

He smiled back and tucked the washcloth over her eyes. "I imagine the light is uncomfortable, even with the curtains closed. Mallory has to have a dark room and no noise when he gets these headaches."

There were sounds in the kitchen and the delicious smell of brewing coffee. A couple of minutes later, Clara walked in carrying two cups. She handed one to her daughter, and the other to Tank. His contained just cream, no sugar.

He gaped at her. "How did you know how I drink my coffee?"

She shrugged and sighed.

He laughed. "Well, thanks. It's just right."

She smiled.

The doctor, John Harrison, was tall, with gray hair and light blue eyes. He smiled as

Clara escorted him into the bedroom, where Tank was sitting beside Merissa on the bed.

Tank got to his feet and the men shook hands.

John opened his bag, got out his stethoscope, and sat down beside the pale woman.

"Dr. Harrison, thank you so much for coming," Merissa said in a weak voice.

"This is how things used to be done, in the old days when I got out of medical school," he said. "I can't tell you how many elderly people who could barely walk almost cheered when I showed up at their doors. Now that I'm old, I understand. It's hard on the joints to sit for an hour or two waiting to see the doctor."

He listened to her chest, checked her vital signs and then looped the stethoscope around his neck. He had her do some very simple exercises and he checked her pupils.

"I haven't had a stroke," she teased.

His eyebrows shot up. "How did you know I thought that?"

"I don't know." She flushed. "These things just slip out." She sighed. "My life would be so much easier if I were normal."

He laughed softly, pulled out a small bottle and unwrapped a syringe. He attached the needle, inserted it into the bottle, pushed out air, filled it to a notch and put

47

the bottle down.

"This may sting a bit." He used an alcohol wipe on her arm before he slid the needle in gently. A few seconds later, he withdrew it. She hadn't even flinched.

"Didn't sting at all. I feel horrible."

"Do you get the aura?" he asked.

"Yes. Usually I just go blind in one eye, with static like you see on a television screen when there's no channel coming up. But this time there were brightly colored lights."

He nodded. "Do you have a family physician?"

"We went to Dr. Brady, but he moved to Montana," she said softly. "We go to clinics now."

"You can consider me your family physician, if you like," he offered. "And I do make house calls."

"That would be so kind of you," she said, with heartfelt gratitude. "You see, we frighten most people, Mama and I."

"I'm not frightened of you. I'm intrigued. That injection will make you sleep. When you wake up, the headache should be gone. But if the headache worsens or you have new symptoms, you must call me."

"I will," she promised.

"And I think you should have a CT scan. Just to rule out anything dangerous."

"I hate tests," she groaned. "But I've had them already. The neurologist didn't find anything like a tumor in the scans. He said it's migraine without a specific cause."

"Do you mind if I contact him?" he asked. "I know we've only just met . . ."

She smiled. "I don't mind at all." It was very nice having a doctor who didn't feel that she and Clara were "peculiar." "I'll write his number down for you." She did, on a piece of paper, and handed it to him. He slipped it into his jacket pocket.

He patted her on the shoulder. "When you're better, I'd like to talk to you about this gift of yours. When I was in college, I did several courses of anthropology. I still audit courses on the internet, to keep up with what's going on in the field. Every community since recorded history has had people with unusual gifts."

"Really?" she asked.

He nodded. "As for psychic gifts, the government once had an entire unit of what were called 'remote viewers.' They were used to spy on other countries. Quite successfully at times," he explained.

"I'd like to hear more about that," she said, becoming drowsy.

"All in good time. If your headache isn't better when you wake up, call me." He pulled out a business card and put it on her bedside table. "My cell phone number is on there. Use it. I never answer the landline phone if I can help it. Only a handful of people know the other."

"That's so kind of you."

He shrugged. "I loved medicine. I still do. I just hate all the nitpicky rules that have reduced it to red tape with pharmaceuticals mixed in."

"Thank you."

"My pleasure."

He left the room, pausing to speak to Clara. Tank smoothed back Merissa's soft hair. "I'll talk to you again, when you're not in such bad shape," he said with a gentle smile. "I hope you get better very soon."

She caught his hand. "Thank you. For everything."

He bent impulsively and kissed her forehead. "You're easy to take care of," he said softly.

"You came to see me. What about?" she wondered.

"You knew I was coming."

"Yes. I felt it."

He drew in a breath. "I talked to the sheriff in Texas. We both remember a man who seemed to have more than one face . . ."

She sat straight up in bed. "That's it!

50

That's it!"

He thought she was having a reaction to the medicine. "Are you all right?" he asked worriedly, coaxing her to lie back down.

"I kept seeing a man sitting at a dressing table, trying on wigs," she blurted out in a rush. "I didn't know what it meant. Now I do. The man who's after you, that's him!"

He felt cold chills down his backbone. "Your mother said you think he's coming here."

"Yes. Soon." She held his hand. "You must be very, very careful," she said, her face drawn. "Promise me."

Her concern made him feel warm inside, as if he were sitting in front of a cozy fire with a cup of hot chocolate. "I promise."

She sighed and closed her eyes. "I'm very sleepy."

"Rest is the best thing for you. I'll come back another time."

She smiled. "That would be . . . very nice."

He got up. She was already asleep.

A man sitting at a dressing table, trying on wigs. At least now, thanks to her, he had some idea of what might be coming his way. He would have to take precautions, and soon. He looked down at the sleeping woman with odd, possessive feelings. He wasn't psychic, but he knew that she was going to play an important part in his life.

CHAPTER THREE

Tank paused to talk to Clara and the doctor when he left Merissa's room.

"She's asleep," he told them.

Clara smiled. "I'm so glad. Those headaches are terrible. You think there may be something bad causing them," she said to the doctor, who looked surprised at her intuition. Clara stared at him with wide, soft eyes that seemed almost transparent. "It's not a tumor," she said in a soft monotone. "There's nothing . . ."

The doctor laughed. "It amazes me, that you can see that."

Clara looked self-conscious. "It comes and goes. I never know when something will pop into my mind. Merissa has a true gift. She can, well, look at something and see what's going to happen. I can't."

"It's a very rare ability," the doctor told her.

"It makes us outcasts," Clara replied. "We

rarely leave the house. People stare and whisper. I hate going to the grocery store. One woman even asked me if I kept a familiar."

"Good Lord," Tank muttered.

"We're pretty much used to it by now." Clara laughed. "And we do get a lot of people who ask us to read for them. That's usually hit-and-miss and I tell them that, but they come anyway. Sometimes we're able to see something that saves lives, or even marriages. It's a good feeling. It almost makes up for the notoriety."

"You handle it well," Tank said.

"Thanks."

"She said her neurologist did tests and gave me his number," he told Clara. "I'll confer with him. But you're right. She showed no signs of having any impairment beyond the migraine. You call me if she doesn't get better," Dr. Harrison told Clara firmly. "I don't care if it's two in the morning."

"I owe you a great debt just for what you've already done," Clara said. She pulled out her purse. He protested but she handed him a large bill anyway.

"Gas money," she told him. "Don't argue."

He just shook his head. "I'm on retirement, you know," he said.

"Doesn't matter. You came here as if we were family, and retirement isn't usually enough to buy food and medicine at once."

He smiled. "All right then. Thank you," he said formally.

She smiled back.

Tank wanted to stay. He hated leaving that sweet blonde woman in the bedroom. He'd felt possessive while he was looking after her. It was a new, and strange, feeling. He'd had brief romances over the years, but he'd never found a woman he could think of in terms of a future together. Now, all at once, his mind was being changed.

It disturbed him, thinking about the chameleon federal agent who had led him into the ambush on the border. He'd dismissed Merissa's vision at the beginning, but after speaking to Sheriff Hayes Carson in Texas, now he was sure she was right.

A few days later, the storm was still annoying everyone, but there were some changes going on at the ranch. All the men had started carrying weapons, even when they weren't riding fence. And whenever Tank went outside, at least two men were nearby, watching — something that Mallory had ordered.

New surveillance equipment was installed by a local company. It seemed to disconcert the man who set up the cameras that so many armed men were walking around near Tank.

"Something going on that you're worried about, mate?" the technician asked Tank. "I mean, men with guns everywhere. You're never alone for a second, are you?"

Tank shrugged. "My brothers are overprotective. Probably nothing, but there may be a threat of some sort."

"And you know this from what, an informer?" the man probed.

Tank pursed his lips. "A psychic."

"Fair dinkum?" the man drawled in a thick Australian accent. He shook his head. "Don't put no faith in them things, mate, they're all bogus. Nobody can see the future."

Tank didn't argue. "Maybe you're right. But we like to err on the side of caution."

"It's your money," the man said, and went back to work.

He was through quickly. "This'll set you right, mate," the installer told Tank with a smile. "This is state-of-the-art stuff. Nobody will be sneaking up on you now. No worries."

"Thanks. It does rather feel like being in prison, however." Tank sighed, looking around at the state-of-the-art camera towers.

"We pay a price for safety," the other man replied. "With your life at stake, this seems a pretty fair dinkum one, you know?"

Tank smiled. "I know." It didn't occur to him then to ask how the man knew his life was on the line, since he hadn't elaborated about the threat to either the woman at the company's office or this installer.

"Well, that should do it," the man replied. "Oh, and I did put a small camera in your office, just to square things up. It's hidden, so you won't have to worry about somebody spotting it."

"Where?" Tank asked, concerned.

The other man put a hand on his shoulder and grinned. "If you don't know where it is, you can't tell somebody, right?"

He laughed. He had a similar appliance in his truck, a Lo-Jack, and where it was installed nobody knew. "I get it."

"Good man. If you have any questions or concerns, you can call us, right?"

"Right. Thanks."

"Just doing my job," he replied, and grinned again.

Why should Tank suddenly think of a play,

with one of the characters complaining that another character "smiled too much"?

Curious, he watched the man climb into a nice, late-model car and drive off. Why wasn't he in a company truck, like most technicians drove?

So he called the security company and asked.

"Oh, that's just Ben." The woman in the office laughed, although she sounded just briefly disconcerted. "He's eccentric. He likes women, you see, and he thinks they're less likely to be impressed by a guy if he's in some company vehicle."

"I see."

"Not to worry," she returned. "I've known him for years. He's just curious, to put it politely. But he knows his job, and he's good at it."

"I'll stop worrying."

"We're happy to have the work," she added gratefully. "It's been a bit slow, lately, with the economy in such a bind."

"Tell me about it." Tank sighed. "We're looking for new markets for our cattle. Everything's slow."

"I guess you're selling off stock."

"Sold it off before winter," he corrected. "And a good thing it was. We're having to truck in feed. This storm is bad."

"I know. I had to get a lift to work with a friend." She laughed. "If he hadn't been able to drive in this, you wouldn't be speaking to me now."

"Good thing your guys can work in this mess," Tank said. "I didn't want to wait for the weather to break to get the system installed."

"Expecting some sort of trouble?" she asked. "Not that it's my business."

"No, nothing out of the ordinary," he prevaricated. "But we had a threat about one of our bulls. Best to be safe."

"Oh." She hesitated. "Not worrying about some sort of attack on people there, then?"

He laughed deliberately. "What in the world would somebody attack us for?" he asked. "I did jaywalk last week, but I hardly think the sheriff's coming by to arrest me."

She laughed, too. "Silly thought. I suppose your cattle are quite expensive."

"And that's an understatement," he replied. "A friend of ours was visited by rustlers a few weeks ago. Had one of his prize bulls taken. Not going to happen here."

"Not with our equipment on the job, I promise you," she replied. "Thanks again for the business. If you know anybody else in need of surveillance equipment, we'd be grateful for the work."

"I'll pass that along."

He hung up.

The storm did break. Snow was still piled everywhere, but the sun came out. Tank had phoned Clara to make sure Merissa was better.

"She's back at work already." Clara laughed. "Would you like to speak to her?"

"Yes, I would, thanks."

There was a brief pause. "Hello?"

Tank loved her voice. It was soft and clear, like a prayer in the wilderness. "Hello," he replied softly. "Are you better?"

"Much. Thanks again for your help. The doctor called in a prescription for me at the drugstore," she added. "He says it will help prevent the headaches, if I can tolerate it." She laughed. "I'm funny about medicine. I can't take a lot of it. I used to take feverfew for migraine, and another herb, but they weren't working."

"Modern medicine to the rescue," he mused.

"Modern medicine is just a reworking of ancient Native American and indigenous folk medicine wrapped up in pills," she pointed out.

"Have it your way." He smiled, then

paused. "When the snow melts a bit, how would you like to go over to Catelow and have supper at that new Mediterranean eatery everybody's talking about?"

Her intake of breath was audible. "I'd love to," she said with flattering quickness.

He chuckled softly. "I like Greek food," he said. "Well, I don't like resinated wine, but that's another thing."

"What is that?"

"The wine?" he asked. "It's an acquired taste, a wine with resin in it. It's quite bitter, but I'm told that many people like it."

"Sounds uncomfortable."

"To me, too. But I love the food."

"I like spinach salad with goat cheese."

"So do I."

She laughed. "We have things in common."

"We'll find more, I imagine. I'll call you in a day or two and we'll set a date. Okay?"

"Okay!"

"Call us if you need anything."

"I will, but we're fine."

"Okay. See you."

"See you."

He hung up, feeling very proud of himself.

A few minutes later, he walked out to the barn, where Cane and Mallory were talking

61

to Darby about arrangements for a new bull they'd purchased. They turned when he came in, wearing a huge grin.

"You win the lottery or something?" Cane joked.

"I'm taking Merissa out to eat," Tank replied.

There were several shocked expressions.

He glared at them. "She won't turn me into a toad if she doesn't like the food," he said sarcastically.

"That isn't what worries us," Cane said quietly.

Mallory moved forward. He put a hand on his brother's shoulder. "Look, it isn't that we don't like Merissa. But we know very little about her family. There have been some stories, some very unpleasant ones, about her father."

Tank frowned. "What stories?"

Mallory glanced at Cane and back at Tank. "Well, that he beat one of his hands almost to death," he said.

Tank was shocked. "He doesn't live there anymore."

"I know," Mallory said. "But . . ."

"But you think maybe Merissa's like that?" Tank said through his teeth.

Mallory removed his hand. "I'm doing this badly," he groaned.

Cane moved forward. "Nobody knows where he is," he said. "There's a warrant, a standing warrant, for his arrest on assault and battery charges."

"If you get involved with her," Mallory seconded, "and he comes back . . ."

Tank understood, finally, what they were saying. He relaxed. "You're worried about me."

They both nodded. "We heard all sorts of things concerning him. He was possessive about his daughter. She was just ten at the time, and he was violent toward anybody who tried to talk to her."

"I wonder why?" Tank asked.

"There were also rumors about what he did to her mother," Mallory added solemnly.

"To Clara?" Tank was shocked. "But she's a woman!"

"A man like that doesn't care," Cane said coldly. "Our doctor told me, in confidence once, that he'd treated Clara for some potentially fatal injuries." He looked at Mallory with a question in his eyes.

"Tell him," Mallory said.

Cane drew a breath. "Merissa was brought in with Clara, with a concussion and a broken leg," he added. "The doctor said she tried to save her mother."

Tank leaned back against a stone pillar

with a rough curse. "Concussion!"

"It could explain some of her strange abilities," Mallory said quietly. "There's no scientific explanation that I'm aware of, but there are many things we still don't know about brain function."

"He hit a ten-year-old hard enough to break her leg?" Tank was talking to himself.

"Yes," Mallory replied. "It's worrying that nobody knows where he is."

"It's been years," Tank pointed out.

"So it has. But it's something to consider. Like that man who helped put you into intensive care . . ."

Tank held up his hand suddenly. "Let's not go into that," he said with a look that wasn't lost on his brothers.

"Okay."

He stood up. "I want to have a look at that tractor that's been acting up," he told his brothers, motioning them to follow him.

They nodded to Darby Hanes, who grinned. He was feeling better and back at work.

Tank started the engine and left it idling.

"I don't think surveillance can pick this up," he told the two of them, "over the noise, and my back's to the camera so they can't read lips. Listen, I don't want to mention anything about our suspicions. Something's not quite right about the company we hired to install the cameras. I can't explain it," he said irritably.

"You been talking to Merissa?" Cane teased.

"I have, but she didn't mention it. No, I just have a feeling," he added heavily.

Mallory didn't laugh. "I had the same feeling," he said curtly. "And I'm not psychic. The guy came in a car, not a service vehicle. He had an Australian accent, but it was put on. I had a friend in the service who was from Adelaide. I know the difference."

Tank lost color in his face. "The rogue federal agent, the chameleon."

"It's possible," Cane said, interrupting.

"Yes, but what do we do about all the cameras? And he might have bugged the phones, as well," Tank said with growing unease. "He had access to the whole house, thanks to my stupidity! I should have mentioned that we hire a company from out of town."

"You couldn't have known," Mallory said gently. "Neither of us thought about the possibility, either. It seemed a logical thing to do."

"Yes, it did," Cane agreed.

"We might have another company come in and tweak the cameras," Mallory suggested with twinkling eyes.

"Not a bad idea," Tank said. "I have a friend who can put bugs in ice cream and you'll never see them. He was working as an independent contractor in the Middle East when I was serving over there. I'll give him a call on my cell."

"Your cell may be bugged," Mallory pointed out.

"I'll buy a throwaway," Cane said. "And use it. We'd all better have some. I'll send Darby into town for them."

"This is ridiculous," Tank muttered. "We hire people to protect us from the bad guys, and they may turn out to be the very people we're watching for."

"Our advantage," Cane said, "is that they won't know we're onto them."

"We could all just be paranoid," Mallory suggested.

The other two looked at him for a minute, laughed and shook their heads. "No."

He shrugged, and grinned.

"Tell the wives," Tank added, "not to say anything about this in the house."

"We will. They're going on a two-day Christmas shopping trip to Los Angeles Friday," Cane pointed out. "Morie's taking Harrison with them. She can't bear to leave him even with Mavie for a couple of days."

"She's a great little mother," Tank said. He pursed his lips. "And I hear you and your new father-in-law have a hunting trip planned for next month up in Montana."

"Heard that, did you?" Mallory chuckled. "We do. Now that he's a grandfather, he's a lot less judgmental and harsh."

Tank didn't want to mention how much Mallory had mellowed. So he just grinned.

"I'll call Merissa back and set up our date for Saturday," Tank decided. "I can be fairly certain that the restaurant won't be bugged."

"I wouldn't make that bet," Mallory replied. "Especially if you told her where you're going."

"I did," Tank groaned. Then he brightened and laughed. "I'll drive her over to Powell instead, and we'll eat at the Chinese restaurant. But I won't tell her until we're on the way."

"Creative thinking," Cane said.

"I'll have my friend sweep the truck before I leave." He paused. "If he's got the time, I might hire him on as a temporary. Nobody has to know what he really does for a living."

"Do it," Mallory said. "Better safe than sorry."

■ ■ ■ ■

Tank sent Darby Hanes into town that afternoon for throwaway phones. As soon as he had his, and it was activated, Tank placed a call.

"Hello?" It was a male voice, deep and quiet.

"It's Tank," he replied. "How are things?"

There was a pause. "Not good. How are you?"

"Fine, so far." He hesitated. "Are you free for a couple of weeks? It's a job, and it pays well."

There was a rush of breath. "How the hell did you know I'm out of work?" came the reply. "Just finished one job and didn't even have another lined up. Bills are piling up, house needs repairs . . ." He was lying through his teeth, but Tank wouldn't know. He didn't speak of his private life to outsiders. He maintained the fiction that he was a starving mercenary, living from job to job.

Tank chuckled. "Great! Well, not about the bills, I mean. But you're hired."

"You're a lifesaver! What do you need done?"

"I've got a rogue fed after me," Tank said. "I just hired a surveillance company to put up cameras and install bugs — but I have a nasty suspicion that the installer will turn out to be the rogue fed who's after me."

"Damn! You do have the worst luck!"

"Tell me about it." Tank sighed. "How soon can you come up here?"

"As soon as you email me a ticket" came the reply. "I haven't unpacked from the last job. It will be a pleasure."

"You aren't working for your . . . for your old boss, I mean?" He bit his tongue. He'd almost slipped and said "your father," but he didn't dare do that. Rourke wouldn't get on the plane. Most people suspected that Rourke was the illegitimate son of K.C. Kantor, the ex-merc millionaire. Nobody said it to Rourke's face. Nobody dared. Besides, if the man was living from hand to mouth, it was unlikely that he had a rich father looking out for him.

"No, the boss and I had a falling out," Rourke replied heavily. It wasn't quite the truth, but it was close enough. "Things have gone from bad to worse. And Tat won't speak to me at all." The last was said with subdued rage. Tat was a socialite journalist who'd gone with Rourke and General Machado to retake Machado's country in South America. Rourke and Tat, his nickname for her, had a very long history.

Rourke had known her since she was a child. They had a rocky friendship.

"Put her neck hairs up again, did you?" Tank asked.

Rourke cursed. "She's gone in with the troops, over in Nganwa," he said, naming a small country involved in a nasty revolution. "I tried to stop her, but she wouldn't listen. It's a bloodbath over there. I know seasoned mercs who won't go near the place!"

"Journalists are usually protected," Tank said quietly.

"Sure they are. Want to hear how many bought it last year on assignment?" he asked pessimistically.

"Sorry to hear she's in danger," Tank said finally.

"Her own damned fault. Stupidity has a price. For two bits, I'd go in and drag her out . . ." He hesitated. Swallowed. "Send me the ticket. I'll be right up."

"I'll email it on my alternate account," Tank said.

"Good man."

"Thanks, Rourke," he said quietly.

"Hey, what are friends for?" came the reply.

Merissa was wearing a soft beige dress that

clung to her slender figure, outlining her pert breasts and tiny waist and flaring hips. She wore flat shoes with it, and her blond hair waved in soft curls around her elfin face. She wore a small Christmas tree pin on the dress and a matching clip in her hair.

She smiled shyly at Tank, who stared at her with open admiration. "If it's too dressy . . ." she began self-consciously.

"I don't very often see women in dresses these days," he replied with a gentle smile. "I think you look lovely."

She flushed and then laughed. "Thanks." She indicated her shoes. "I can't wear high heels. I suppose this looks peculiar . . ."

"It looks fine." He didn't question the odd remark. "Ready to go?"

"Yes." She peered into the living room. "See you later, Mom. Lock the doors," she added firmly.

Clara laughed softly. "I will. Got your key?"

"Yes."

"Have fun."

"Thanks."

Tank stuck his head in the door and grinned. "I'll take good care of her," he promised.

"I know you will," Clara replied.

Rourke had arrived the day before. He got to work at once on the security cameras, swept the house for bugs — and found several — and swept the truck just before Tank got in it for his date.

"We're going to Powell to have supper," he told her. "Sorry, but we've had a hitch in our security."

Merissa was very still. "It was him. The man in the suit."

He glanced at her quickly. "Well . . . yes, we think so."

"How ironic," she said breathlessly. She shook her head. "He's very confident."

"He is, but it will be his undoing," he said coldly.

She didn't speak. Her face was drawn.

He stopped the car at a red light as they approached Powell. "What do you see, Merissa?" he asked very softly.

She swallowed. "Something bad."

"Can you be more specific?"

She glanced at him. "I don't know." Her face contorted. "It's just a feeling right now. I can't . . . I can't see what it is."

He reached across the seat and caught her

soft hand in his. "It's all right. We'll handle it."

She felt a jolt all the way to her feet at his touch. His hand was big and warm, callused from work. She looked down at it in the light from the streetlamps. It was a beautiful hand, very masculine, with neatly trimmed and clean flat nails.

"You have beautiful hands," she burst out.

He chuckled. "Thanks. Yours aren't bad, either."

She grinned.

He felt the same electricity that she did. It was comforting, to have that physical contact with another human being. Tank had imagined himself in love a couple of times, but it had never been this intense. He wanted to protect her, take care of her. She was a strong, capable woman. She could support herself, and did. But she made him feel taller, stronger.

"What are you thinking?" she asked suddenly.

He squeezed her hand gently. "That this is one of the best ideas I've had in years."

She laughed. "Thanks."

"You're comfortable to be around."

"Not many people in Catelow would agree with that."

"They don't know you. People are afraid

of the unknown, of anything that isn't scientific."

"Well, this certainly isn't scientific," she agreed. "I've spent my life seeing things that terrify me." She glanced at him. "So many people want to know the future. But if they could see what I see, they wouldn't. It's never good to know what lies ahead."

"I have to agree."

"I mean, it's one thing to have a handle on the weather, or what fashions will be in vogue the next year, or if you're going to meet someone who will change your life. But to want to know what's going to happen to you in a year, two years . . . You should never want to know those things."

He rubbed his thumb gently over the back of her hand as he drove. "You never talk about your father."

Her hand jumped, as if it had been jolted by electricity.

He looked toward her. "Sorry. I didn't mean to upset you."

She swallowed. "You've . . . heard things."

He pulled into the parking lot at the Chinese restaurant and cut off the engine. He turned to her. "Honestly, yes, I have." He searched her eyes, huge in that pale face. "You don't have to talk to me about him if you don't want to. We barely know each other."

She hesitated. "He was . . . brutal."

"Was?"

She bit her lip. "We haven't seen him in years," she said. "We don't know where he is. But we're always afraid that he might come back." She closed her eyes and shivered. "He was a big man. He was so strong . . . !"

"He hurt you."

She looked up at him with tragic eyes. "Me, and Mama," she agreed heavily. "I was so happy when he left. She threatened him. She told him what would happen if he stayed in Catelow. She knew, you see, and it wasn't only a premonition. He beat up one of our farmhands and almost killed him. Mom told him that the man would press charges and he would go to jail. It's the only reason he left."

"I see."

She drew in a breath, and shook her head. "No, you don't. I lived in terror all my life that he would kill my mother." She closed her eyes. "Once, I got brave, and tried to stop him."

"With almost fatal results," he added.

Her eyes were huge. "You know?"

"Catelow is a very small town, Merissa,"

he pointed out. "Yes. I know." His expression hardened. "If I'd been here then, he'd never have touched either of you."

Her face lightened, and her eyes widened. "He would have been afraid of you."

He searched her eyes. "Are you? Afraid of me?"

She swallowed. "Not so much anymore," she said. "A little, maybe."

His face softened. "A little?"

She shifted on the seat. "Not in the way you mean. You . . . confuse me. You make me uncomfortable. But not in any way I've felt before. . . ."

While she was talking, he unfastened his seat belt, and hers, and moved closer. "Uncomfortable?" he asked, propping his hand on the door beside her ear.

"A . . . little," she stammered. He was very close. She could smell the spicy cologne he wore, feel the heat from his body. His lips were at her forehead. "Just . . . a little," she amended.

He laughed softly. "Just a little?"

She struggled to keep her breathing steady, but it was a losing battle. One of his hands came up and rested against her cheek. His thumb worked at her soft lips, parting them very gently.

"I like making you . . . uncomfortable,"

he whispered as his head bent. "Just a little."

His chiseled mouth traced her lips, teasing them apart very tenderly, so that he didn't frighten her. She was very nervous. Her hand came up to touch his, and it was ice-cold. He didn't need a program to know that she wasn't used to having a man this close. It made him feel more protective than ever.

"Easy, now," he whispered, and his lips parted hers so that he could ease between them. "Easy . . . does it."

His mouth moved down onto hers. It was unfamiliar. It was disconcerting. But after a minute, it became more familiar, more comfortable. Very soon, her lips relaxed. Her body relaxed.

She liked it.

He drew her closer, but slowly, gently. He wrapped her up against him like fragile treasure and worked on her mouth until he made her hungry for him.

She reached up, around his neck, and clung to him quite suddenly as the hunger flashed in her like lightning. She kissed him back with the same urgency that he kissed her.

But very soon, it became clear that he was going to have to start undressing her or stop kissing her. It had been a very long dry spell.

He drew back, flattered that he had to uncouple her hands from his neck and ease her away from him.

He smiled gently at her embarrassment. "Don't worry. It's all perfectly natural."

"It . . . is?"

"Yes. It is." He brushed back her hair, loving the feel of it. "We should go inside."

She swallowed. She could still taste him on her lips. He tasted of coffee and mint. She smiled slowly. "I guess so."

He chuckled. He got out and helped her down. He held her hand all the way into the restaurant.

CHAPTER FOUR

"Why did you change your mind about where we ate?" Merissa asked when they were halfway through huge plates of chicken lo mein, which they discovered was a mutual favorite. "I mean, I'm not complaining, I love Chinese food. But why?"

"Same reason I hired a man to sweep my truck for bugs," he said heavily. "It seems I hired the bad guy to put in a surveillance system for me."

"Oh, my gosh!" she exclaimed.

"I'm usually more careful," he said with a smile. "But I had no idea he was that close. You see, your premonition was right on the money. You really do have a gift."

"I hate having it," she replied.

"This time, it might save my life," he said. "I'm grateful."

She grimaced. "I was so afraid, turning up at your door in a snowstorm." She laughed. "But I felt I had to tell you."

"If you hadn't, I'd be in a world of trouble right now," he pointed out. "I had no idea that I was even a target after so long."

"You wouldn't have been, I think, except for the politician running for federal office," she said. "He's trying to get rid of any embarrassing loose ends before the campaign heats up. Imagine what his adversaries could do with information like his friendship with a drug cartel."

"Yes."

"This man you hired, to look for the bugs your adversary placed," she began. "There's a woman. She's in very great danger." She bit her lip.

"She's a photojournalist covering a war in Africa," he supplied, not even uneasy now about her gifts.

She nodded. "An unexpected thing will save her life," she said slowly. "A necklace, of all things."

"She'll be all right?" he asked, concerned.

"She won't die," she amended.

That sounded ominous.

She drew in a breath. "Someone told a lie. It's what separates them. He believed it." She sipped hot tea. "It was said to protect her, but instead it destroyed her happiness." She looked up at him. "She loves him so much," she said heavily. "It's a shame."

He wondered if he should tell Rourke.

"Don't," she said, as if she'd read the thought. "Don't say anything to him. Things are at a crossroads right now. If he acts too soon, she could die. Everything is connected. We live in a silver web of activity, binding all that lives on the earth." She laughed again. "I sound like a tree hugger. Well, I am a tree hugger. But we're much more connected than people think."

"A butterfly flaps its wings and there's a typhoon?" he teased.

"Something like that, yes."

He leaned back in his chair and studied her warmly. "You're amazing," he said. "I've never known anybody like you in my whole life."

"I hope that's a compliment."

"It truly is," he confessed. He smiled. "And tonight is a beginning. Isn't it?"

She started to say something. Her eyes grew opaque. She lost color. Her green eyes were terrified when they met his. "We have to go home. Right now! Please!"

He didn't bother to ask what was wrong. It was enough that she knew something was urgent. He got up and paid the check and then led her out to the truck.

"At my house or yours?" he asked as he

started it.

"Mine. And please, hurry!" she said. "It may be too late already!"

He didn't spare the engine.

They pulled up in front of Merissa's cabin and ran onto the porch. Merissa worked her key in the lock, fumbled and finally opened it.

"Mom!" she called frantically. "Mom!"

There were sounds of movement. A door opened. Clara came out into the hall, a little foggy, laughing.

"Here I am. What's wrong?" she asked when she saw their worried faces.

"I . . . had a feeling," Merissa said, hating to put it even into words, for fear it might come true.

"A feeling?" Clara asked gently, and now she was frowning, too.

Merissa relaxed. She laughed. "I'm sorry. I'm so sorry." She turned to Tank. "I rushed you home for nothing!"

"It's always good to check," Tank replied gently. "I'm beginning to put a lot of confidence in your 'feelings.' "

She smiled at him warmly. "Thanks."

"What sort of feeling?" Clara asked, because she knew that Merissa didn't give way to panic.

"I don't know. Something dangerous.

Something planned." She closed her eyes. "Soon. Very soon." She opened her eyes. "I don't know what!" she groaned.

Clara hugged her. "Don't worry, honey. We'll be okay."

"Just in case," Tank said slowly, "I'm going to put a man over here, to keep an eye on the place."

"That would be so kind of you," Clara began.

Merissa frowned. "Do I smell smoke?"

They split up, going from room to room. All of a sudden, the fire detector in the back bedroom went off like an explosion.

Tank ran ahead of the women, rushed into the room and stopped dead. There was smoke coming from an extension cord. Beside it, a squirrel was squirming in agony.

"Oh, dear," Clara murmured. "I forgot to close the flue in here . . . Squirrels love to come in the cabin and build nests in the ceiling." She grimaced. "Is he dead?"

Tank picked him up. The squirrel was shivering. "He's not dead, but he's going to need some attention. I have a friend who's a wildlife rehabilitator. I'll call him as soon as I get home. Have you got a shoebox and an old towel?"

Clara rushed to get them for him so that he could transport the injured squirrel.

"I'll unplug it."

"Be careful, honey," he told her.

She glanced at him and flushed prettily. She laughed and eased the plug out of the wall.

He loved that blush. He loved calling her pet names. She was the sweetest woman he'd ever known.

"You think he'll be okay?" she asked, gently touching the head of the injured squirrel.

"Careful, he may bite," he said.

"Oh, they never bite me. I've picked up all sorts of injured things, even a snake, once. I had to put a bandage on his back. Weed eater got him," she said ruefully.

"You aren't afraid of snakes?" he asked, curious.

"I'm terrified of them," she said. "But he was bleeding and obviously in pain. So I picked him up. He didn't seem to mind, even when I started putting antibiotic ointment and a big Band-Aid on him. I had to take him to a wildlife rehabilitator, too. I wonder if it's the one you know?"

He chuckled. "Probably. There aren't too many of them around Catelow." He paused. "What sort of snake was he?"

She blinked. "I don't really know. He was quite large."

"Color?"

She described it.

He burst out laughing. "I don't believe it. I just don't believe it. That's a rattlesnake, you crazy woman! They're deadly poisonous!"

"Are they? He was very tolerant. He didn't even rattle when I put him in the box and took him to the rehabilitator. I guess that explains why he was upset when I wanted him to let the snake go. He didn't tell me."

He was amazed, and it showed. "Truly gifted," he murmured.

"Animals like me, I suppose," she said shyly. "I have to shoo the birds away from the feeders. One stood on my wrist while I filled up the tube feeder."

"I like you, too," he said softly, searching her pale eyes.

Her lips parted on a quick breath. "You do?"

He smiled.

"I mean, you're not afraid I might turn you into a frog or something in a temper?" she asked, not quite facetiously.

"You don't have a cat."

"Excuse me?"

"Everybody knows that witches keep cats," he pointed out. "Look it up."

She burst out laughing.

"Should I tell him about the two stray cats we feed every morning?" Clara teased as she came back with a shoebox and a piece of towel.

"Shh!" Merissa said quickly, putting her finger to her lips.

They all laughed.

Tank made holes in the top of the shoebox while Merissa held the squirrel.

"You're going to be just fine, don't worry," she told the little animal. It looked up at her from wide, dilated eyes. It was still shivering.

"I think it's in shock," Tank said. He took the squirrel and put it gently in the box with the towel and closed it up. "I'll call my buddy right away."

"You'll let us know?" Merissa asked.

He smiled. "Of course."

"I hope they don't eat the wiring in the attic," Clara said nervously. "I'm going to close the flue right now!"

"At least he's a boy squirrel. We don't have to worry about any babies in a nest inside that the mother couldn't get to," Merissa said. "They say if it's a mother squirrel and you close her access, the babies will all die. It's so sad."

"True. But so are electrical fires." Tank glanced at the wall where the cord had been plugged in. "Don't use that until I can get one of my men over here to check the wiring."

"Okay," Merissa said. "Thanks. I'm terrified of fire."

"Me, too," Clara seconded.

"Not much danger of that, just from a blown extension cord, especially when you're standing beside it when it blows. But it's always best to be cautious. I'll take our friend home with me. I'll call you tomorrow," he told Merissa.

She grinned. "Okay."

He grinned back. "Good night."

They went out to the porch to see him off. He waved as he went down the driveway, still covered with the remains of the snowstorm.

They went back into the living room. The small Christmas tree they'd put up that day was beautiful with its colored lights. Clara didn't have them set to flash because it gave Merissa headaches. It was pretty just the same. Clara put an arm around Merissa's shoulders. "So now I can see which way the wind is blowing, and I don't even need to be psychic." She laughed.

Merissa leaned her head against her mother's. "I'm so happy. I never expected to find anyone who'd like me the way I am."

"I thought I had, once," Clara said quietly. "I made a terrible mistake. And you paid more for it even than I did."

Merissa was very still. "Dalton knows."

"What?"

"He knows, about what Dad did. He said if he'd known us back then, my father would have gone to prison for it."

"I lived in terror for so many years, afraid that Bill would return, that he'd find us, that he'd want to get even with me for divorcing him," Clara confessed.

"Do you know where he is?" Merissa asked worriedly.

Clara shook her head. "The last I heard, from his cousin who's still in touch with me, he was working on the docks in California. I hope he stays there."

"So do I," Merissa replied. "Oh, so do I!"

Tank drove the squirrel to the rehabilitator. It was necessary, because law prevented any veterinarian from treating a wild animal. That had to be done by a trained rehabilitator, and there were so few that many injured animals died. The rehabilitators were so overworked that many just stopped answering their phones in self-defense, not having realized the incredible number of injured wild animals they were signing up to treat.

The law was in place to protect animals and the public, but it seemed to Tank that it was designed to let wounded wildlife die. Like so many other little-known laws, its good intentions sometimes were outweighed by its tragic consequences.

"At least this one will live," Tank told Greg Barnes, his friend.

"Yeah, he's just shocked and burned a bit." Greg chuckled. "A couple of days rest and some good food, and he'll be back out chewing up electrical cords again." He put the squirrel in a clean cage with water and food. Nearby were many other cages, containing a raccoon with a bandaged leg, a wolf with a leg missing, even a raven with a broken wing.

"What happened to all of these?" Tank asked.

"Kids with guns" came the irritated reply. "A teenager shot the raven for sport. I had words with him and his father, and court action is pending."

Tank shook his head. "And the wolf?"

"Ate two of a rancher's calves. He was trapped. He lost the leg and would have died if I hadn't found him. People and wild animals just don't mix."

"Ranchers have to live."

The rehabilitator nodded. "So they do.

Nobody wins in a situation like this. The rancher is being fined for trapping the wolf. It's an endangered species. The rancher said his calves were also endangered, but it won't help him." He glanced at Tank. "Most of the people who write law concerning wild animals have never seen one." He had a strange, wicked look on his face. "You know, I have this recurring daydream about putting a couple of these legislators in a room with several hungry wolves . . ." He sighed. "Well, never mind. But I guarantee it would change attitudes. The survivors would probably legislate for change." He put his hand to the wolf's muzzle through the cage and stroked it. The wolf didn't seem to mind. "Not you, old fellow," he said gently. "There are sweet wolves and mean wolves. Sort of like people." He glanced at Tank. "But in the wild, a wolf is going to do what comes naturally, whether it's kill and eat elk or cattle. The trick is to make sure the numbers aren't so big that the habitat can support the pack and they don't resort to raiding cattle ranches."

"Don't tell me. Tell Congress."

"Wouldn't I love to tell Congress how I feel about what goes on in the real world out here. How do you tell a wolf it can't cross a property line? Or a raven that if it goes to ground hunting a rabbit it's likely to be shot in lieu of a target?"

"At least you're trying to help," Tank pointed out.

Greg smiled. "Trying to. Yes." He waved an arm around the room full of cages. "I have two more rooms like this." He cocked his head and pursed his lips. "Ever wonder why I'm not married?"

Tank chuckled. "Not really. I don't know a lot of women who'd like to share space with a wolf. Even one in a cage."

"Got a cougar in the other room. A ferret and a couple of skunks. All victims of trapping." He shook his head. "The raven was a special case, I mostly do mammals."

"Who brought him to you?"

He grimaced. "The boy's mother. His dad thought it was great, how he hit the raven on the fly. His mother was horrified."

"Good for her. I like to target shoot, but I don't do it with animals. Well, except deer, in hunting season," he amended. "I love venison."

"Me, too," Greg confessed. "That's rather a different case. Not enough forage for an overpopulation of deer, so we hunt the excess to keep the herds healthy. Can't explain that to outsiders, either. We're killing Bambi."

"Bambi can kill you with those hooves," Tank commented. "They're like razor blades."

"Indeed they are. Deer are powerful, especially the bucks, with those big racks."

"Think the squirrel will live?"

"If he doesn't it won't be my fault," Greg said. He smiled. "I love animals."

"Maybe someday you'll find a woman who does, too."

He shrugged. "Or not." He eyed Tank. "You got this squirrel from Merissa Baker, didn't you?" he asked.

"No comments about curdling milk," Tank said defensively.

"Oh, I didn't mean it like that," Greg replied. "She's got this way with animals, is what I meant," he said. "Brought me a snake one day that she'd bandaged. She was afraid the bandage wouldn't stay on." He whistled. "Biggest damned timber rattler I ever saw, and it was lying in her arms like a baby. Minute I touched it, it tried to strike at me. But I bandaged it and nursed it back to health and turned it loose."

"She told me about that." Tank laughed. He shook his head. "Some gift."

"Some gift. There are people among the Cheyenne tribe here who have it. I've seen them gentle wild horses with just light touches and tone of voice. You know," he added, "maybe there's something to this theory that everything has a soul."

Tank held up both hands. "I have to go."

"Just thinking out loud, is all." Greg chuckled. "Anyway, your squirrel is going to be fine. Might not be a bad idea to truck him up north a few miles to turn him loose. For the sake of the wiring in Merissa's house, that is."

"I was thinking the same thing!"

Tank went back home. He was still laughing about the snake.

"What's funny?" Mallory asked with a grin.

Tank smiled. "Merissa once took a snake to Greg Barnes for treatment."

Mallory shook his head. "I'll bet she hates snakes, too."

"She does, but that isn't what makes the story curious. It was a timber rattler."

Mallory's eyes grew larger. "It didn't bite her?"

"Greg said she brought it in, holding it in her arms, and it just laid there. Until he tried to work on it, that is, and it struck at him." He laughed at his brother's expression. "She has a way with animals."

"A timber rattler." He sighed. "Well, that's

one for the books."

Tank nodded and smiled.

Mallory was watching him with interest. "Things heating up, are they?"

Tank was surprised. "How would you know that?"

"You're my brother. It isn't like you to take an interest in a woman. Well, it's not an everyday thing, at least." Mallory was alluding to his own wife, Morie, in whom Tank had been briefly interested before he realized that Mallory's antagonism to her was concealing a growing passion.

"I love Morie like a sister," Tank said quickly. "Just in case you wondered."

Mallory clapped him on the shoulder. "I know you better than that."

"We had a very nice supper," he recalled with a smile.

"I like the food at that place, too," Mallory began.

"We went to a Chinese place in Powell," Tank corrected.

Mallory's eyebrows lifted. "Why?"

He shrugged, and jerked his head toward the base phone on Mallory's desk in a corner of the living room. "Just wanted a change."

"I see." And Mallory did see. He was aware of the bugs.

Just as he said that, Rourke strolled in, one brown eye twinkling beside the one with the eye patch. His blond hair was thick and combed. He was wearing khakis, a habit from South Africa, where he lived, and he looked very smug.

"Fourteen bugs," he said. "I tweaked them all. He'll be listening, alternately, to ball games from San Francisco, police calls from Catelow and pings from the International Space Station." He grinned.

They laughed. "Well, that's a relief. I was afraid to say anything out loud," Tank told him. "In fact, I took my girl to a restaurant in Powell because I was afraid they might have bugged the one in Catelow since I mentioned it in front of the phone." He hesitated. "I'm probably paranoid."

"You're not," Rourke commented. "They probably did have someone standing by to slip a bug under the table wherever you sat. Someone working as a temporary waiter."

"You're good," Tank mused.

Rourke shrugged. "Years of practice. I used to work for Interpol, a long time ago. But the pay was somewhat less than I earn with small arms in dangerous places."

"Hazardous work," Mallory commented.

Rourke nodded. "But it's what I do best." He sighed. "There's a revolution going on in a country near mine. Near Kenya. I was on my way there when you called for help." He smiled at Tank's guilty expression.

Tank knew about Rourke's friend, Tat. He almost mentioned what Merissa had told him but he paused. She'd warned him to say nothing or it might cost the photojournalist her life. He kept his silence.

"Sorry about that," Tank said gently.

Rourke shrugged again. "No big deal. I can go later. It's not as if the war will be over in a day or two. Sad case. The president of the country is Harvard-educated, he's brilliant and he has a feel for politics. His opponent comes from some dusty backwater village and he can't even sign his own name." His expression became grim. "He's ordered women and children butchered for daring to help the government forces, in ways I can't even tell you about. It's like tribal warfare back in the 1800s, only worse." He looked at Tank. "Even having been in a war in the Middle East, you have no idea how warfare is conducted in such places. I've been shot at by eight-year-olds with AK-47s."

"Child soldiers." Tank's expression was eloquent. "People who employ them should be tried and shot."

"They will be, when the president is back

in his office. And he'll prevail. I'm certain of it. He has the backing of most of the Western nations." His smile was sarcastic. "His country is almost floating on oil, you see. Some of his advisors are spec ops people from a country I won't name."

Tank sighed. "At least he has help."

"A lot of it. But meanwhile, whole villages are being burned out, their populations decimated. Crops are destroyed before harvest, so the refugee population grows daily. Borders are closing around the country, so there are tent camps set up everywhere. It's the most heart-rending thing I've ever seen."

"War is ugly," Tank agreed. "Thanks for taking care of the bugs," he added, changing the subject. "I was starting to twitch every time I looked at the phone."

Rourke smiled. "I know that feeling."

He turned. "I've got to talk to our electrician. I want him to go over to the Baker house and fix an electrical problem that the squirrel caused."

"Is the squirrel returning when it's mended?" Rourke wondered.

"Nah. Greg's going to release it a few miles north."

Rourke pursed his lips. "Does a squirrel have built-in GPS?"

Tank burst out laughing. "I don't know. Maybe I should look that up before he has time to release the varmint."

"Not a bad idea," Mallory added. He made a face. "I wish Morie and my son would come back. I'm lonely."

"I imagine Cane is, too." Tank chuckled. "He'll be missing Bodie, especially since she's pregnant. He paces and paces, worrying about her."

"Shopping trips." Mallory shook his head. "I don't know why they can't shop in Catelow."

"Big Paris fashion boutiques and fancy baby boutiques on the go in Catelow, are there?" Rourke asked with a bland expression.

"Well, not so much," Mallory replied with twinkling eyes.

"Good point," Tank replied. He was thinking of Paris fashions and how they'd look on Merissa, with her neat, trim figure.

"You need to bring Merissa to dinner when they get home," Mallory commented as they wandered out of the house toward the bunkhouse.

Tank's heart jumped. He smiled. "That's a good idea."

Mallory just laughed.

■ ■ ■ ■

The electrician went to the Baker home, but midway there, he hit something and had to pull off the road. He got out to see what had stopped him and found, of all things, a spike strip, like policemen used to trap fleeing criminals, lying across the asphalt. He pulled it to the side of the road and left it, then called Darby Hanes.

"Can't you just change the tire?" Darby asked, surprised.

"I've got four flats," the electrician, Ben, muttered. "I don't carry four spare tires on this thing."

"Good Lord, what'd you hit?" Darby exclaimed.

"A spike strip," Ben said disgustedly. "I can't imagine why the police left it here for people to run over!"

"What police? You're out in the country. And I haven't heard anything about a chase."

"I know."

"Call the wrecker. I'll be right there."

"No need, Darby. I'll go with the truck and wait while they get the tires on it. I'll phone the Bakers and explain."

"Well, okay. That might be best. While

you're there, get them to check the battery. Replace it if you need to. Truck's been hard to start lately."

"I noticed. I'll do that."

Ben sighed and called for the truck to be towed. As an afterthought, he tried to phone Merissa and explain the delay, but her phone didn't seem to be working. No matter, he'd phone from the mechanic's shop later. Surely it wouldn't take that long for the mechanic to do the job.

"There," the electrician said with a smile. "All done."

Merissa grinned. The man had been thorough. He'd checked all the phones and the wiring, and replaced the outlet where the squirrel had bitten the extension cord through and caused the short. He'd even checked out Merissa's computer, just to be safe. Since it was so important to her job, he added, it wouldn't hurt to make sure it was in good working order. She'd agreed.

"That's so kind of you,' she told him. "Thanks a million. I'd be happy to pay you . . .'"

He waved payment away. "It's just my job. I'm glad to help."

She walked him out to the porch. He was driving a black sedan, nothing fancy. She wondered why he hadn't come in a ranch truck, but perhaps he had somewhere personal to go and didn't want to use the ranch's gas for it. She wondered why the man gave her an uneasy feeling. Probably, she reasoned, she was getting paranoid. He was personable and seemed very kind. Still . . .

"Well, thanks again," she said.

He turned and smiled. He was tall and slender, with brown hair and dark eyes, very dignified. He didn't look like a ranch hand at all. "My pleasure," he said. He climbed into the car and drove away.

"What a very nice man," Merissa said to her mother.

"Yes. The Kirks have been good to us." She hugged her daughter. "I'm so glad that we still have each other. If Bill hadn't gone away when he did . . ."

"Don't think about it," Merissa said, hugging her close.

Clara sighed. "I can't help it. You know, San Francisco isn't that far away, and Bill works for a shipping company on the docks, Meriwether's. If he knew we were still here, if he ever tried to return . . . !"

"He won't come back," Merissa said softly. "You told his cousin that we were living in Billings, didn't you?"

"Yes." She relaxed. "Yes, I did. And I know he doesn't have caller ID, so he wouldn't notice the area code or the number. I'm sorry. It's just that I've lived in fear all these years that he'd want revenge, that he'd try to do something awful to us."

"He won't come back," Merissa assured her. "He won't."

Clara drew back and smiled. "You're right, of course."

"Of course! So let's go have supper."

"That is an excellent idea," Clara agreed, leading the way into the kitchen.

Later, Tank phoned them. "I'm sorry Ben didn't make it over there," he said. "He had to go with the truck and wait while they replaced the tires. The mechanic was swamped, so it took a long time. He said he tried to call you and couldn't get through."

"Odd," she remarked. "The phone didn't ring."

That was puzzling, but the snowstorm did make the power and phone service a little sporadic lately. "Well, anyway, he'll get there first thing in the morning."

"Ben?" Merissa asked, stunned. "Who's Ben?"

"Our electrician," he replied. "The one

who was coming over to replace your wall outlet."

"But . . . the electrician came," she faltered. "He checked out everything, even my computer, and redid the wiring . . ."

"I'll be right over," Tank said curtly, and hung up.

Merissa looked at the phone with a puzzled expression. She wondered why Tank sounded so upset. Then she remembered what he'd said. His electrician hadn't come? So who was the nice man who'd fixed the wiring?

CHAPTER FIVE

Merissa met Tank at the front door. He got out of the ranch truck with another man, a tall, blond man with one eye and an eye patch. "But he already fixed the wiring," she began.

Tank put his finger to his lips. He looked at the other man and nodded. The man with one eye grinned at Merissa and went past her into the house.

"Don't say a word," Tank told her. "But come with us and show Rourke what the man worked on."

She went pale. "It was the man who's after you, wasn't it? I knew there was something wrong about him. And I didn't even realize . . . !"

She was heartsick.

He drew her into his arms and hugged her close. "It's all right," he said softly. "Don't worry about it. We'll make every- thing right. Come on, honey."

He held her hand and led her back into the house. Clara was standing in the hall with Rourke already.

Merissa led the men through the house, pointing out everywhere her visitor had been. It took a long time. Rourke used some odd instrument to pinpoint every small, unnoticeable change. He removed several components, even one from Merissa's own computer tower, a flash drive she hadn't even noticed, hidden in the back of the computer, in a place she never used.

Finally Rourke loaded all the bugs into a small bag and carried them out to the bed of the pickup truck.

He came back inside grinning. "He was efficient," he mused. "But the work was just a little sloppy. I suppose he thought your man might show up sooner than he expected," he told Tank.

"A good thing he didn't," Tank replied. "There might have been trouble."

"Just what I was thinking," Rourke added. He smiled at Merissa. "Everything is fine," he told her when he saw her expression. "Most people wouldn't have suspected him of foul play. He seems to be quite good at disguise."

"He was polite and he had nice manners," Merissa said heavily, sitting down at her desk. "I didn't even realize . . ."

"Hold it," Rourke said. He had an instrument in his hand and it was flashing. He motioned Merissa out of her chair. He got down on one knee, looked under the desk and extricated a small device.

"Hi, pal," Rourke said into it. "Sorry about the earache, mate." And he smashed the device with his shoe. He chuckled. "Missed that one. He'll have a hell of an earache, I hope."

Merissa ground her teeth together. She wasn't used to espionage of any kind, and it disturbed her. The man had rung alarm bells in her head, but she hadn't felt that intuitive something that told her the whole situation was wrong. That was unusual. But, then, her gift was sporadic, which was why it was so difficult for scientists to accept the validity of such unusual abilities.

"I should have seen it, though," she pointed out.

"You're not infallible," Tank said fondly, and with a smile. "I don't mind. It makes you more like the rest of us. We make mistakes, too."

"Seen what?" Rourke asked, frowning.

Tank hesitated. "She sees things. She knows things before they happen," he said reluctantly.

"Ah, yes." Rourke wasn't weirded out. He just smiled. "I have this old chap who works for me, on my place in South Africa. He has a gift like that. I learned long ago to listen when he made warnings."

Merissa was fascinated. "You don't think I curdle milk, then?"

He burst out laughing. "Not at all. I'm rather used to psychic phenomena. Africa is a place of the supernatural, you know. We're surrounded by it. Many of the native people still cling to old beliefs and ancient ways. They're wiser than we are. We think we own the world. They know we don't, that there are forces far more powerful than our modern devices."

She was fascinated. "I've always loved reading about Africa. There are webcams all over that you can plug into and watch wildlife in real time."

He nodded.

"It's very nice for people who can't go there," she said. Her eyes took on a merry gleam. "And there's always YouTube," she added. "I've been to all sorts of mysterious places through the eyes of personal video cameras."

"Why would he plant bugs here?" Tank asked suddenly.

Rourke glanced at him. "Because he

knows you have an interest . . . here."

Tank felt sick to his stomach. He looked at Clara and Merissa, recalled the anguish they'd been through at the hands of Merissa's brutal father. Now he was putting them in danger, just by being close to them.

Merissa walked up to him and looked up into his eyes. "Some things happen because it's part of a plan, one we don't know about, can't know about. Life is a test. Life is lessons. People come into our lives at certain times, for certain reasons."

"Predestination," Rourke mused, nodding his head.

"Well, sort of," she faltered. "I mean, the future isn't set in stone. I think it can be changed by decisions we make. But I think there's some overall plan for our lives. We call it God," she said, nodding toward her mother. "Other people call it fate or luck or chance. But I do believe in it."

"So do I," Tank replied, and looked deeply into her eyes for so long that she flushed a little.

"Did you say anything in here that you would have minded him hearing?" Rourke interrupted, looking from one woman to the other.

"Nothing at all." Clara laughed. "Just general conversation."

Merissa nodded. She didn't want to re-mind Clara that they'd been talking about her father. But that wasn't what the shadowy eavesdropper was interested in. He wanted to know about Tank, about his movements, where he was, what he was doing. He was planning tragedy for Tank, not for Merissa and Clara. So she kept her silence.

"We'd better go," Rourke said.

Tank nodded. He touched Merissa's cheek with his finger. "Don't worry, everything's back to the way it was."

"He did a pretty good job on the wiring, coincidentally," Rourke told them. "If he hadn't added the bugs at the same time, I'd call it perfect."

"He wasn't expecting a surveillance expert to check his work, I imagine," Tank said, tongue-in-cheek. "Oh, Greg's going to mend your squirrel and truck him up north to release him," he added. He smiled. "The little guy's going to be fine."

"Thank goodness." She sighed.

Tank lifted his forefinger. "No saving snakes."

She put up both hands, palm out, and grinned. "It's winter. No snakes to save."

"Good point."

He followed Rourke down the steps and into the truck. He waved as they drove off.

"Saving snakes?" Rourke queried.

Tank chuckled. "That's a story and a half. Let me tell you about it." He did, all the way home. Rourke almost fell out of the truck laughing.

Merissa worried about the conversation she and her mother'd had — the one about her father. She knew the criminals weren't going to be concerned with her, but it disturbed her that they'd mentioned her father's employer, and his location.

"You don't surely think they'd call him for some reason?" Merissa wondered aloud, having explained her fears to her mother.

"Sweetheart, why would they?" Clara asked reasonably. "They don't have any quarrel with us."

"They wired our house . . ."

"To get information about Dalton," Clara said sadly. "I'm sorry about that, but it doesn't put us on the firing line. They're just desperate for any tidbits on his movements. It doesn't concern us."

"I suppose you're right," Merissa replied.

"Of course I am. Want to watch the news with me?" she asked.

Merissa shook her head. "I think I'll work for a while."

She smiled. "Good idea. Take your mind

off things."

"Just what I was thinking."

She went into her small office and sat down at the desk.

Tank was watching the news when the doorbell rang. He was alone at the house. The wives had returned home, and then they had all flown to Denver for a cattle show. It had been planned for a while, but it was a good thing, under the circumstances. Tank had worried about having family members in the way, in case the rogue agent made a move.

Christmas was a few days in the future, but he didn't mind being by himself. Rourke was around, and so were plenty of cowboys. It wasn't as if he was alone. Now that the snowfall had stopped, there was a window that allowed them out of town. At least, temporarily.

Mavie opened the door to two gentlemen wearing dark suits. One was slender and olive-skinned with long black hair in a ponytail. The other was blond with dark eyes. Both were unsmiling.

She raised her eyebrows and looked wary. "We haven't seen any flying saucers."

They burst out laughing at the "men in black" assumption. She grinned. "Can I help you?"

"We're here to see Dalton Kirk. Is he in?" the dark-haired one asked politely.

"Yes. Come in out of the cold."

Dalton, hearing voices, came into the hall. He frowned. Were these more of the bogus fed's accomplices?

"I'm Jon Blackhawk, Senior FBI agent from San Antonio, Texas," the dark-haired one said politely. "This —" he indicated his companion "— is Garon Grier, he's SAC at my office." They both produced credentials for his inspection. He handed them back.

"SAC?" Dalton asked, frowning.

"Senior Agent in Charge," Garon replied. He smiled. It looked as if he didn't do it often. "We heard about your visitor. We'd like to talk to you. We're friends of Sheriff Hayes Carson, from Jacobs County. He's involved in a case we're working."

"Come in and have a seat," Dalton said, leading them to the living room. He turned off the television. "Mavie, can you bring coffee, please?"

"Certainly. It'll be right up," she said politely.

The two men sat down on the sofa, facing Dalton in his easy chair. "We've done some checking," Blackhawk said. "I know this is an unpleasant memory for you to revisit,

112

but we need to speak to you about what happened when you worked for the Border Patrol in Arizona."

Dalton took a breath and managed a faint smile. "Not a subject I revisit often," he agreed. "But I can tell you what I remember."

"Please," Grier added.

"There was a man. I'd forgotten until a friend of mine —" he didn't name Merissa or the circumstances under which she knew about the man "— brought it up. There was a DEA agent who came to me about a possible incursion in my territory. He said a shipment of narcotics was being brought across by men in paramilitary uniforms and he needed assistance to stop them." His eyes narrowed with memory. "He was in an unmarked car. I was in my patrol vehicle. I followed him to the site. It was dark, but there was a full moon, so I could see the movement. I got out of my vehicle and when I saw the perpetrators, I realized that I needed backup. But when I went to call it in, he stopped me. He said that he had other agents in place, I just needed to go in with him to support them."

"He said there were other agents there?"

"Yes. I had no reason to distrust him. He had proper ID. I always check," he added.

"Checked, that is. Anyway, I pulled my service weapon and we went in sight of the suspects. He called out first that we were federal agents, for them to stand down and put their arms on the ground."

He blinked. "The rest . . . is still a bit hazy. I was shot, but not by the suspects. The shot seemed to come from behind me. It hit my lung. I went down. I remember looking up at this flashy Hispanic man. He had a gold-plated automatic aimed at me and he was smiling. He said that it was stupid to tangle with a cartel the size of his, and that I wouldn't have the chance to do it again. I remember it felt like being hit by a fist, several times. I lost consciousness and came to in the hospital."

"How did you get there?"

Tank managed a smile. He felt as if there was bile in his throat. The memory was still sickening. "Of all things, I honestly believe it was one of the mules who called an ambulance. He slipped back when the other men were driving away. The other man, I vaguely remember, was cursing because he'd called for help. They argued. I passed out before they left. I talked to dispatch when I got out of the hospital. The 911 operator said the Hispanic man actually apologized and said that if he could have stopped it, he would have. He said that he and his family would pray for me." He shook his head. "They must have, because the doctors said they'd never seen a man in my condition live to tell about it."

Blackhawk winced. "I know about gunshot wounds. My brother worked for us, and for the CIA. Over the years, he was shot at least twice, and one wound was life-threatening. It was rough on the family as well as on him."

"My brothers almost went crazy," Tank recalled quietly. His eyes fell. "So did I. I didn't deal with it well." He shrugged and managed a smile. "I'm still not dealing with it all that well." He shook his head. "I was in the hospital for weeks."

Grier's dark eyes were icy. "These people think of their adversaries as insects. They don't mind killing anyone — women, children, it's all the same to them. The only thing they care about is the money."

Tank laughed shortly. "I noticed. The guy had a gold-plated automatic, for God's sake!"

"Did Sheriff Hayes tell you how he and his new wife escaped the kidnappers?" Blackhawk asked with a smile in his black eyes.

"He did tell me some things about it, but

not all the details," Tank replied.

The two visitors exchanged glances. "One of the kidnappers owned the house where they were kept. He had an outhouse with, get this, a gold-plated, jewel-encrusted toilet paper holder. She used it to cut through their bonds."

Tank laughed. "I don't believe it!"

"Neither did they." Grier shook his head. "I thought I'd heard everything. I used to work with our Hostage Rescue Team," he added. "I do know about hostage-taking. In many cases, the victims are dead in the first twenty-four hours. Hayes and his wife were very lucky."

"Which brings us to you, and the purpose of our visit," Blackhawk added, leaning forward. "Hayes Carson arrested a major player in the cartel, which was founded by the late, great drug lord they called El Ladron. The guy was carrying gold-plated hardware. Thing is, Hayes Carson was in the company of a supposed DEA agent. When people started asking questions about the man, and started digging into his identity, things popped. A bogus secretary got a job with Carson's office and managed to get her hands on the computer — she erased evidence of the man's presence at the arrest. When they hired an outside consultant to try to recover the evidence from the hard drive, he was killed."

"This sounds big," Tank said quietly.

"It is big," Grier added. "Obviously somebody doesn't want the agent identified. We want to know why."

"Especially since it seems he's been feeding information to the major drug cartels for several years, as a rogue DEA agent," Blackhawk agreed.

"If you can remember anything, you need to tell us," Grier said. "We have reason to believe there may be a connection between the rogue agent and a politician who's running for office."

Tank stared at them, frowning. He'd heard all this, but he did have a question. "What does that have to do with the cartels?"

"One of them seems to be feeding money to his campaign, hoping for better access across the border with his election," Blackhawk said solemnly. "It's an ugly business. And we also have reason to believe that the rogue agent has a background in assassination."

"This just gets better and better," Tank said, shaking his head.

"What can you tell us?" Grier asked.

"For one thing, your rogue fed posed as a surveillance firm installer and bugged my damned house," Tank said.

Grier looked around worriedly.

"No worries" came a good-natured voice from the doorway. "I fried them. The chap's good, but he leaves a lot of nasty footprints!"

Blackhawk glared at him. "Rourke. What the hell are you doing here?"

"Working," Rourke said with a grin. "You boys are a long way from home."

"You know Rourke?" Tank asked the men.

"Yes," they said in unison, and not in a happy tone.

"Now, now." Rourke chuckled. "I don't step on your toes. At least, not much." He sobered. "This chap is quite good. He's efficient and he has all the aspects of a chameleon. If he has a background in assassination, Cy Parks has a man working for him who might know something about him."

"Carson."

"The sheriff?" Tank asked.

Blackhawk shook his head. "Not the same Carson. This one is Lakota." He made a face. "We have a mutual cousin."

"He's Native American?" Tank asked.

Grier nodded. "Damned good at his job. He was employed by the government at one point. But he didn't fit comfortably in a conventional unit, so they transferred him to spec ops. He worked with us on one job." He shook his head. "Scary fellow."

"Bad attitude," Blackhawk agreed. "Most snipers miss occasionally. This guy — never."

"We'll talk to him when we get back home," Blackhawk said. He cocked his head at Rourke. "I thought you were bogged down in that job in South Africa."

"I made enemies," Rourke said shortly, and he didn't smile. "I hate damned politicians. They're arming eight-year-old kids and sending them out with automatic weapons, too doped up to care what they shoot."

"Run for public office and put a stop to it," Grier suggested.

Rourke made a sound deep in his throat. "Not in that country. All I want for Christmas is to see the rebel leader hung by his entrails."

"Bloodthirsty," Blackhawk muttered.

"Not if you saw what he did to a village near the capital," Rourke replied.

"How do you know Kirk here?" Grier asked him.

"I was on special assignment back in the day when Tank was serving in Iraq."

"Tank?"

Tank grinned. "I killed one. They stuck me with the nickname and I've had it ever

119

since. I came out of the army and landed a job with the border patrol." He looked at his two visitors. "I never want to wear a badge again."

"Well, the job does have a few drawbacks," Blackhawk said mildly, and smiled. He glanced at Grier. "Our wives forget what we look like from time to time."

"You married?" Grier asked Tank.

"Not yet." Tank laughed. "Haven't really thought about it much." He was thinking about it now, but he wasn't going to share those very personal thoughts with his guests.

"Can you describe the man who led you into the ambush with the drug cartel?" Grier asked.

"Yes. He was a tall blond man with black hair, short, had a British accent and a Texas drawl and red hair and spoke with a Massachusetts accent," he rattled off, tongue-in-cheek.

They blinked.

"Same suit, different face, hair color, complexion and accent," Tank told them. "The guy who came out here to install the surveillance cameras was the same height, but everything else was different. He's a chameleon."

"I'm beginning to realize that," Blackhawk replied. "The descriptions we're getting of him are just the same. His height seems to be the only constant."

"No," Rourke interrupted, shoving his hands into the pockets of his khaki slacks. "There's another. He's a master of disguise. Even in a field of spies, that talent would stand out enough to be conspicuous. That's your key. That's where to start looking. And Carson would be your best bet to find a trail."

"Not to mention the politician who's lining up to go to bed with the drug cartels," Tank added. "Might not be a bad idea to put a tail on him."

Blackhawk pursed his lips. "Not bad at all."

"Which is why we've already done it," Grier said.

"Way ahead of me," Tank said. "See why I'm not in law enforcement anymore?"

"What bothers me is why he's after him," Rourke said, indicating Tank. "He can't really identify the man. If he could, the would-be assassin would have no problem just killing him outright." He hesitated. "And if he was here on your place, why not just shoot you down in your own front yard?"

Tank stared at him. "There were witnesses when he was here. We had several cowboys working in and around the house, and our men go armed in winter. Wolves," he explained.

"It's illegal to shoot a wolf," Blackhawk reminded him.

"Yes, it is, but if a rabid one goes for my throat, I'm shooting him and the charges be damned," Tank replied firmly.

Both men chuckled.

"He bugged the phones at the Bakers' home, too," Rourke reminded Tank.

"The Bakers?" Grier asked.

"She's a . . . friend of mine," Tank said.

"With rather special skills," Rourke said.

Tank gave him an irritated glance.

"What sort of skills?" Blackhawk asked.

Tank hesitated.

"Tell them," Rourke said firmly.

Tank sighed. "She's psychic. I don't mean like those people on television who charge money to tell you things you want to hear. She's the real thing. She came over here in a blizzard to warn me that a man was going to try to kill me because of something I didn't remember. She described the shooting, every detail. She didn't even know me when it happened, and she sure as hell wasn't there," he added firmly. He shrugged. "Spooked me, I can tell you. She told our foreman, Darby Hanes, to take someone with him when he went to cut a tree that had fallen on the fence line. He didn't want to, but I made him." He paused. "Tree fell on him and he became stuck. He would have died if he hadn't taken another hand along."

Blackhawk just nodded. "We have people in our community in Oklahoma with that gift. Science won't believe it exists. But it does," he added quietly. "I've seen it work. She might have saved your life."

"And put herself on the firing line," Grier interrupted. "If he's after you and he knows about her gift, she may be in danger, as well."

"I'm taking care of that," Rourke told them. "Nobody's hurting her. I promise you."

Grier's eyes were narrowed. "I still don't understand why he's after you," he said thoughtfully. "Sure, you might be able to describe his height, remember something about the way he looked or walked or stood. But he's paranoid about getting rid of anyone with any sort of memory about him. He had a computer expert killed in Texas for trying to recover an image off a hard drive in Sheriff Carson's office. He's gone to great expense trying to bug your house." He frowned. "It doesn't make sense."

"What did your friend say again, about the reason?" Blackhawk prompted Tank.

"She said he was after me because of something I didn't remember."

Grier glanced at his companion. "Perhaps a hypnotist."

Blackhawk nodded. "I was thinking the same thing."

Tank frowned. "Excuse me?"

"We've done it out of desperation a time or two in murder cases. Sometimes you see things but don't remember them. Like a license plate number or an identifying mark. Little things solve big cases," Blackhawk said.

Grier nodded. "Would you be willing to do it, if we could get someone up here?"

"Certainly," Tank agreed. "But I'd already promised Sheriff Carson I'd fly down there to talk to him in person."

"We could set it up at his office," Grier replied. "In fact, I know a hypnotist in San Antonio who's worked with us before on cases."

"Let me wait until my brothers get back from that conference in Denver," Tank asked. "I can't leave the ranch with no one in charge here." What he really meant was that he couldn't leave Merissa. The stalker had been in her house. God knew what he might do if she was alone, without Tank's protection. Mallory and Cane would make sure nothing happened to her, or Clara, in his absence.

"Not a problem," Grier said. "Think you can make it before Christmas?"

"Yes. I'll make my arrangements and get in touch with you when I'm coming," Tank told them.

"That's a deal."

They finished the coffee, complimented Mavie on its strong perfection, shook hands with Tank and left.

"Is something going on that I shouldn't know about?" Mavie wanted to know.

Tank shrugged. "A lot, probably, but we don't keep secrets from you," he added with a smile. "They want me to see a hypnotist. They think I might remember something about the man who shot me."

Mavie shivered. "That might not be a good thing, boss. You remember too much as it is."

"I was thinking the same thing." He smiled. "I'm going to get some paperwork going in the office."

"I'll clean up the kitchen, then I may go watch television before it's time to make supper."

"You and your soap operas." He rolled his eyes.

"Getting harder to find one to watch, they're cancelling so many of them." She sighed. "I miss the old days and the old soaps." She shook her head. "These new ones are heavy on intimate stuff and spare on relationships."

"Sort of like the movies." He studied her. "You know, Hollywood producers never seem to notice what keeps drawing people back to movies like *The Sound of Music* and *The Day the Earth Stood Still* and *Ben-Hur*. It's because they were powerful stories about people, and you could take your children to see them. Except for cartoon movies, what sort of films can you take children to see these days?"

"I loved *Star Wars.*" Mavie sighed.

"Yes, well there are rumors that they're going to make the new ones more adult-friendly."

Mavie glowered. "I can see where that's headed, if it's not just rumors. I guess *Star Wars* will just be for grown-ups now."

Tank laughed. "They will never do that. Imagine having to give up on all that merchandising for kids."

"Well, I hope you're right." She threw up her hands and went back to the kitchen, muttering about the world in general and modern movies in particular.

CHAPTER SIX

"You're going to Texas!" Mallory exclaimed when he got home.

Tank nodded. "I need to talk to the sheriff down there and compare notes. Maybe we both saw something that we don't remember and discussing it will pop it out."

"It's dangerous," Cane said quietly. "For you to go alone."

"I'm not taking Rourke with me," he told his brothers. "In case you wondered. He's needed here, to keep an eye on you and the Bakers."

"But, Tank . . ." Mallory began to protest.

"Not to worry," Rourke interrupted as he came into the room. "Sorry, didn't mean to intrude, but I've got it covered. He won't be going alone."

"You're not coming with me," Tank said shortly.

"No. But I have someone who'll be at the airport when you get there."

"Who?" Tank asked.

"Nobody you know. Nobody you'll recognize. And nobody will recognize him, either. But he'll be watching. If you get into any trouble at all, you'll be safe."

"Thanks, Rourke," Mallory said. "I was concerned."

"Yeah, me, too," Cane replied.

"I'm a grown man," Tank protested.

"Yes, but you're our brother, too," Mallory said, "and we worry."

He grinned at them. "Nice of you."

"We'd miss the piano playing," Cane said with a twinkle in his eyes. "Even if it is pretty sad compared to Mallory's."

Mallory grinned. "Truer words were never spoken."

Tank threw a napkin at him.

He booked a flight online and then he drove over to Merissa's house to see her.

"I'm going to Texas," he said while they drank coffee in her kitchen at the little white table. Clara, discreetly, left them alone.

"To see Sheriff Carson." She nodded.

He laughed wryly. "Nothing gets by you."

"Not much, anyway." She sipped coffee.

"Do you see anything?" he asked.

She searched his eyes. The look was long and intent and she blushed and laughed.

"No. I mean, I don't see anything bad."

He reached across the table and took her hand in his. "You know," he said, "I could really get addicted to that pink blush. It makes me feel dangerous."

She laughed. "You're not dangerous. Well, maybe a little."

He smoothed his thumb over her soft palm. His expression hardened somewhat. "You already know about the way I was shot."

"Yes."

He turned her hand over and looked at it instead of her. "There are scars. Some of them are pretty bad. I never wear cutoffs, even in summer. Or go bare-chested."

"You think the scars would matter to me?" she asked softly. She smiled. "Silly man."

His eyes jumped up to hers. "Are you sure? Or are you just guessing?"

She started to speak when Clara came to the door carrying her purse. "I have to run to the store. I'm out of walnuts!"

Tank stared at her.

She grimaced. "Well, it's winter and we feed birds. We feed lots of birds," she explained. "There's this gorgeous woodpecker —"

"Yes, he drills on the wall outside every

morning until we put walnut halves on the fence."

Tank blinked. "Walnuts?"

Clara laughed. "We buy walnuts in bulk. The woodpecker loves them. There are two pairs of them. And of course we have the little birds that stay year-round." She sighed. "But I'm out of walnuts and he's outside my bedroom window right now. Can't you hear that?"

They listened. There was a loud drumming sound, like wood being hit with a nail over and over again.

"It's him," Clara explained. "He won't stop until he gets fed, and I've nothing to feed him. So I have to run to the market."

"Be careful," Merissa said.

"I'm always careful. I won't be ten minutes." She waved and ran out the door.

"Don't run, there's ice!" Merissa called after her.

"Okay!" Clara called back. There was the sound of a car door opening and closing, and then an engine that eventually fired up.

Merissa winced as the car made it out of the yard. "I had a mechanic check it out for me," she said heavily. "It starts only when it wants to."

"I'll have my mechanic come over and see about it."

"Oh, no, please. You've done so much for us already . . . !"

He smoothed over her hand. "I have to take care of my best girl," he said softly. He tugged on her hand. "Come here," he said softly.

That deep note in his voice melted her. She got up from her chair and let him pull her gently down onto his lap.

"You need to see what you're getting into," he said quietly. He unbuttoned his shirt and pulled it away from his muscular, hair-covered chest.

She was so fascinated with this view of him that she didn't notice the scars.

That rapt stare made him laugh. He'd been uneasy about showing her what the bullets had done, but she didn't seem to find him unpleasant. In fact, her stare was flattering.

He drew her hand to the muscles under the thick, soft hair. "Here." He drew her fingers over the thick scars where the bullets had gone in. Two had hit him in the lung and collapsed it. Another had passed under his rib cage. Two had hit his legs, in the thighs, and it had taken several surgeries to remove splintered bone and repair muscle.

"I've never touched a man like this," she

faltered.

He smiled. "I like that."

"You do? Really?" she asked softly. "I was afraid . . . Well, you know, some modern men think it's really stupid that women don't pass themselves around like drinks at a bar."

"I'm not one of them. I'm pretty old-fashioned myself."

She traced around one of the scars and winced. "This must have been horribly painful, Dalton," she said.

He liked the way his given name sounded on her lips. She was soft and warm and sweet. He looked at her mouth and ached to catch it under his. The way she was touching him was very arousing.

He bent and took her lips softly under his. "You taste like black coffee," he whispered, chuckling.

She smiled under his lips. "So do you."

He drew her head down against his shoulder and looked long and deep into her eyes until she flushed at the intensity. He didn't smile. Neither did she.

He looked at her mouth, pretty and slightly red from the pressure of his lips. "It's been a long time since I felt so much hunger for a woman's touch," he whispered. "A very long time."

His mouth pressed down on hers, gently parting her lips, moving under them with a slow, steady pressure that grew harder and hungrier by the second.

He lifted her closer, feeling her soft hand tangling in the thick hair on his chest while the kiss became so passionate that she moaned.

His hand found the hem of her T-shirt and moved under it, up to the frilly little bra that covered her. He unfastened it and found the firm, hard-tipped flesh with his fingers.

She gasped, but she didn't protest.

"Trust me," he whispered at her mouth. "But not . . . too far."

He pulled up the hem and before she realized what he meant to do, his mouth opened on her breast, taking all of it inside, working the nipple hard with his tongue while he suckled her.

She cried out, a sound that penetrated his spinning brain as if from a distance. She tasted like the sweetest sugar on earth. His free hand went down her back, into the waistband of her jeans and around, over the soft flesh on her hip, around to the front, to her belly.

"Dal . . . ton?" she whimpered.

"Dear God," he groaned.

He stood up, carrying her down the hall to her bedroom. He kicked the door shut behind him.

"Mama will be home . . . soon," she choked out in a voice that she almost didn't recognize.

"I'll hear her," he lied.

He slid her down on the bed and stripped her to the waist, throwing off his own shirt at the same time.

He smoothed his body down over hers, shifting her legs so that he could sink down between them, while his hair-roughened chest buried her soft breasts under it.

His hand went under her hips, lifting her into the sudden hard thrust of his body. "Beautiful," he whispered, looking at her breasts as he moved roughly against her hips. "So beautiful!"

He was causing sensations within her that she'd never known. The pleasure was shocking. It lifted her body in an arch as she struggled to get even closer. She hadn't the will to protest what he was doing to her. She loved the weight of him, the feel of him so intimately close.

"It feels . . . so sweet," she gasped as he fed on her breasts.

"Imagine how it would feel inside you," he whispered at her mouth. "Hard, and deep . . ."

She cried out. He smothered the sound under his devouring lips while his hips moved insistently on hers. She could feel him growing even more potent by the second.

"Merissa," he groaned. "It's been so long . . . !"

He unzipped her jeans. He was pulling them down when the sound of a car pulling up out front with its roaring engine shocked them into stillness.

"No," he groaned again, shivering.

She held him tightly, kissing his neck. "It's all right," she whispered. "It's all right."

"That's what . . . you think."

He managed to roll off the bed and went into her bathroom.

She got dressed quickly, opened the door and went into the kitchen. She peered into the window, seeing her disheveled reflection. Well, it might look as if they'd been kissing, but her mother wouldn't suspect anything more. She hoped. She dabbed water on her face and wiped it with a paper towel.

The front door opened.

"I'm back," Clara called.

"I'm in here," Merissa called. She smiled at her mother. "Dalton's in the bathroom,"

136

she whispered.

"Ah." Clara put the walnuts on the counter. "The car's making funny noises," she said sadly. "I don't know what to do."

"I do," Dalton said from the doorway. He didn't look disheveled at all. His hair was combed and he was smiling. "I'm sending one of my mechanics over tomorrow to have a look at it. But this time, he'll come with Darby Hanes. So if anybody else shows up and claims to be sent by us, you call the ranch house first. Okay?"

"Okay. Dalton, you really shouldn't," Clara began worriedly. "I mean, you've done so much already . . ."

"We take care of family," he told her. And he looked at Merissa in a way that made her cheeks go red.

Clara started to speak but didn't.

Dalton just chuckled. "I'm going to be a pest," he told her. "Sorry. But your daughter is like flowers to a bee. Can't stay away," he said, and his voice dropped an octave as he looked at her.

"I don't mind," Merissa said, her own voice full of soft meaning.

Dalton winked at her. He checked his watch. "I have to go," he said. "I need to pack to get ready for the Texas trip."

"You're going to Texas?" Clara asked.

"Yes. I'm going to talk to Sheriff Carson and a couple of feds about my run-in with the drug cartel."

"Not alone?" Clara continued, concerned.

Tank chuckled again. "Rourke's got a buddy who's going to cover me like tar paper," he told her. "I'll be fine."

"In that case, I won't worry." She smiled. "Have a safe trip." She lifted her head and groaned. "He's still at it!"

They heard the tapping on the wood outside Clara's bedroom window.

"The woodpecker." Clara laughed. "I'd better go feed him before he breaks into the house."

She took a package of walnut halves, opened it and walked toward the back of the house.

When they heard the back door slam, Tank pulled Merissa close and kissed her with a new tenderness. He drew back, smoothing his big hand over her blond hair.

"We're going to be very good together," he whispered.

She flushed. "Listen, I'm very . . . I mean I . . . I can't . . ."

He hugged her tight. "I won't ask you to. That's a promise. I have something more permanent in mind."

"Permanent?" she asked at his chest.

He smiled and drew back. "We'll talk about it when I get back from Texas. Okay?"

She brightened. "Okay."

He laughed and shook his head. "I wish I could take you with me. Listen, you watch where you go. Be aware of your surroundings. Rourke will be watching, but he can't be everywhere." His eyes pinned her. "I want you safe."

"I will be," she promised him. "You be careful, too," she added. She bit her lower lip. "Airplanes are scary."

"I've been riding around in airplanes half my life." He laughed. "It's safer than driving. Really."

"Okay. Have a good trip."

"I will."

He kissed her again, hungrily, let her go and went out without looking back.

Merissa was still staring after him when her mother came back into the kitchen.

She put a comforting arm around her daughter. "He's the one."

"Yes," Merissa said, hugging her back. "He's the one."

Tank was disconcerted by his powerful reaction to Merissa, and, especially, hers to him. She really was hungry for him; that was evident. He should probably take a step back before rushing in headfirst, but caution was the last thing on his mind.

Then he remembered Vanessa. She'd come to work for the brothers, babied them, petted them. Tank had gone overboard for her. And then they found out that she was a thief, a woman with no particularly fine feelings at all. He'd trusted her and he'd been, like his brothers, betrayed by her.

But Merissa was different. People locally knew her. She might have a strange reputation, people might even think she had supernatural leanings, but she was respected. She wasn't the sort of person who'd betray him. Of course she wasn't.

He had to stop thinking that way. He'd learned the hard way that women couldn't be trusted. Before Vanessa, there had been another heartbreak. He was a sucker for a sweet smile; that was the problem. But this time was different. Very different.

"You look pensive," Mallory said when he came in the door.

Tank made a face. "I'm getting in over my head," he said.

Mallory smiled. "Happens to all of us. And then you get a baby and you go all crazy and buy closets full of baby clothes and furniture and big plastic toys . . . !"

"Oh, stop it, I'm not even married yet."

Tank chuckled.

"She thinks you're hot," Cane remarked as he entered the room. "Mavie says Merissa looks at you like she could eat you with a spoon."

Tank actually flushed. "She did? She does?"

They laughed.

"It's nice to see you with somebody we approve of," Mallory commented.

"People call her a witch," Tank reminded him.

"She's uniquely talented," he replied. "There are some unusual people in the world. We got lucky and found one in our neighbor. Well, two of them, Merissa and her mother," Mallory added. "You know," he said thoughtfully, "we might have lost Darby if Merissa hadn't had that premonition."

Tank nodded. "That was pretty shocking. Until then, I never really believed in any of that psychic stuff."

"Neither did I, honestly," Mallory said. "But she knew about your attacker, too. You might be dead as well if she hadn't interfered." He shook his head. "She's quite a woman."

"Not bad-looking, either," Cane added, laughing. He held up both hands when Tank glared at him. "Hey, I'm happily married and about to become a father."

Tank laughed. "Sorry."

There had been a bit of a rivalry between Cane and Tank over Bolinda, Cane's wife, before they were married. It had been a rocky relationship, and at one time Tank had even flirted with her. But once he knew how Cane felt, he backed off.

"I like her," Cane added, smiling gently.

"When you get back, Morie wants to have her over for dinner one night, after Christmas," Mallory said. "It would be nice for the wives to meet her."

"I agree," Tank said. He sighed. "Well, I'd better get packed. I hate leaving. And Merissa was nervous about my flying. I usually enjoy it, but now it makes me concerned."

"Driving takes longer," Cane pointed out.

"So it does."

"He just doesn't like being out of control," Cane told Mallory. "He'd fly the plane if they'd let him."

"I can drive a tank," Tank protested. "If I can do that, I'd be able to pilot a plane. I'd just need a few lessons." He grinned.

They shook their heads and walked off.

He wondered who Rourke had watching

him at the airport. He waited on the concourse gate to board. The man would probably be on the plane with him. But most of
the passengers seemed to be families. There
were a couple of businessmen in fancy suits.
One of them was carrying a laptop in a case.

He drew Tank's eyes. That man was tall,
streamlined but muscular. He walked with
a peculiar gait. Funny, to notice the way a
man moved, but Tank had worked with a
special forces group in Iraq that was assigned to a mission near his unit's command
post. He'd seen that walk before. It was
common among men who hunted men. It
was hard to put into words, but he recognized it when he saw it.

The man carried himself perfectly erect,
no slumping there. He had jet-black hair
that he wore in a ponytail down his back. It
was as black as a raven's wing. He wasn't
bad-looking. Women seemed to find him
interesting. He smiled at one, a sophisticated
woman by the look of her, and she seemed
absolutely mesmerized by him.

He noticed Tank's covert scrutiny and
glanced at him from black eyes under heavy
dark eyebrows. He had a lean face, deep-set
eyes and a chiseled mouth. He looked
dangerous. Odd, for a businessman.

Tank lifted his eyebrows, refusing to be

intimidated. The man pursed his lips and actually grinned before he turned his attention back to the woman who was approaching him with a big smile.

Even in his best bachelor days, Tank had never been able to attract women like that. Well, some men just had the gift.

He thought about Merissa and smiled to himself. He wasn't going to be interested in attracting women again, he decided. He had his own. His own. That made him feel warm inside, safe, protected. It had happened so suddenly that he hadn't had time to think about the impact it was going to make on his life.

Merissa was innocent, a person of faith with high ideals. She wasn't a woman for casual relationships. But he liked that. He wasn't a rounder. He was feeling his age, although he was only thirty-two. He was growing used to the idea of having Merissa around. Maybe a child. A little boy who'd look like him, or a little girl who'd look like her. He recalled the very hot and heavy intimacy they'd shared on her bed, and how he'd almost died from the agony of having to walk away from her. Yes, they were going to be explosive together in bed. And he liked her. That was an important part of marriage.

Marriage! There. He'd actually said the word in his mind, the word he'd avoided for years. But it didn't seem to hold the quiet terror it once had. Settling down seemed as natural as kissing Merissa's soft mouth. He actually looked forward to it.

He wished he could have taken her to Texas with him. But she had her work, and she'd told him she was behind. There would be plenty of time for trips later on.

They were boarding business class now. He went onto the gangway, smiling at the flight attendant who was waiting down the ramp at the door of the plane. She checked his ticket and indicated his seat assignment.

He hadn't planned to go business class, but his brothers had insisted. He didn't fly anywhere enough to make it exorbitant this once. In the spring he'd be on planes a lot, going to seminars, visiting other ranches, visiting congressmen to lobby for better laws for the cattle industry. He'd be working on brochures for their own spring sales and planning the big twice-a-year cattle sale on the ranch. He was going to be busy. So this trip would be something like a working vacation for him. He'd talk to the sheriff, but he also had plans to visit a ranch in Jacobsville to check out some Santa Gertrudis cattle to add to the brothers' breeding stock. They had a very small seed herd of the native Texas strain. He wanted to pursue it. A good bull wouldn't be a bad idea at all. New blood every two years kept their breeding herds viable.

As he took his seat, he noted that the ponytailed businessman took a seat across from him. The flight attendant made a beeline for him and offered him anything he wanted. She was also grinning from ear to ear, like the woman who'd flirted with him in the airport.

Tank just shook his head. The man had a real gift.

It wasn't a long flight. At least, it didn't seem long to Dalton. He read a couple of magazine articles, dozed for an hour or so and listened to the flight attendant telling the businessman across from Dalton about her whole life. He smiled to himself. The guy really had something. The flight attendant was very pretty.

When they landed, Dalton hefted his carry-on from the overhead compartment and got in line to baby-step out the door. No matter how organized the crew was, it was still a free-for-all trying to get off a plane.

As he approached the exit, he noted the

flight attendant slipping a piece of paper to the businessman. He chuckled to himself.

A driver was waiting for him at the entrance to the concourse, holding up a sign with "Dalton Kirk" on it.

He raised an eyebrow. His brothers, no doubt. He wondered why they thought he needed a limo to get to his hotel. San Antonio wasn't that large a city, but apparently it was large enough to house a limousine service or two.

But as he started toward the man holding up the sign, the businessman suddenly bumped against him.

"Sorry," he said loudly. But under his breath, he said, "Don't go near the guy with the sign, it's a trap."

"My fault," Tank replied.

He kept walking, not even looking toward the man with the sign. Once they were outside the airport, the businessman drew him to one side.

"Rourke sent me," he told Tank. His face was very somber. "He didn't say anything about a driver waiting for you here."

"I thought my brothers did it for a surprise," Tank replied, looking around.

"If they'd done that, I'd know about it," the other man replied. "I left my car in overnight parking. I'll drive you down to Jacobsville. Boss is expecting you. You're going to stay with him."

"Boss?"

"Cy Parks," the man replied. "He owns one of the biggest . . ."

". . . Santa Gertrudis cattle ranches in south Texas," Tank finished for him. "In fact, he was on my list of people to see. I want to talk to him about a new bull." He hesitated. "But I promised to check in with the local FBI office . . ."

"Later," the man replied, looking around them with narrowed eyes. "If they sent someone to the plane, they'll be watching. Let's go."

For the first time, Tank noticed a bulge under the man's jacket.

"You packing?" he asked as they moved quickly toward the parking lots.

"Yes." He didn't say anything else.

Jacobsville was just a few minutes drive down the road, through some beautiful country. "It must be really pretty here in the spring," Tank remarked as he looked across the flat horizon with small groves of trees and the "grasshoppers," or oil pumpers, dotting the landscape.

"One landscape's pretty much like another," his companion replied. He glanced at Tank. "You should have questioned who I was, you know," he said. "If that rogue agent is on the job, he'll know Rourke is working for you and that he said he'd have somebody at the airport."

Tank was very still. His eyes narrowed as he looked hard at the man driving the car.

There was a patient sigh. "I am the real deal," he replied. "I'm just saying that you shouldn't have assumed I was."

Tank chuckled. "Okay. Point taken."

He turned off the main road down a long ranch road between two white-fenced pastures with two levels of electrified wire in between. There were sleek, red-coated cattle eating at several points where hay had been provided.

"Nice cattle," Tank remarked.

"Boss only stocks the best" was the reply. "We had to put out surveillance cameras here as well because somebody walked off with one of his prize bulls in the middle of the night."

"Did they catch the perp?"

The tall man pursed his lips and glanced at Tank. "I caught him."

"With the bull?"

"Fortunately. Rustling still carries a heavy penalty here in Texas, and we had proof.

He'll be serving time for the indefinite future."

"You're a tracker," Tank murmured with narrowed eyes, and nodded when the other man glanced at him with surprise briefly visible. "I served in Iraq," he explained. "There was a spec ops team assigned to my unit. Funny, the things you remember in a combat zone, but I remember how one of those guys walked. It's a gait you don't see in many people."

"Cash Grier, the local police chief, has it, as well," the man agreed.

"Grier." He frowned. "Wasn't he a government assassin?"

"Yes, he was," the man replied. His black eyes were full of secrets as they met Tank's.

Tank cocked his head. "Am I seeing a similarity about which I shouldn't speak?" he asked.

"Absolutely."

He pulled up at the steps of the ranch house. It was sprawling and had paved flagstones leading to the front porch. There were mesquite trees around the compound, a huge barn out back, fenced pasture and a garage. There were stables out near the barn.

The tall man got out of the car. Tank followed him to the front porch, where a man with silvering black hair and green eyes was waiting.

"Cy Parks," he introduced himself, holding out a hand.

"Tank Kirk." They shook hands.

"Tank?" Parks asked, amused.

Tank shrugged. "I killed one in Iraq. The name stuck."

"Come on in. Lisa made a cake and coffee. We can talk before the kids get back from a friend's Christmas party," he added with muffled laughter. "Once they're home, it gets harder to have a conversation."

"I've got a new nephew back home." Tank laughed. "We're up to the eaves in big plastic baby toys."

"We've moved on to the next level of those," Parks said, indicating scattered games and spinning toys and little pedal cars. "Good thing it's a big house."

"You're telling me!" Lisa Parks laughed. She came out to greet them. She had green eyes, like her husband, but blond hair and she wore glasses. She was a pretty woman, still slender after two children. "Come in and have coffee and cake." She glanced at the tall man. "I know. You hate cake, you don't drink coffee . . . you'd rather be dragged behind a mule than sit around talking to people all day."

151

The man gave her an enigmatic look.

"How about checking out that truck we noticed earlier?" Parks asked the man. "Take one of the boys with you. Just in case."

The man glowered at him. "I invented stealth."

"I know that. Humor me."

The other man sighed. "You're the boss."

"Oh, and Grier called," Parks added darkly. "It seems you've upset his secretary. Again."

"Not my fault," the man said with the first strong emotion he'd shown since Tank had met him. His eyes flashed. "She starts it and then runs to her boss to tattle when she can't take the heat."

"This is not my problem," Parks replied. "Take it up with Grier."

"Tell him —" he indicated Tank "— not to be so trusting. He never even asked me for ID."

"What good would that do?" Parks muttered. "You never carry any. Which reminds me, I also had a call from a sheriff's deputy who stopped you for speeding yesterday . . ."

"Tell you about it later," the tall man said. "I'll check on the truck." He held up a hand when Parks started to speak. "I'll take one of the boys with me," he said with irritation.

He walked out of the room.

"Sorry about that," Parks said when he'd gone. He shook his head. "He's head of the class when it comes to risky operations, but he's a pain every other way."

"Who is he?" Tank asked.

"Carson."

"Is he related to your sheriff, Hayes Carson?" Tank pressed.

"Well, see, we don't know if Carson is his first name or his last name," Parks replied. "In fact, if you hack into government mainframes, you discover that he doesn't even exist."

Tank blinked.

"It's a long story. Right now, let's just eat cake. My wife —" he smiled at her "— makes the best pound cake in south Texas."

"Flatterer," she teased as she put the cake on the table and passed out plates and forks and a knife. "Well, don't stand on ceremony, dig in. I'll just get the coffee!"

CHAPTER SEVEN

Tank liked Cy Parks and his wife. They were surprisingly down-to-earth people, despite Parks's unconventional background. He, along with local doctor Micah Steele and counterterrorism teacher Eb Scott, had formed a small unit of mercenaries who went all over the world as part of their jobs. They were taught, in turn, by a group of legendary fighters, now retired, whom they still kept in touch with.

Eb Scott's school drew pupils from all over the earth. He taught all sorts of subjects, including small-arms instruction, defensive driving, hostage rescue and demolition. There were rumors, unsubstantiated of course, that the occasional government agent benefited from Scott's instruction.

"Is there anything you guys haven't done?" Tank asked Parks when they were strolling through the barn to look at some of his prize yearlings.

Parks shrugged. "We never took over a country." He chuckled. "But one of our locals, Grange, did. He used to work for Jason Pendleton, but he's got his own place now. His father-in-law manages it for him while he's occupying the Military Chief of Staff position in Barrera, over in South America."

"I understand the president of Barrera has family locally, too," Tank remarked.

He nodded. "His son is Rick Marquez. Rick's a lieutenant of detectives with San Antonio P.D. now, and his mother still runs Barbara's Café in town. Good food. Almost as good as what my wife cooks."

Tank nodded. "That was good cake."

"She's a wonder." He glanced at his companion. "You married?"

Tank shook his head. He smiled secretly. "But I have prospects."

Parks chuckled. "Good for you."

"I appreciate the hospitality," Tank added. "I travel a lot for the ranch. You get sick of hotels, no matter how good they are."

"Tell me about it."

Tank sighed. "I just hope your sheriff has some ideas about how we can track down this guy before he offs one of us," he said quietly.

Cy nodded. "You're worried about your family."

Tank agreed. "And not just my family — my girl," he added softly, referring to Merissa. "She's the one who warned me. This rogue agent bugged her phones, as well as the ranch. Rourke's got his eye on all of them, but it's still unsettling."

Cy clapped him on the shoulder. "I know how it feels, believe me. But we've got plenty of people trying to ferret out his identity. He can't hide forever."

"I hope you're right," Tank said.

Tank enjoyed Cy's two little boys. They were smaller versions of their father, both with dark hair and green eyes. They wanted to know all about Tank's ranch and what sort of cattle he ran. He got a kick out of listening to them hold forth on the subject of genetics. Obviously they were already headed in the direction of becoming ranchers when they grew up.

Tank called Merissa early the next morning.

"Anything going on that should worry me?" he asked her gently.

She laughed breathlessly. She hadn't expected him to call, and she was all aflutter at the sound of his voice. "Not much," she said. "Your man came and fixed the car for us. Thank you so much."

"You're welcome. You're sure he was our man?" he added worriedly.

"Oh, yes. Rourke came with him," she added. "He's a very interesting person."

Tank ground his teeth together. "He's my friend, but he's a merc," he began.

"You aren't . . . jealous?" she asked shyly.

"Jealous?" he burst out. "Of course I'm jealous! You're my girl!"

There was a soft gasp. He could almost hear her heart beating. "Oh, that sounds . . . very nice."

He grinned from ear to ear. "Does it?"

"I like Rourke a lot. But not in that way," she said primly.

He chuckled. "That sounds very nice, too," he repeated her words.

She laughed.

"I love to hear the way you laugh," he said softly. "I miss you."

There was an indrawn breath. "I miss you, too. You aren't going to be there a long time, are you?"

"No, just today. I'm going to talk to the sheriff later . . ." He paused as a car pulled up out front. He peered through the curtains. It was a squad car. He grinned. "Speak of the devil." He laughed. "It's the

sheriff. I have to go. You take care of yourself. I'll see you soon."

"Yes. You do the same. Bye."

"Bye."

He hung up and went outside. Cy Parks
joined him on the porch.

A tall blond man in a uniform got out of
the Jacobs County Sheriff's Department
vehicle and came toward them.

"Tank Dalton?" the man asked with a
smile as he studied Cy's companion.

Tank grinned. "Sheriff Carson?"

"Hayes." He shook hands. "If it's not too
early for you, I thought I'd ask if you could
come over to my office for a chat."

"Go ahead," Cy told him. "If you need a
ride back, I'll send one of the boys."

"No need." Hayes grinned. "I'll bring him
back."

"Thanks."

"No problem."

Tank climbed into the patrol car with Hayes
and they drove to the sheriff's office.

"How's your arm?" Tank asked him.

Hayes grimaced. "Still painful. I'm doing
physical therapy and hoping I'll regain at
least partial use of it, but things are unsettled right now." He shook his head. "I've
been shot before, but I never had conse-

quences like these."

"I know what you mean," Tank replied quietly. "I had injuries that required multiple surgeries. It was a few months ago, but I still get jumpy if there's a car backfire."

"Law enforcement is not a job for the weak of heart."

"I totally agree," Tank said. "That's why I market cattle now."

Hayes laughed. He led the way inside the building to his office, and offered Tank a seat. "I like my coffee strong."

"Me, too."

"Good thing, that's the only way you'll get it around here." He produced two cups of coffee and put Tank's in front of him. "There's cream and sugar . . ."

"I don't want either."

"Same here."

Tank leaned back in the chair. "Did you ever catch the would-be assassin who shot you?" he asked.

"Not yet," Hayes said with evident irritation. "We've put pressure on everybody we know. I even had my father-in-law ask around." He leaned forward with a grin. "That's how you indicate you're really desperate — you involve a drug lord in your investigation. But my wife's father has a good heart. He's just in an illegal business."

He shook his head. "He doesn't seem to run out of applications for jobs on his horse ranch in Jacobsville. But just between you and me, I think a lot of the applicants are undercover narcs." He chuckled.

"That wouldn't be a surprise."

Hayes sipped his coffee. "We identified the shell casing," he said. "Unfortunately the bullet's still in me. The surgeon refused to remove it. He said it would complicate my recovery if he went in digging around delicate tissue."

"I'm still wearing one of mine, too," Tank replied. "I remember reading about Doc Holliday of O.K. Corral fame — they said when they examined his body, he was carrying several ounces of lead . . . bullets that doctors had just left in him."

"In those days, the late 1800s, it would have been lethal trying to remove them," Hayes agreed. He put down the coffee cup. "I'm still trying to understand why this man, whoever he is, targeted you and me. Neither of us can actually describe him. We don't know who he is, or who he works for." He frowned. "My office computer was destroyed, and when I had one of Eb Scott's computer techs try to recover the hard drive, he was killed." His eyes narrowed.

"What is this guy trying so hard to cover up?"

Tank shook his head. "I have no idea. But he's good at what he does. I had a friend of mine, Rourke, come up and check my place for bugs. It turns out that the surveillance company I hired was bogus. Their consultant, who was supposed to plant surveillance equipment, bugged everything, too."

Hayes shook his head. "I can't remember a case like this, not in my whole life."

"I wasn't in law enforcement that long, but neither can I," Tank said. "There hasn't been another attempt on your life?"

Hayes shook his head. "Well, that's not quite true," he added with a short laugh. "It seems El Ladrón, before his untimely death, hired a new assassin to come after me."

"And . . . ?"

Hayes's eyes twinkled. "He hired a guy who worked for my father-in-law briefly. He's gone back to Houston, but he still keeps in touch, just in case the assassin wants to take me out."

"They didn't know who he was?" Tank exclaimed.

"Nope."

"It wasn't Mr. Parks's employee, the other Carson?"

"No. Now there's an interesting case,"

161

Hayes mused. "He actually blew up El Ladron with a couple of hand grenades down in Mexico. The Mexican government did take a brief interest in the case, but we have a DEA agent who's related to the former president. He made a couple of calls for us and they dropped the inquiry."

Tank just shook his head. "This is one odd case."

"Indeed it is."

"I understand that Carson doesn't carry ID and can't be found in a database anywhere," Tank replied.

"He's an enigma. I owe him my life. So does my wife." Hayes shook his head, too. "He has some unique skills. In fact, he just went on our honeymoon with us before he went to shepherd you down here. In a separate room," he added with a chuckle. "He's thick with Cash Grier, which leads to an assumption I probably shouldn't make."

"That he works, or worked, for the government in covert assassination," Tank said, nodding at Hayes's surprise. "I happened to mention to him that I noticed his gait. It's one I saw in spec ops people in Iraq. Men who hunt men walk that way."

Hayes nodded. "I know. If you ever see Cash Grier walk, it's an experience. He's still skilled with a sniper kit. In fact, a couple of years back, he took out a kidnapper who was holding a DEA agent's child hostage. Did it from an astonishing distance, in the dark. Amazing."

"His wife was a movie star, wasn't she?"

He nodded. "They have a little girl, so he's not so much into dangerous occupations as he was. They have Tippy's younger brother living with them also. He's just fourteen. He and Cash go fishing together and they game online. They're best friends."

"Nice for him. For both of them."

"Yes."

"You said she sees things," he began.

"She has premonitions," Hayes told him. "They're uncanny. Saved Cash's life a time or two."

"My . . . friend," he said hesitantly, "sees the future, too. But she's never certain exactly what she sees. Sometimes it's clouded. Like the guy who's stalking me. She saw him sitting in front of a mirror trying on wigs. We concluded that he's good at disguise."

"That reminds me. I had Rick Marquez ask his father-in-law if he could check into that for us."

"His father-in-law?"

Hayes nodded. He grinned. "Runs the CIA."

Tank whistled.

"Anyway, he found a whole list of undercover agents from several agencies who have a reputation for their use of disguises. So I'm afraid it's going to take a long time to narrow it down to even a handful."

"Another dead end," Tank agreed. He sighed. "I could stand in the center of town and wait for him to come shoot me."

"From what we've been able to put together, he avoids crowds when he's planning a hit."

"Which would explain why he didn't just shoot me in the front yard of my own ranch when he came out to put in the surveillance devices," Tank told him. "He did seem disconcerted that we had so many armed men just standing around."

"Good thing," Hayes said. "I don't think he'd have minded killing you face-to-face."

"Nor do I. But if it hadn't been for Merissa, I wouldn't have been expecting it." He shook his head. "She didn't even know me. She came walking up to the back door, in a blizzard because her car wouldn't start, to tell me I had to be careful. She said it was because of something I didn't remember."

Hayes frowned. "Was she more specific than that?"

"Not really. It comes and goes with her. She said that I knew something that I wasn't aware of knowing, and it posed a risk to the man."

"Nebulous."

"Yes. But even so, it probably saved my life."

"What do you remember about the man, the supposed DEA agent, who led you into the ambush in Arizona?" Hayes asked.

Tank sighed. "I remember that he wore a suit. It's still sort of hazy. He was medium height, nothing remarkable about his features. He was the sort of guy you wouldn't even notice on the street."

Hayes was remembering. "Yes. The guy I remember was pretty much the same. But he had a marked Texas drawl."

"I think it was the same guy, after I was shot, who was giving a drug mule hell for calling 911 for me — he had red hair and a Massachusetts accent. But he was dressed the same." He shook his head. "I thought I was hallucinating."

"Nice of the mule to call for help."

"Yes. Unexpected. I don't even know who he was. I owe him my life. I hope they didn't kill him for it."

"You never know. I've heard of whole villages wiped out just for revenge against one man who lived in it."

"So have I."

"My wife and I saved one man from El Ladrón," Hayes recalled. He laughed. "My wife held an AK-47 on him and never knew if it was even loaded — but she bluffs well. Anyway, he didn't want to hold us hostage, but his bosses knew his family and threatened to kill them if he stepped out of line. Carson, who works for Cy Parks, got his family out of Mexico."

"So he does have at least one soft spot?"

"Not sure about that," Hayes said. "He doesn't seem to care about much. Although, he does have something of a reputation with women."

"Deserved." Tank chuckled. "I saw him in action at the airport. He draws them like flies to honey."

"Draws them, yes. But he's not a sentimental man."

"I wouldn't have thought so, either."

"How about your brothers?" Hayes asked. "This must be hard on them, too."

"They worry. My older brother Mallory has a new son."

Hayes smiled. "I like kids. My wife has a little brother and sister who live with us. They light up the place. We're hoping to have one of our own."

"You said something about Cash Grier's secretary having a photographic memory, and that she saw the rogue agent," Tank said. "Any help there?"

Hayes shook his head with a long sigh. "She had a police artist draw the man she remembered. But the nose was different, the hairline was different . . ." He grimaced. "The only thing familiar was the ears."

"Now ears are a pretty good identifier," Tank replied. "You don't usually try to disguise those, even if you use makeup or wigs."

"That's true." Hayes agreed. "Maybe we should issue a BOLO for a pair of ears."

"It's not so far-fetched," Tank assured him. "I'd really like to have a look at that sketch."

"That's one of the reasons I asked you to come down here. Just a sec." Hayes picked up the phone and called Cash Grier. After a brief conversation, he hung up. "He's got a few free minutes. Let's go over to his office and have a look at that sketch."

Tank smiled. "Now you're talking."

Cash's secretary, Carlie Blair, had wavy dark hair and green eyes and a pert smile. She greeted Tank as if he'd been her neighbor all her life. She pulled the sketch out of a nearby filing cabinet and handed it to him.

"That's the best the artist could do," she explained. "It's not perfect. I think the nose was a little longer and thinner, and the chin had more of a square look."

"How about the ears?" Tank asked.

She blinked. "The ears?" She looked at the sketch and slowly nodded. "Yes, he certainly got those right. I remember because he had sort of a notch in one, as if he'd been cut and it had healed but left a scar."

Tank's jaw was clenched. "Yes," he said. "I remember now. It was his left ear. And he wore an earring in it, a small gold circlet."

"Yes!" she agreed.

"I remember the earring myself," Hayes said. He frowned. "Odd, I'd forgotten that." He scratched his head. "It was overshadowed by the shirt he was wearing. It was paisley, I think."

"I remember the shirt, too." Tank laughed. "It must be a favorite piece of clothing, if he was still wearing it when you saw him."

Carlie was frowning. "It was gold paisley," she recalled, closing her eyes so that she could focus better. "With beige and brown patterns."

"Yes," Tank agreed. The memory came back along with the pain. He was looking at the shirt when the bullets hit.

"Well, I've got a favorite shirt," Carlie remarked. "I wear it at least twice a week. Of course, it's not paisley. It's a black T-shirt with a green alien face and it says, They're Coming! under it." She grinned.

"She likes to wear it if we get visits from feds," Cash Grier remarked as he joined them, glowering at his secretary. "She's unconventional."

"But I can type, I have a pleasant phone personality and I can find anything you lose, Chief." She grinned even more broadly.

He shook his head. "Yes, and you can spell. It's just that mouth . . ."

"What do you mean?" Tank asked.

Carlie looked past him and her face took on a sarcastic expression. "Well, look what walked in the door. I need to start a fire out back. Got any spare hand grenades on you?" she added.

The newcomer was Carson, Tank's shadow on the plane.

He gave Carlie a glowering stare. "Something wrong with matches?" he asked. "Or don't you know how to use them?" he added with a bland smile.

"I can use a Glock," she retorted. "Wanna see?"

"She cannot use a Glock," Cash Grier

interjected. "The last time she tried, on the firing range, she hit two windshields and a tire, and the cars weren't even parked on the range."

"It was a horrible accident," Carlie defended herself.

"Yes, it was. You picked up a gun."

"Your coffee will have salt tomorrow morning in place of sugar," Carlie assured Cash.

"If I fire you, your father will make me the subject of his next two sermons," Cash said grimly. "But I'll risk it."

"Sermons?" Carson asked, frowning.

"Her father is a Methodist minister," Cash explained.

Carson's expression was indescribable. He narrowed his eyes as he looked at Carlie, who avoided him and went back to the drawing on her desk.

"Don't worry, religion isn't contagious," she told Carson without quite looking at him.

"Thank goodness," Carson drawled. He looked at Tank. "Did you recognize the face in the drawing?"

"Not so much," Tank replied. "But we've all agreed that the ears are the one thing we all remember about him." He turned to Hayes. "You should talk to those two feds,

Jon Blackhawk and Garon Grier . . ." He frowned and looked at Cash. "Grier?"

"My brother," Cash said. "He's always been FBI. I worked with, shall we say, less structured government agencies."

"Covert," Carson said with a mock cough.

"Look who's talking about covert," Cash said pointedly.

"Takes one to know one," Carson shot right back. But he grinned. So did Cash.

"I've already talked to Blackhawk and Cash's brother," Hayes told Tank. "Which reminds me, they wanted me to tell you that they can't set up that hypnotist they wanted you to see. He had a family emergency and is out of town. Maybe another time."

"Another time," Tank agreed, secretly relieved.

"It turns out that he —" Cash indicated Carson "— worked with an associate of mine from Brooklyn, New York."

"Should we ask what sort of work?" Hayes mused.

"It would be safer not to," Cash told him.

Tank shook his head. "I've never been in a place where so many people were ex-feds."

"Or ex-mercs," Cash added. "We've cornered the market on them."

"It's a good place to retire, or that's what Cy Parks always says." Hayes chuckled.

"He's a nice fellow," Tank remarked. "I was perfectly happy to stay in a hotel, but he insisted."

"He knows you're in the market for a new bull," Cash said with a big grin.

"Well, I am, actually," Tank had to agree.

He went back to Carlie's desk and took another look at the man. "He really is a chameleon," he remarked. "But why is he so worried about what we might remember? I couldn't pick him out on the street. Well, maybe that scarred ear would give him away, but there's nothing else really memorable about him."

"Maybe it's something that doesn't readily show," Carson remarked, joining him. "Or maybe he's just paranoid."

Hayes shook his head. "He killed a computer tech who tried to restore his image on my computer."

Carson's black eyes narrowed. "Yes. He was a friend of mine," he said tautly. "Sweet kid. Never hurt a fly. Knew everything about computers." His face set in hard lines. "I'd like to meet the man who popped a cap on him."

"He feeds people to crocodiles," Cash said in a mock whisper, jerking his head toward Carson.

Carson glared at him. "It was hungry.

Poor old thing hadn't been fed in days."

"So it was an act of charity. I see," Hayes mused.

Carson shrugged. His expression went even tauter. "The man tortured Rourke's friend, a female photo-journalist covering the assault on Barrera. She'll carry the scars for the rest of her life."

"I don't doubt that Rourke helped you feed the croc," Cash replied.

Carson's black eyes met his. "Sometimes you do what feels right, even if it's not quite legal."

"Well, it wasn't in my jurisdiction, so I'm not concerned," Cash told him. He wagged a finger at him. "But you feed anybody to a crocodile in my town, you're looking at life behind bars."

"No problem," Carson said. "I like whiskey."

"Life . . . behind . . . bars. Whiskey." Tank burst out laughing. It was a play on words that almost got by him.

Carson actually grinned.

"And it would be nice if you stopped wearing that damned knife in public," Cash told the younger man, indicating the huge Bowie knife strapped to his hip. "It makes people nervous."

"Makes her nervous, you mean," Carson

replied, jerking his head toward Carlie.

"I don't like knives," she muttered under her breath.

"Men with guns walk around in here all the time, you don't mind them," Carson retorted.

"I've never seen a gunshot wound. I have seen the result of a knife fight." She gave him a long look. "I had nightmares . . ."

He frowned. "When was this?"

She averted her eyes. "My father was attacked a few months ago by a man with a knife. We don't know why. He was lucky, because it went in just at the waist and didn't even nick a vital organ."

"Who would attack a minister?" Hayes asked, shocked.

"We don't know," Carlie replied sadly. "Just some crazy guy, we think. Sometimes, I think the whole world's gone mad."

"It does seem so, from time to time," Tank had to agree. "Did they catch the man?"

"Not yet," Cash answered for her. "But we're still looking."

"I don't like knives," Carlie reiterated, glaring up at Carson. "Especially that sort." She indicated the Bowie. "It's scary."

"I'll start wearing a suit so I can conceal it from you," Carson promised dryly.

"Why would you carry something that

big?" Hayes wondered.

"Snakes," Carson said, deadpan.

"Good luck going after a sidewinder with a knife," Tank told him. "You'd get bitten before you could reach him with it."

"Not if it was thrown," Carson returned. He looked so confident that the others just shrugged and let the subject go.

"Do you remember anything else about the man?" Tank asked Carlie as he studied the sketch. "Anything you didn't tell the police artist?"

She was thinking, hard. "I'm not sure. That's basically what he looked like," she added, nodding at the portrait. "He was very friendly. Personable. I remember he talked to me about sharks."

"Sharks?" Tank probed.

"He said that they were misunderstood, that people just assumed they were dangerous. But that they really weren't. It was just when they were hungry, they killed."

"What an odd thing to say," Hayes remarked.

"I thought so, too," Carlie agreed. "He said that he liked to swim with them in the Caribbean, in the Bahamas."

"Now that might be interesting," Hayes said.

She laughed softly. "I'd forgotten, until

just now." She glared at Carson. "He reminds me of a shark. That's why I thought of it."

Carson's eyebrows arched. "A shark? Me?"

"Dark and lithe and stealthy and dangerous," she returned. "Attacks when you least expect it, from cover."

"An apt description. Not of you," Tank told Carson with a grin. "But it would fit the perpetrator." His expression became grim. "He led me into an ambush that almost cost me my life. And he did it so easily, with such finesse, that I never suspected a thing. She's right about his personality," he added, alluding to Carlie. "He put me at ease the minute he walked into my office. He seemed just like one of the guys."

"I got that impression, too," Hayes said. "He put himself right in the middle of a drug bust." He frowned. "Something else I remember, I had two armed deputies with me. They came up unexpectedly when they heard the call go out over the radio about a traffic stop involving narcotics." He looked at Tank. "He was shocked to see them. That was just before the other feds showed up."

"He might have been planning the same thing for you that he did for me," Tank suggested.

"Yes, but there was no reason for him to want me dead." Hayes tried to make sense of it. "He was in on the arrest. He went to my office with me and waited while I filed the report on my computer, along with a photo my deputy took at the scene of the arrest and one of all of us with the drug haul and the confiscated gold-plated weapons. I wasn't the only law enforcement officer at the bust."

"I don't think he meant to kill you. Not then, anyway," Carson interjected with narrowed eyes. He perched himself on the edge of Carlie's desk, to her obvious dislike. "I think it was something that happened after both shootouts. Something connected, but apart from them."

"He was obviously in with the drug cartel," Hayes replied. He nodded slowly. "He was trying to protect his people from arrest. He failed in my case, but not in yours," he told Tank.

"Yes, but he has no reason to come after me now," Tank said slowly. "I haven't even spoken about the case since I gave my last report, just before I resigned from the job."

Cash Grier leaned against the wall, arms crossed, deep in thought. "Attempted assassination," he said, nodding toward Hayes. "Kidnapping, for no apparent reason." He

177

glanced at Tank. "Armed assault, followed much later by stalking and surveillance. He's after something that happened as a result of both shootings. Maybe not the shootings themselves at all."

"What?" Hayes asked.

Cash shook his head. "I don't know. But there is a feverish political race going on right now for a congressional seat vacated by the unexpected death of our senior Texas U.S. senator. There's a special election coming, although someone will be appointed to fill out the rest of his term, which ends this year. There are rumors that the leading candidate has ties to the cartel over the border, and that at least one rival candidate has been blackmailed to quit the race."

"I had heard about that," Tank said. "You think there may be a connection?"

"There just may be," Hayes said. "Especially if the man we remember could be part of the drug cartel."

"We know he is," Cash replied. "The problem would be proving his connection. If he's close to the candidate, that might be enough incentive for him to get rid of any witnesses. Also, he was a rogue DEA agent, a mole. I'm sure he was passing sensitive information to his cronies."

"Maybe somebody found him out," Tank

guessed.

"Yes," Cash replied. "But who he is —
that might be the heart of the problem. If
we find out his identity, and it can link him
to the cartel and the candidate for the Senate . . ."

"That would be a motive for murder,"
Hayes agreed. "A very good one."

CHAPTER EIGHT

"I have a strange feeling that all this is somehow connected to that special election in the Senate race," Cash said with narrowed eyes.

"So do I," Carlie piped in.

Carson gave her a mocking look. "Now you're psychic?" he drawled.

She smiled blithely. "If I was, you'd be wearing the hilt of that big knife in your mouth," she said sweetly.

He lifted an eyebrow and gave her a look that made her blush. Her antagonism hit him on the raw and he retaliated. "Sorry," he said. "But if that's flirting, it won't work. I like my women —" he gave her a cool stare "— prettier, and more physically perfect."

Carlie's face fell like a rock, although she didn't lower her gaze. She gave him a belligerent stare.

"That was uncalled for," Cash Grier said coldly to Carson. "Apologize. Right now."

Carson seemed to realize that he'd stepped over a line. "Sorry," he told Carlie with a face like stone. "He's right. It was uncalled for."

Carlie averted her eyes. She was painfully aware of her lack of attractions. Her sense of morality wouldn't let her play around with men, and she had less than visible assets, physically. She was more sensitive about her body than most women, for reasons she wasn't sharing in a public venue. It shouldn't have bothered her that Mr. Womanizer there didn't like her. She should be grateful not to be a target. Still, it stung to have her deficiencies pointed out in public. Especially in front of men. She mumbled something and excused herself to go make coffee.

"Dammit!" Cash snapped at Carson with blazing dark eyes. Tank saw immediately the danger in the man that was carefully concealed most of the time behind a pleasant personality. The anger seemed oddly out of proportion to what Carson had said. "What the hell were you thinking?" he demanded.

Carson shifted restlessly. "Wasn't thinking," he said through clenched teeth. It was a rebuke he wouldn't have taken from any other man. But he respected Grier.

"Obviously," Cash replied tersely. His eyes

narrowed. "There are a lot of things you don't know. Snipe at her again and you'll deal with me. Understood?"

Carson jerked his head up and down, once.

"When is the special election?" Tank asked, to break the tension.

"In the spring," Hayes remarked.

"That does give us a little time to investigate," Cash said, apparently over his anger. "But not a lot."

"I'd wiretap every damned Texas DEA agent's phone," Carson interjected with cold eyes.

"Great idea," Cash said. "You go find us a judge to sign the warrant."

Carson sighed. "Okay. I get the point."

"Besides that, we don't know if he's still with the agency in some satellite office somewhere," Hayes added. "There's a good turnover in every agency these days because of funding. Maybe he even quit the agency once he realized we had a photo of him on our computer."

"There has to be some way we can trap this chameleon," Tank said curtly. "Listen, we know he's targeting me, even though we don't know why. We know he's targeting you, too." He indicated Hayes. "But you have powerful connections. Maybe he's not willing to tangle with your new father-in-law. But I'm on my own. I don't have a network behind me."

"You do now," Cash said.

"Indeed," Hayes agreed.

"Thanks," Tank said, smiling.

"You're also forgetting that the late El Ladron's men hired your father-in-law's temporary employee to kill you," Carson told Hayes. "If they're plotting anything, he'll be the first to know."

"Assuming they haven't rumbled him," Cash told him. "Never underestimate an organized network of criminals."

"Good advice," Hayes seconded.

"But the point is, regardless of by whom," Tank interjected, "I'm being actively targeted. Rourke's got my back. But it wouldn't hurt to bring in a little help. Do we know somebody in the FBI or Eb Scott's group who has some free time and would like to hire on as a cowboy in Wyoming?"

There were amused glances between the other men.

"I can ride a horse," Carson said surprisingly.

"You'd need to talk to Cy Parks about that," Hayes remarked.

"Like Mr. Parks would miss him," Carlie said under her breath, and she didn't look at Carson when she spoke. "Coffee's up," she added as she sat down at her desk.

"Why don't you go?" Carson shot at her, embarrassed by his former outburst and angry that she'd made him look like an idiot in front of the other men. "You seem to know how to do everything. Can you ride a horse?" he added sarcastically.

She glared at him. "Yes, I can," she said. "And use a lasso and even shoot a gun if I have to."

"No more talk of shooting guns, please," Cash groaned. "First you have to learn how, especially after the last fiasco at the firing range."

She glared at him, too. "I could learn if somebody would teach me!"

"Don't look at me," Carson drawled with pure venom. "I'm not teaching you any-thing."

"Mr. Carson . . . or whatever your last name actually is . . . I was not speaking to you," she said icily.

"You couldn't pronounce my last name," he returned, dripping even more venom. "It's Lakota."

She flushed and averted her eyes.

He saw that, frowning. Why should his heritage provoke such a reaction?

"Lakota?" Tank asked softly.

Carson nodded. "I grew up on a reservation in Kyle, South Dakota," he said.

"No wonder you're so good at tracking," Hayes remarked.

Carson glared at him.

Hayes held up both hands. "I'm not stereotyping. I mean, growing up in relatively rural places, like Jacobsville, or rural South Dakota, people learn to use their senses more, and most rural men hunt and track."

"I see." Carson relaxed a little.

"Touchy," Cash Grier remarked with narrowed eyes.

"You don't know me," Carson replied quietly. "Or you'd understand why." He turned to Tank. "You can hire me on for a few weeks. I'll do some checking, make some inquiries. In your part of Wyoming, I won't even raise eyebrows much. There are communities with native people all over the place."

"Not so many as you might think," Tank began.

Carson smiled. "That's because you don't know where they are. I do. I have Cheyenne cousins."

"In that case, I'd love to give you your very own horse and a new rope." Tank chuckled.

"A new one? Gee, thanks," Carson said sarcastically.

"You can stretch it between a tree and the rear bumper of a truck and it'll work really nicely," Tank assured him.

All the men laughed.

"I'll talk to Mr. Parks about it tonight," Carson assured Tank. "But I don't think he'll mind. He has plenty of other employees to look after things. And it's Christmas in three days. He can call it a holiday vacation."

"I'd better get back there, it's late," Tank said, glancing at his watch.

"I'll drive you," Hayes said.

"We'll talk again," Cash said, shaking hands. They wished each other a Merry Christmas. Cash smiled and went back into his office. Tank and Hayes said their good-byes to Carlie and walked out.

That left an embarrassed, heartsick Carlie at her desk alone with a ravenous wolf.

Carson stood over the desk looking down his straight nose at her. "Well done," he said coldly. "I felt like a slab of meat on a grill."

She looked up at him without her usual tartness. Her eyes showed the wound. "Don't you have something earthshaking to do elsewhere?" she asked in a subdued tone and pulled out a file from her lower drawer.

It humiliated her that her hands were shaking.

He saw that and felt even smaller. He hated her. It was so odd; he didn't usually dislike women, even plain ones. But she antagonized him. She confused him, unsettled him. He didn't like having his calm shattered. Besides that, she looked a little like Jessie . . .

His face closed up. His black eyes narrowed, stabbing at her.

"Do you mind?" she gritted. "I have work to do."

"You could always call the chief out to protect you," he drawled.

She looked up at him with quiet pride. "I can defend myself, thanks."

He had sharp eyes. He was used to dealing with hazardous situations, with dangerous people. He saw more than most people did. His eyes strayed to her shoulder, where the T-shirt was a little tight, just over the fleshy part of her arm. Odd, the way the shirt fit. There was a wrinkle, as if the flesh underneath wasn't quite smooth . . .

She put her hand over her shoulder defensively. "Was there something else you wanted?" she asked harshly.

His eyebrows arched. "No. There's nothing here that I want, or ever will." He even smiled. He turned and walked out the door.

Carlie shivered. She'd seen where his eyes were. She rubbed the scar self-consciously. She'd really have to go back to button-up shirts. Or make sure her T-shirts and sweaters were big enough not to draw attention to certain things.

She turned on the computer and focused on the task at hand.

Tank was on his way back to Wyoming the next morning. He didn't like being away from the ranch. More specifically, he didn't like being away from Merissa. He'd missed her like crazy. He couldn't wait to get home, to see her, to touch her, to kiss her . . .

Across the aisle, Carson had yet another admirer, a blonde flight attendant with a smile so big that it seemed to go from ear to ear. He really did know how to lure women. But it was a shame he'd been so cruel to Cash Grier's little secretary. She might not be pretty, but she had a livewire personality and a good sense of humor, and she seemed to be a person of faith; that alone was rare in this jaded world. He wondered why Carson was so antagonistic toward her. So he liked pretty women. That was no excuse to make cruel comments about a woman who wasn't.

Carson was an odd duck. He never seemed to fit in anywhere. He was a maverick who hated authority. But it had amused Tank to see how much he respected Cash Grier. One word from the police chief and Carson had shut up immediately.

The men had something in common, probably a covert background that gave them a point of reference as well as a mutual respect. It had occurred to Tank that Carson didn't seem to mind leaving Texas for a while, either. He wondered if it had anything to do with Cash's secretary.

Rourke met them at the airport. His blond eyebrows met above the black eye patch over one eye, and the brown eye twinkled.

"What the hell are you doing up here?" he asked Carson as he shook hands with Tank.

"Hunting." Carson grinned.

Rourke chuckled. "Welcome, then. I could use the help."

"He's my latest hire," Tank said meaningfully. "I have a lot to tell you."

"Let's go back to the ranch. I have a few things to tell you, too," Rourke said, and that wasn't a pleasant tone in his voice.

"What's up?" Tank asked when they were in the double-cabbed ranch pickup on the way

189

to the ranch.

"It's Merissa Baker," Rourke said.

"What the hell . . . !" Tank burst out. "Is she hurt? Is she all right?"

"No," Rourke said.

"Then what . . . !"

Rourke pulled the truck over into a convenience store parking lot and turned to Tank. "Some things have happened since you've been away. Clara's ex-husband showed up at their cabin. He claims that it's his and he has the papers to prove it."

"Does he?" Tank asked coldly.

"It's up to her to prove he isn't the owner," Rourke said. "And somehow a whole file of her important papers went missing."

"I thought he'd been gone for years," Tank said. "Why would he come back now?"

"That's a very good question" was the reply. "I don't know. He moved into the house with them. Clara's terrified of him. Merissa is trying to stay out of his way. I went over to check on her and he literally blocked the door and refused to let me speak to her."

"Head that way," Tank instructed. His expression and tone of voice was harder than Rourke had ever heard from Tank.

"Now that's amazing," Rourke said as he

pulled back onto the highway. "You know, that was exactly what I was going to advise."

"You packing?" Tank asked him.

"Always," Rourke replied.

"So am I," Carson said from the cramped backseat.

"Bowie knives don't count," Rourke jibed.

"They do if you know how to use one," Carson said haughtily.

The two men in front laughed, but there was no real amusement. Tank was worried. He knew what the man had done to the women in his family, and it disturbed him that they were at his mercy. Well, that was something he was about to fix. Right now.

The truck pulled up at the front of the house and the three men got out. As they approached the house, a tall, powerfully built man with thinning black hair and a mean expression came out to meet them.

"I came to see Merissa," Tank said pleasantly.

"I'm afraid she's not available," the man said with an arrogant look.

Tank went right up to him. "You don't know me," he told the man with a cold smile. "My name is Dalton Kirk. My brothers and I own the Rancho Real. We have a whole damned team of corporate attorneys with a little time on their hands. If I don't get in that house, right now, I'll have my private investigator do some digging. You say you own the place, right? Prove it!"

The man was less aggressive now. In fact, he shifted his belligerent posture and lost his arrogance. "Hey, no problem, you can see her if you want to. No need to go calling attorneys, for God's sake. Merissa, come out here!"

The tone of his voice made Tank furious. He held in his rage and waited, not too patiently, until a subdued, worried Merissa came out onto the porch. She looked ragged. Her eyes had dark circles under them and she was obviously distressed.

"Come here, honey," Tank said softly and held out his arm.

She ran to him, sobbing, to be enclosed hungrily in his embrace.

"It's all right," he whispered. "It's going to be all right."

She clung closer.

"What the hell is that all about?" the man on the porch growled. "I haven't hurt you!"

"Make him let Mama come out here," she whispered urgently in Tank's ear, so that the man couldn't overhear her. "Please, Dalton!"

Tank smoothed her hair and kissed her

forehead. "Don't worry." He let her go. "I want to talk to Clara," he said out loud.

Now the man really looked unsettled. "She's indisposed."

"Rourke," Tank said, nodding toward him.

Rourke pulled back his wool jacket and disclosed a holstered .45 automatic. At the same time, Carson moved to his right and pushed back his own jacket, showing the big Bowie knife.

"Are you . . . threatening me?" the man stammered.

"I want to see Clara," Tank told him. "Whether or not it's a threat depends on whether or not she comes out here." He pulled out his cell phone. "Our sheriff, Cody Banks, is a good friend of mine. I have his number on speed dial."

Now the man was really unsettled. He swallowed. "She had a fall," he said quickly. "She has a few bruises. It ain't my fault!"

"Clara!" Tank called shortly.

The door opened. Little Clara, nervous and shivering, came into view. There were bruises on her face.

"Come here to me," Tank said softly. "It's all right," he added when she looked with evident fear at her ex-husband. "Come on. He isn't going to touch you!" He glared at the man as he said it, and his expression was dangerous.

Clara ran down the steps, almost stumbling. Tank put his arm around her. "You okay?" he asked softly.

She sobbed. "I am now, thanks."

He hugged her and then let her go. He pushed the speed dial on the phone. "Cody?" he asked when his friend answered. "We've got a little situation here, and I need some help."

"Hey, there's no need for that!" the man on the porch yelled. "No need at all!"

Rourke walked up on the porch. He stood beside the man and looked down at Clara. "Did he strike you, Mrs. Baker? Please don't be afraid to answer me. He will not touch you again. You have my word on it."

Clara drew in a shattered breath. "Yes. He beat me up because I asked him to leave," she said in a defeated tone.

"That's a damned lie!" the man yelled. "She fell! You tell him you fell, Clara, or you'll regret it!"

"Terroristic threats and acts," Rourke said quietly. "Assault and battery. My, my, you are going to be in trouble."

"Like hell I am," the man said nervously and tried to make a run for it. Rourke had him on the floor in a heartbeat, and cuffed.

"You carry handcuffs around with you?"

Carson asked in a shocked tone.

"Hey, you never know when they might come in handy," Rourke told him. "No, actually, I bought them a week ago, with other . . . intentions in mind."

"You let me go! I want to go!" the man groaned. "It wasn't even my idea to come back here, but I've got an outstanding warrant in San Diego and he threatened to go to my parole officer!"

"He, who?" Rourke asked, jerking him to his feet.

The man hesitated. He actually looked afraid.

Tank joined Rourke on the porch. "Who?"

"Don't know his name," Baker said miserably. "He wore a suit. Said he was a fed and he could lock me up for ten years. He said to come here and say the house was mine. Don't know why. He paid for the plane ticket. Listen, I don't want no more trouble! I just want to go home!"

"Not just yet," Tank told him acidly. "First there's a little matter of assault and battery and some missing paperwork."

"Damned paperwork's under the mattress in the spare bedroom," he grumbled. "And I'm sorry I hit her, but she told me to get out." His face flamed. "Ain't no woman alive talking to me like that on my own place!"

"It's not your place," Merissa said with cold pride. She was shaking but her voice was almost steady. "It's ours. And it will suit us both very well if we never have to see you again."

"You won't," Tank assured her. He looked at the man with icy eyes. "He's going to jail for a long, long time."

"He'll get me a lawyer," Baker told him. "He'll pay for it. He'll say those women lied."

"You want to take a look at Clara's face and run that line by me again?" Tank demanded.

"Well, I ain't going to jail!"

He broke away from the men and took off out the back of the cabin.

"Carson, you're quicker than I am," Rourke began.

Just as Carson started to the side of the cabin, there was a loud report.

Tank swore once, violently. "Stay with Clara and Merissa," he told Rourke. He and Carson ran around to the back of the cabin. Just down the trail there was a crumpled body.

Carson went down on one knee. He felt for a pulse he knew he wouldn't find and got to his feet again. "Better call the coroner," he told Tank, and deliberately stood in front of him. "Judging from the size of the exit wound, it was a high caliber rifle. Get out of here, quick!" he added. "Go! He isn't after me!"

Tank went around the side of the house and up onto the porch. "We'd better get inside," he said.

"Bill?" Clara asked worriedly.

"Dead," Tank said bluntly. "I'm sorry."

Clara wept quietly. "I'm sorry he's dead, but only because he was once my husband. He was the most cruel human being I've ever known."

"I can understand why," Tank said, looking at her ravaged, bruised face. "I'm sorry I wasn't here." He put an arm around Merissa, who was shaking, and held her close. He pulled Clara to his other side. "It's going to be all right," he said softly. "Nobody's hurting my girls on my watch."

They both sobbed. He just held them closer.

The sheriff came first, followed by EMTs, and a deputy stood watch over the remains until the coroner was able to get there.

Sheriff Cody Banks was furious when he saw Clara's face. "Any man who would do that to a woman should be shot," he muttered furiously.

"That's why I phoned you," Tank said. "I meant to have him arrested for it. But he ran, and someone took him out. The same someone," he added heavily, "that I think is after me."

"You want to run that by me again?" Cody asked.

Tank nodded. "You can come to supper. We'll tell you everything we know." He indicated his two male companions. "There's a lot going on."

"I wouldn't mind supper," Cody replied with a grin. "I'm so tired of burnt eggs and half-cooked bacon."

"You're not married?" Rourke asked.

Cody shook his head sadly. "You know that new strain of flu that's going around, the deadly one? She was a doctor. She was treating a patient in a hospital down in Boulder. She died."

"I'm sorry," Rourke said softly.

"Me, too," Cody replied. "It was over a year ago, but it takes some getting used to. We'd only been married two years."

Tank looked at Merissa and imagined how he would have felt in Cody's position. It was devastating.

"What about Clara and Merissa?" he

asked the room at large. "Are they going to be safe here?"

"You want a gut reply, no," Rourke said abruptly. "If he's brazen enough to kill one of his own accomplices, he'll kill anybody. He brought Clara's husband back here for some reason that we don't know. But it means he's targeted them. Maybe he knew the man's past and hoped he'd kill them." He shook his head. "Whatever the reason, they're in as much danger as you are."

"They can come and live at the ranch," Tank said. "We've got three spare bedrooms. It's a huge place."

"It's such an imposition," Clara protested.

"Yes," Merissa added worriedly.

Tank just smiled. "Lots of room and good company. You can play with Mallory's baby, too," he added.

Clara and Merissa just melted. "Their little boy?" Merissa asked, and her eyes lit up. "I love babies."

Tank looked absolutely smitten. He sighed and smiled to himself.

"Babies!" Carson's face was harder than stone. He turned on his heel and walked away. It was such an odd reaction that Tank and Rourke exchanged curious looks.

"Well, if you want my vote," Cody added, "I think it's a good idea to get the women out of here. This place is too isolated for comfort."

"I don't know," Merissa said after a minute. "I mean, we've been here all this time alone and he hasn't tried anything. He's bugged the phones, but he didn't try to hurt us."

"That's true," Clara said. She sighed. "I just don't understand what he wants from us."

"To torture him, of course," Rourke said, jerking his head toward Tank. "To make him nervous, unsettle him, keep him off his guard. Maybe keep him from remembering something the enemy doesn't want remembered."

"Enemy." Cody chuckled. "War term."

Rourke shrugged. "I've spent my life fighting small wars all over the world, in and out of the military. Force of habit."

"Then if he's just trying to unsettle us, it won't matter if we stay here," Merissa said softly. She looked up at Tank worriedly. "I'm sorry, it's a generous offer, really it is. But I'm uneasy around other people. I just don't . . . socialize all that much. And if I'm upset, I can't work."

Tank was disappointed. And worried. "You'd have a room all to yourself."

She nodded. "Yes, but you have a big family. They're very nice," she added, holding up a hand. "But I'm a solitary person." She looked very worried. "I'm odd, you know. I don't fit in with other people."

"You fit in with me," he pointed out and he smiled.

She smiled back. "Of course. But . . ."

"Don't force her," Clara said softly. "We've both had too much of that in our lives, both physical and verbal."

"Okay," Tank said at once. "I won't." He looked at Merissa with a speaking expression. "But I'm going to worry."

Merissa smiled. "We'll be okay."

"Yes, they will," Carson said quietly, returning to the porch. "I'm moving in here."

"What?" three voices said in unison.

Carson glared at the two men. "Rourke can't stay here and watch you, too," he told Tank. "Besides, how do you think the rogue agent knew about her husband?" He indicated Clara.

"He bugged the phones," Tank said. "But we found all the bugs, right?" he asked Rourke, who'd done the sweep.

"We were talking about Bill before you found them," Clara confessed sadly. "Including where he worked. I'm sorry. It was my fault."

Tank put an arm around her. "Nothing is your fault," he said gently. "The man was an animal. The world is better off without him. I'm just sorry about the way it went down."

"Me, too," Clara said. "Shot down like an animal . . . and just before Christmas." Her eyes teared up.

"It will be all right, Mama," Merissa said, hugging her close. "We all have to face what he did. He was violent and he hurt us. He hurt other people, too. His end was like his life, a mirror of the damage he did." She closed her eyes. "I'm sorry, too. Whatever else he was, he was still my father. But at least we don't have to live in fear of him anymore."

"It's just, the way he died," Clara said. She wiped her eyes. "He had a girlfriend, didn't he? Should we try to find her?"

Tank and Cody Banks exchanged meaningful looks. There might be clues to the man's identity in Bill Blake's circle of friends in California. "That's not a bad idea," Tank said.

Cody nodded.

"I have a friend who lives in San Diego," Rourke said. "I'll get him on it. If you have a contact there in the sheriff's department," he told Cody, "that would help. His friends and acquaintances might be able to point us to clues about the rogue agent's identity."

"I agree," Cody said. "Good thinking. I'll get on it."

A van pulled up in the driveway and a man in jeans and a sweatshirt got out, along with a younger man who stayed in the van. The coroner was tall, with thinning hair and a sad face.

"The coroner," Cody introduced. "Mack Hollis."

"Hello," he greeted them. "I understand there was a death?"

Cody nodded. "My man is standing over the body. I'll show you where it is."

The two men went around the house. The man in the van climbed out and followed closely behind.

Clara's face was very pale. "I don't want to be out here when they bring him around . . ."

"He'll be in a body bag," Tank said gently. "You won't have to see him. But we can go inside if you'd rather."

"I'd rather," Clara said gently.

Carson followed Tank and the two women into the house. The women looked at him with curiosity and a little uneasiness.

"I'll be a model houseguest," Carson told them politely. "I'll be outside most of the time, observing, setting up a perimeter. I'll only need a room to sleep in at night."

Merissa was nervous. It showed.

Carson actually smiled. "I haven't ever hurt a woman."

Merissa relaxed a little and managed a smile in return. "Okay."

"You can have the guest bedroom," Clara said gently. "It's sort of cluttered . . ."

"Leave it that way. I don't mind clutter. Now if you'll excuse me, I'll get to work." He nodded to Tank and Rourke and went back outside.

"Well," Rourke told Tank, who was irritated, "he's got a point. You're the danger magnet right now. If you stay here, you put them in even more danger."

"I know that," Tank gritted. "That doesn't mean I like it."

Merissa went right up to him. "We'd feel safer with a man here, especially after what just happened," she said. "It's okay."

He relaxed. He smoothed his big hand over her hair. "I worry."

She smiled. Her eyes were soft with affection. "I like that."

He chuckled.

Cody came back into the cabin a few minutes later. The women had made coffee, and

Rourke and Tank were sharing a pot with them.

"Coffee?" Merissa asked the sheriff.

"Sorry, no time," he replied. "We've got him loaded up and our investigator is out there doing the walkaround with a crime scene technician. It will take a little time to complete, but they won't bother you," he told the women. "The investigator will need to speak with you. And I'll need a report. If I give you the forms, can you fill them out and have them dropped by my office?"

"Certainly," Clara said for both of them. She teared up again. "He was a bad man. But when we first married, he was so gentle and kind . . ." She shook her head. "I never understood what changed him."

"Life happens," Cody said quietly. "I am sorry for your loss."

"Thank you," Merissa said.

Cody looked at Tank. "What time is supper?"

Tank chuckled. "Six sharp. You don't have to dress. We're informal."

Cody grinned. "Okay. See you then."

Tank and Rourke stayed until the investigator was finished and the women had given their information to him. The crime scene technicians packed up and left with him, with trace evidence, photographic evidence and measurements intact.

"I'll get home," Tank said. "I hate to leave you, both of you, here." He sighed. "But Carson's right. I don't want to make you a target. It's me he's after."

Merissa hugged him. "Thanks for caring."

"Silly woman," he teased. He bent and kissed her gently, in front of them all. "I have to take care of my girl."

She beamed. "Don't go out alone."

He grinned. "Never." He glanced at Rourke. "He wouldn't let me."

"Dead right," Rourke replied. "And don't be afraid of Carson," he added gently. "He's not what he seems. He's a good man. He'll take care of you."

"He's very . . ." Clara searched for words.

"Yes." Rourke laughed. "He's very everything. But he'll never let you down."

"Okay," Merissa said.

"I'll call you later," Tank told Merissa. He kissed her again and he and Rourke left the cabin.

On the way home, he stopped by a local jewelry store. Christmas was almost on them, and he meant to get her something very special indeed. She liked rubies. He smiled as he picked out a set of rings.

CHAPTER NINE

Merissa found Carson hard going as a houseguest. He never said a word. He nodded as he passed them when he got up in the morning, but he was constantly out and about on the property. He checked out all the rooms. There was an attic, too, but Merissa assured him that it was only a crawlspace and a ladder would be required to access it. They didn't even have a ladder.

The second day he was there, Merissa got up the nerve to ask him if he wanted coffee when he started out the door.

He paused, glanced at her wary expression and retraced his steps. He was much taller than she was, about Dalton's height. But he was much more somber and uptight.

"It's okay if you don't," she said quickly. "I just wanted to offer. I mean, you don't eat meals with us or . . . We wouldn't mind, you know, there's always extra food . . ."

He liked her shyness. It was unusual. Well,

Cash Grier's vicious little secretary was shy when she wasn't verbally assaulting him. He hated the memory of her. He hated having hurt her . . .

Merissa swallowed, because he looked suddenly angry. She had a terror of angry men, learned at a very early age from her father.

Carson saw it and forcibly relaxed his expression. "I appreciate the offer of food, but I have meals at the Kirk ranch, so that I can keep Dalton up-to-date." He smiled. "He really has a case on you."

She smiled back, and her whole face lit up. "I sort of have a case on him, too," she confessed. "He's . . . very special."

"He feels the same about you." He hesitated. "I would like coffee."

She beamed. "I just made a fresh pot. It's rather strong," she said hesitantly.

"I like coffee that needs to be cut with a knife," he told her.

She was amazed at the difference it made when he smiled. He was an odd sort of man, reclusive and introverted. But she sensed tragedy about him. Great tragedy.

Her eyes became that odd opaque shade that indicated she was seeing things far away and back in time. She poured his coffee and put it in front of him. She sat down with her own. Her expression was troubled.

He was quick. He knew about her special gifts. "You know things about me," he said quietly.

"Yes," she confessed.

"And not gleaned from any conventional source."

"That's also true." She looked at him with true compassion. "I'm so sorry, for what happened to you."

His face hardened for a moment and then suddenly relaxed. He stared into the black coffee. "I've never spoken of it," he replied quietly. "My parents are both dead, and I had no siblings. I have a cousin or two spread around in the Lakota and Northern Cheyenne reservations. Nobody close. Not anymore."

"Losing the child was the worst of it," she said in a soft monotone, her eyes far away. "She lied to you." Her face tautened. "But it wasn't your fault," she said suddenly, staring right into his shocked eyes. "He was drinking . . ."

He drew in a sharp breath.

"You didn't know," she said, nodding. "You should check the police report. It was why he wrecked the car. He didn't mean to kill her, or himself."

"I chased them," he gritted.

"Of course you did. You were young and in love, and she'd hurt you. It's not a good thing, but it's a human thing. It was a mistake. But you're still punishing yourself for it. What sort of life is that?" she asked gently.

He bit his lower lip, almost hard enough to draw blood.

"I know. You don't speak of such matters to anyone. But I'm . . . not like other people," she faltered. She swallowed. "I know things. I see things. I'm outside, looking in. I don't belong to this world, except in a disassociated fashion. I'm an outcast. Like you," she added with a sad smile.

He looked at her with his true face, the one he never let show. It was vulnerable and still and sad. "Her cousin told me the child was mine. She was seven months pregnant, but she didn't want me. She wanted him. He beat her, abused her . . . treated her like dirt. It didn't matter. She wouldn't leave him. I couldn't make her see sense. He came to her house and saw me, and ordered her into the car. He jerked her in, with no consideration for her condition, and sped off. I thought . . . he was going to hurt her. She had my child inside her. I chased them, trying to save her." His eyes closed. "He hit the side of the bridge. It was made of wood and the car went through it. They dropped into the river, far below. They found the bodies downstream the next day."

"I'm so sorry," she told him, and meant it. "It destroyed your life."

"Yes," he said tautly. "I decided that variety was better than commitment." He looked world-weary. "But it's not. At the end of the day, I'm still alone."

"We're all alone, inside ourselves," she said, her voice quiet and soft. "I've lived that way, too. Well, not with the variety thing." She laughed. "My mother and I are people of faith. We don't walk in step with the modern world."

He cocked his head and studied her. Innocence. It was as clear as day. It reminded him of Carlie's face, as guileless as a child's. He remembered what he'd said to Carlie and it shamed him all over again.

Merissa frowned. "There was an attack," she said in a monotone. "With a knife. She tried to save him . . ."

"She? Who?"

"She works for a man in a uniform," she said. She blinked. "I'm sorry, I can't see any more than that. But there are secrets, deadly secrets. She doesn't even know some of them. Her father . . ." She cleared her throat. "It went away."

He knew who she was seeing. Carlie. He remembered the odd fit of her T-shirt at the shoulder and her fear of his knife. He remembered what she'd told them about her father being attacked with a knife. Maybe she'd gotten in front of him, been cut. And he'd said he liked his women prettier and more physically perfect! He almost groaned.

"You have . . . a remarkable gift," he managed after a minute.

"A gift and a curse," she replied. "I hate most of the things I see. It's what saved Dalton, though," she told him. "I told him that he was under threat because of something he didn't remember. He had no idea."

He nodded. "His assailant would probably have killed him if you hadn't given him the warning." He hesitated. "What do you see, in my future, if you don't mind my asking?"

She studied him for a long time. Her eyes took on the opaque look once more. "Your past will mar your future," she said quietly. "It makes a wall, between you and something you want. Something you're afraid to want."

He frowned. "Do you know what it is, exactly?"

She drew in a breath. "Sorry. It doesn't

work that way. It's like I can see the pattern of things, but not the substance. Sort of like seeing the skeleton, with no flesh on it."

He smiled. "Well, I guess I'd better lie about my past when whatever it is presents itself," he said with a twist of his lips.

"Lying is never a good idea," she pointed out. "Even when it's painful, the truth is the best path."

"Perhaps," he said. He finished his coffee and got to his feet. "Thank you," he said solemnly.

"For what?" she asked.

He smiled. "For being a good listener."

She smiled back. "I might add that I never speak of personal matters to people who aren't involved with them. I won't tell anyone what I know about you." She pursed her lips. "Not even the crocodile thing, overseas."

"That wasn't really me. It was Rourke. I just assisted."

"Why did Rourke feed a man to a crocodile?" she asked curiously.

His face went taut. "The man in question tortured a young woman — a personal friend of Rourke's who's a photojournalist. He used a knife on her. She'll carry the scars forever, unless she decides to have plastic surgery. Right now, she won't talk about it. She calls them badges of courage."

"What a brave young woman," Merissa said.

"Very brave. Rourke's known her since she was a child. He hates her most of the time, God knows why. But he went berserk when she was kidnapped."

"Yes. I saw her," she replied. "I told Rourke what I saw."

He raised both eyebrows.

She just smiled.

He shook his head. He got the idea. She didn't talk about her readings.

"I'll get back to work. Sing out if you need me," he said.

"I will. Thanks," she added gently. "For taking care of us."

"I'm just working the perimeter." He laughed. "I don't think you're really in any danger, either of you. I think he's just pulling Dalton's strings, making him dance." His eyes went cold. "He's a piece of work, this guy, whoever he is."

"I wish we knew why he's targeting Dalton," Merissa said worriedly.

"No idea?" he asked her.

She shook her head. "I can't see things that closely. In this case, I wish I could!"

He nodded. He left her to her thoughts.

Later in the day, Merissa had a phone call. "Tough luck. About your father, I mean," a voice with a thick Cockney accident said.

"Who is this?" she demanded, but she knew. It was obvious. "Why did you send him here?" she added.

"If your boyfriend had stayed away, your father might have solved a problem for me."

"What problem?" She was looking out the window, wishing Carson would come in.

"I don't want you telling Dalton anything else. I don't want you warning him, Witch Woman," he added in a cold, merciless voice.

"You can't stop me unless you kill me," she said angrily.

"I don't have to threaten you. There's always mommy."

Her heart stopped. Clara had driven into town to shop. "What have you done to her?" she exclaimed, terrified.

"Relax. She's safe. At least, for today." He paused. "I want you to stop reading Kirk's future. You tell him anything else, about me, about the past, and your mother will pay for it, do you understand me?"

She swallowed hard. "Yes."

"I'll know. Your boy Rourke may have removed all the bugs, but I have a couple he won't find."

"There's someone else," she told him in the monotone she employed when she was reading someone, when she touched some nebulous force that supplied her with intelligence that came from God knew where. "Someone who knows all about you. You think he's dead, but he's not, he's . . ." She shut up quickly. "Even if you kill Dalton, the other man will tell. Men are looking for him right now."

"Which men? Where?" he demanded.

She blinked. "I don't know," she said. Her voice was racked with pain. "It's not like reading a book or watching a movie. I just get feelings, impressions." She hesitated. "You should go away right now, while there's time," she said huskily. "I can see your future. If you were a friend, and I was reading for you, I wouldn't even tell you, it's so horrible . . ."

"That's just pathetic," he spat. "You think I believe all that hoodoo? It's just made up things!"

"If you truly believe that, then why do you want me to stop telling Dalton things?" she asked reasonably.

There was a pause. Carson walked in and

she gestured at the phone frantically, hoping he'd understand.

He was quick. He went into her office.

"I don't believe it," the man on the phone said angrily.

"Neither does Dalton," she assured him.

"Sure. But you warned him I was after him," he replied. "You knew."

"Yes, I knew, but I don't know why and neither does Dalton! What do you want?"

There was a pause, as if she'd surprised him with the sincerity in her tone.

"Well?" she persisted. "You're targeting a man for something that he doesn't even know," she said angrily. "It's the other man you'd better worry about. He knows you . . ."

This time there was an intake of breath. "Well, I'll be damned," he said to himself. "I know who you're talking about. Thanks, kid. I'll take care of that little problem right away!"

He hung up.

Merissa stared at the phone with horror. She'd sent him out to kill a man by telling him about his future. She didn't know who the man was, she couldn't warn him. Whoever it was, he was going to die because of her!

Carson came in, hesitating.

She looked at him with horror as she hung up the phone.

"I've got a trace on the call," he told her. "What did he say?"

"I told him that he had another man to worry about instead of Dalton, a man who knew him and would tell what he knew. I don't know who it is, but he'll die because of me!" she moaned. "I've killed him!"

Carson moved closer. "You haven't," he assured her. His black eyes narrowed. "Did he threaten you?"

"He threatened my mother," she said miserably. "He says if I tell Dalton anything else he'll know it. He says Rourke didn't find all the bugs . . ."

He held up a hand and motioned her outside.

"Yes, Rourke did," he said deliberately. "The man lied to you. He can't hear what's going on in here. It's perfectly safe to talk."

"You're sure?" she replied, playing along.

"Positive. Come here a minute, I want you to look at something."

She followed him off the porch and out into the yard.

"I'll get Rourke over here to do another sweep," Carson assured her.

"But what about the man . . . ?"

"We'll try to find him," Carson said. "I'll

make some phone calls. It's not your fault. You were trying to save your mother."

She looked world-weary. "I'm so tired of all this," she said. "Will it ever end?"

"Yes, it will. I promise you, it will."

She smiled sadly. She wasn't convinced.

Clara came home and Merissa spoke to her in the yard, telling her what had happened in her absence.

"Maybe we should move in with the Kirks," Clara said worriedly.

"It's Christmas day after tomorrow," Merissa said softly. "I don't want to impose on their family that way. We're going to be all right," Merissa promised. "I know it's scary, but I trust Carson. He's a good man."

"He's a very odd man." Clara laughed. "But if you trust him, I will, too." She hugged the younger woman. "My poor baby. It's been such a traumatic few weeks. We should look forward to spring. I mean, we always get good times after bad ones. Don't we?"

Merissa nodded. She sighed. "I hope so."

"We won't say anything in the house that concerns Dalton or spies or bugs or anything else," Clara assured her. She was somber then. "People in town are talking about Bill's death," she said. "We're going to be the subject of gossip again. And what do we do about his funeral, sweetie?" she added.

"Will it be up to us to bury him, or does his girlfriend want to take care of the arrangements? Could we ask Sheriff Banks to call her?"

"I think we might," Clara replied. "That terrible man, to send him back here and subject us to the horror all over again." She closed her eyes. "He killed Bill."

"I may have helped him kill someone else," Merissa said with anguish, and explained.

"Perhaps if I tried to help you with a reading of my own," Clara pondered.

"Would you?" Merissa asked. "You're better at some things than I am. It might help. Whatever you find out, we could tell Dalton." She shook her head. "I'm afraid the sheriff thinks we wear pointy hats and dance naked around bonfires in the deep woods."

"He's a nice man," Clara responded. "He's just very normal. The paranormal has no place in his life."

"That's like most people."

"Oh, I ran into Dr. Harrison," Clara said. "He asked about your headaches."

"They're better," Merissa replied. "I do wish they'd go away, though," she grumbled as they went into the kitchen. "I just got a refill on my prescription medicine yesterday and stuck it in my bedside table. I don't know what I'd do without those capsules."

"At least you have something that works now. Carson said he's driving over to see Dalton." She pursed her lips. "Might you like to go with him?" she teased.

Merissa's face lit up. "Might I? I'll get my coat!"

She went to the front door. "Carson, can I go, too?" she called.

He threw up a hand and motioned her to the car he was driving.

"I'll just be a minute!"

She grabbed her coat, kissed her mother and ran out to the car. Carson opened the door for her, smiling at her surprise.

"My mother had excellent manners," he explained as they drove to the Kirk ranch. "She taught me courtesy."

"It's very nice in a man," she said.

"Works wonders with women," he quipped.

She stared at him quietly. "Women will be your downfall," she said. "Sorry. I didn't mean to pipe up like that." She flushed.

"No offense taken," he replied. He glanced at her. "What do you mean, though?"

"Your past will affect your future," she

repeated what she'd told him once.

"You mean I'm going to meet some innocent little thing who'll think I'm a rake and avoid me because of it?" He laughed.

It wasn't really funny, what she'd seen in her vision. But it was perhaps better not to tell him all of it. "Something like that, I'm afraid," she said instead. However, it was going to be much more serious than he ever realized. He didn't seem to think of his wild lifestyle as a problem. It would become his worst one.

They drove up at the Kirk ranch and Dalton turned from a conversation he was having with one of his men. When Merissa got out of the car, he was smiling from ear to ear as he came to meet her.

"What a nice surprise!" he exclaimed, and hugged her. "I was coming over to see you later," he teased. "Saved me a trip."

She smiled. "I have a little problem."

He looked immediately at Carson.

"Hey," Carson said indignantly, "I don't poach."

Tank looked embarrassed. "Sorry."

Carson just chuckled. "I need to talk to Rourke."

"He's in the house. Go ahead."

He nodded and left them alone.

"It's nothing like that," Merissa told him softly. "Carson is . . . not what he seems. The other man called me, the one who's stalking you."

"What did he say?" Dalton asked at once, concerned.

"He said that if I tell you anything else about him, he'll know, and my mother will pay for it." She ground her teeth together. "Then I slipped up and told him there was someone else, someone he thought was dead, who knows much more than you do and who was about to tell people." Her eyes teared up. "He'll kill the man, and I don't even know who it is or how to warn him. Carson said he'd make some phone calls." She looked up at Tank. "I don't want someone innocent to die because of me."

He drew her close and hugged her. "We'll find out who it is and warn him. Don't take it so to heart. You might even be wrong, for once," he teased.

"I don't think so."

He lifted his head. "You worry too much."

She grimaced. "Not so much anymore, I wore out my nerves on you, thinking about that man killing you."

He touched her mouth with the tips of his fingers. "I'm hard to kill. Honest."

She managed a smile.

"Come on inside."

"I can't stay long," she said worriedly. "Mama's by herself. I'm afraid for her . . ."

Even as she spoke, Carson came down the steps and went toward his car. "I'm going back over to the Bakers. Can you bring Merissa home?" he asked Tank.

Tank grinned. "Of course."

"Thanks. See you."

He drove off with a wave.

Tank took Merissa into the house. The whole family was in the living room, playing with Mallory and Morie's little boy on the carpet. Even Bolinda, visibly pregnant, was sitting on the floor beside her husband, Cane. They looked absolutely fascinated.

There was a huge, brilliantly decorated Christmas tree in the corner of the room, with gaily wrapped presents piled up to the second limb around it. The tree was artificial, Tank had told her, because Morie had allergies that kept them from having a live tree.

"The tree is beautiful," she whispered.

He chuckled. "Morie puts them up on Thanksgiving eve," he told her. "And they stay up until New Year's Day."

"We're always late with ours. But we usually take them down the day after Christmas."

"I could come and help you take it down," he offered with a smile. "I can reach the top to get the star off without a ladder."

She laughed softly. "We don't have a star. But that would be nice."

He grinned from ear to ear. The others, hearing voices, looked over at them.

Merissa glanced up at Tank worriedly.

"It's all right," he said softly, putting an arm around her. He walked her closer to the sofa.

Four people and a baby looked at her.

She flushed and moved closer to Tank.

His arm tightened.

"Have a seat and an ugly, nonbiodegradable but functional highly colored plastic baby toy, and join in the fun," Mallory invited with a grin, handing her a rattle.

It broke the ice. Merissa burst out laughing as she took the toy from him.

"Sit down," Morie invited with a smile. "We don't bite, honest."

"And nobody's going to make sarcastic remarks," Bolinda added gently.

Merissa sat down, Tank dropping to the couch beside her. "You were always kind to me in school, when a lot of people weren't," she said to Bolinda. "I had to drop out and

225

be homeschooled eventually because I couldn't take it anymore."

Bolinda reached up and patted her arm. "Different is not bad. You have a real gift. We're all grateful that you were able to warn Tank in time to save his life."

"Amen to that," Mallory agreed, and Cane nodded. "We're sort of used to him. Even if I can play the piano better than he can," he added dryly.

"Challenge. Challenge!" Cane piped in.

"Yeah. You think you're better than me, you can prove it," Mallory said haughtily.

Tank flexed his fingers and grinned at Merissa, who was laughing. "Okay."

He went to the piano. "Requests?" he called out.

"Anything except Rach Three," Mallory said sourly, alluding to the almost impossible-to-play Rachmaninoff 3 composition by the great Russian composer.

"Jealous," Tank told Merissa in a stage whisper. "I can play it and he can't."

"I could play it if I wanted to," Mallory muttered.

"I love 'Send in the Clowns,' " Merissa said softly.

Tank's eyebrows lifted.

"Did I say something wrong?" she asked worriedly.

"It's his favorite," Cane said gently and laughed.

"Oh!" She flushed as she met Tank's soft, searching eyes.

"Similar tastes in music," he teased. "Not a bad thing at all. Okay. Here goes."

He began to play. Merissa closed her eyes to drink in the sweet beauty of the song. It was timeless, ageless, haunting. Her mother had a recording of it sung by Judy Collins, inherited from Merissa's grandmother, who had loved it dearly. Merissa had fallen in love with the recording long ago. Even without the words, the melody was exquisite.

Tank finished. Merissa wiped her eyes. He grinned.

"Okay," he invited Mallory, who was holding his son and grinning. "Your turn."

Mallory kissed the little boy and handed him over to a beaming Morie. "On my way."

Tank got up and sat beside Merissa on the sofa. Mallory flexed his own fingers, gave Tank a smug grin and launched into his own favorite, the theme from *August Rush*.

Merissa sat entranced while he played. When he finished, she clapped.

"Sorry," she told Tank.

He only laughed. "No need. He really is

better than me. I just like to pull his chain occasionally. Bravo, Mallory," he added, and he clapped, too. "I yield to a maestro."

Mallory made him a mock bow. Then he went back to playing with the baby.

"Coffee?" Morie asked, surrendering the baby to Mallory again as she got to her feet.

"That would be very nice," Merissa said.

"Come with me," Morie invited, smiling.

Merissa smiled at Tank and went to join the other woman in the kitchen.

"You can be in charge of mugs." Morie laughed. "They're in the cupboard, there."

Merissa went to get them. They were thick white mugs. She looked at them with surprise. The Kirk ranch was massive. She expected bone china, at the least.

Morie saw her expression and grinned. "We don't use the good china except at Christmas dinner," she confessed. "Nobody likes hand washing every single piece of it, you see. Those —" she indicated the mugs "— go very nicely into the dishwasher and never crack."

"You aren't what I expected," Merissa confessed shyly. "I mean, I knew Bolinda from when I was very young, and she was always kind. But people say you're from a very powerful ranching family in Texas. I thought . . ."

Morie put an arm around her shoulders impulsively and hugged her. "We're just people," she pointed out. "My dad's just as much at home in a dented pickup with torn seats as he is in a Jaguar. He and my mother raised my brother and me not to be snobs," she added with a chuckle.

"I didn't mean it like that," Merissa said softly, and smiled.

"I know." Morie sliced pound cake and put it on a platter. She glanced at Merissa. "We all know what happened over at your place. I'm so sorry. Just before Christmas, too."

"I still don't understand why the man would do something so horrible. He sent my father to terrorize us." She closed her eyes and shivered delicately. "You have no idea what he did to us, to my mother and me, before Dalton came and the others came and rescued us. He said he was going to kill me. . . ."

Morie hugged her close and rocked her. "It's all right. He'll never hurt you again."

She shivered. "The man shot him dead, right in our backyard." She pulled away and wiped at her eyes with a paper towel Morie passed to her. "Why kill him?"

"Apparently he'd served his purpose," the older woman said quietly. "Or some purpose that only he knew. People like that aren't quite sane, I think."

Merissa nodded. "He's dangerous. The most dangerous person I've ever heard of. He said he'd be listening, and if I told Dalton anything else about him he'd kill Mama."

Morie grimaced. "If it helps, these things do finally get resolved. One way or another." Her eyes were sad. "You heard about Joe Bascomb, didn't you?"

"Everybody did," the other woman said. "It was so brave of you, going out to find Mallory after Bascomb had kidnapped him and left him to die. He could have killed you."

"I knew that," Morie said. "But I would have had no life without Mallory."

It was said in a matter-of-fact way. Merissa saw the love in the other woman's eyes for her husband as she glanced through the doorway of the kitchen past the dining room into the living room beyond, where Mallory was sprawled on the carpet with their son.

She looked back at Merissa. "You would have done the same, if it had been Tank," she said perceptively.

"Of course," Merissa said without a pause. She drew in a breath. "He's my whole world now. I can't imagine life without him in it."

Morie smiled. "You won't have to, from what I've seen," she told her. "You watch, he'll come through that door any minute. He can't stand to be away from you. He's been mooning around here all day trying to find an excuse to go and see about you . . . See?" she whispered.

Tank appeared in the doorway, hands in his jean pockets, eyebrows raised. "Are we ever going to get coffee, you think?" he mused.

The women laughed.

"We're putting it on the tray now, with cake," Morie said. "Want to carry it in for us?"

He grinned. "My pleasure." He glanced at Merissa with a look in his eyes that made her just melt.

He put the tray down on the coffee table and drew Merissa to his side on the sofa.

"I like mine black," he told her. He smiled.

She laughed. "I like mine with cream and sugar."

"It doesn't matter. You like 'Send in the Clowns,' " he teased. "We'll find other things in common, too."

"Yes." She leaned over to pour the coffee for him.

All too soon, she had to leave. Tank drove

her back to her home, but he stopped a little way from the cabin, put the truck out of gear and removed their seat belts. While she was wondering why, he pulled her across his lap and kissed her with a starving passion.

She reacted to it at once, her arms around his neck, her body straining to get as close to him as she possibly could.

His hand went under her blouse, searching for soft flesh to explore. His mouth teased around her lips until he roused her. The kiss was deeper, slower, hungrier than any they'd shared before. He groaned.

"I'm sorry," she whispered, feeling his anguish.

"We should get married," he blurted out.

CHAPTER TEN

Merissa drew back from him with a faint gasp. "What?" she stammered.

He ground his teeth together. She looked so shocked that he was embarrassed, and suddenly his confidence about her feelings for him took a nose-dive. The set of rings in his pocket was burning a hole in the material of his coat now. "I didn't mean to say that," he lied. "I'm sorry. I got in over my head a little too quickly."

"It's . . . all right," she said, moving away from him, back to her own seat. She fastened her seat belt for something to do. "No harm." She tried to smile. For an instant she'd thought he meant it, and her heart sailed up into the sky. Now he was busy backtracking.

"I'm really sorry . . ."

"Oh, you don't have to apologize," she assured him urgently. "I know men sometimes say things they don't mean when they, well, you know." She flushed. He seemed really regretful about what he'd said. She only wanted to ease the embarrassment. "I'm not ready to get married, anyway," she lied. "So it's fine. Really."

He didn't look reassured. In fact, he looked puzzled and then almost offended. He put his own seat belt back on, put the truck in gear and drove up to her porch.

He cut off the engine. "I'll walk you inside," he said quietly. "I want to make sure Carson's here."

"Okay."

They moved into the house in silence, not touching, not speaking. Merissa was concerned. He must be terribly embarrassed to have blurted out such a compromising proposal. He had been vague about the future, but he'd never said anything about marriage. She was crazy about him, and he seemed to have feelings for her. But it was one thing to feel passion for someone, quite another to consider spending the rest of your life with her. She wanted Tank to be sure. And she wanted a proposal that came when he wasn't out of his mind with desire.

So she didn't say anything about their former conversation.

"I'm home," Merissa called.

Clara came out of the kitchen. "So I see.

Hello, Dalton," she greeted with a smile.

He nodded, but he didn't smile. "I just wanted to make sure everything was okay," he told the women. "I'll check back tomorrow. Have a good night."

He left without even looking at Merissa.

"What happened?" Clara asked worriedly.

Merissa drew in a breath. "I'm not sure. And I can't talk about it right now," she added gently. "I'm sorry."

Clara hugged her. "Have a nice cup of hot chocolate while I peel potatoes for supper. Carson's outside working on some project of his. He won't tell me what it is."

"Is he near the house?" Merissa asked, curious.

"Not really," her mother said. "He was going to start putting up surveillance devices at the boundaries of the property. Why?"

"I just wondered." She had an uneasy feeling, but she didn't want to put it into words. She drew in a long breath and rubbed her temple.

"Not another headache?" her mother asked worriedly.

"No," she said. "Well, not yet, anyway."

"You do know where you left your prescription medicine?"

"Of course," Merissa said, and smiled wanly. "It's in my bedside table, where I always keep it." She cocked her head. "You think I'll get one, don't you?"

Her mother was noncommittal. "You look worried and Dalton looked, I don't know, upset."

Merissa averted her eyes. "We had a little . . . misunderstanding."

Clara patted her shoulder affectionately. "It's early days yet," she said gently. "You don't really know each other. Time will take care of that."

Merissa shrugged. "I hope so."

"Things are usually a little rocky at first. But he's very fond of you. He doesn't make any secret of it."

Merissa nodded. She glanced at her mother. Clara had made her a cup of hot chocolate. She put it in front of her at the table. She poured potatoes into a big bowl, got a knife and sat down to peel them.

"It takes time for people to grow together and trust one another," she told Merissa. "He's been alone for a long time."

"He's very rich," Merissa said through her teeth.

"And you think he'll consider you a gold digger — is that a proper modern word?" Clara laughed. "You're the least mercenary person I've ever known."

"Still, it's a very different lifestyle than ours."

"He's a rancher. He loves animals. He loves the land. He's like us. So are his brothers and their wives."

Merissa made a face. She sipped the hot chocolate and sighed with pure contentment. "Nobody makes this like you do."

"Thank you, dear." She was quiet.

"You're thinking about my father, aren't you?" she asked.

Clara nodded. "I loved him once," she said. "It was a horrible way to die, a horrible thing to do, to bring him back here and sacrifice him." She lifted her eyes to her daughter's. "He was evil. But even a dog shouldn't die like that."

"I know." Merissa stared into the hot chocolate. "That man should die like that. The one who sent my father back here, who's trying to kill Dalton."

Clara's knife was still. "You should never wish such things on anyone," she said in her soft voice.

"I know," Merissa replied. "It's unnecessary. I've seen his death. It's . . . more horrible than you could even imagine." She shivered.

"Let's talk about something more pleasant."

"I hear that some fabulously wealthy man is putting together a manned mission to Mars and he wants volunteers," Merissa said with a grin. "All I need is a space-suit . . ."

"You can't go."

"Why not?"

Clara laughed. "You have a very nice future ahead of you, right here in Wyoming. And no, I won't tell you what it is."

Merissa grimaced. "Well, it doesn't contain Dalton, I'm sure of that. He almost left a trail of fire behind him getting out of the driveway."

Clara didn't say a word. She just smiled.

It was almost inevitable; the migraine. It came on an hour or two after Merissa's odd conversation with Tank.

She was sitting in the living room with her mother, watching the news, when she began to feel the effects.

She rubbed her temple with obvious pain. It was like a knife in her right eye. When she opened it again, her field of vision in that eye looked like the static on a television station that was temporarily off the air.

"Oh, dear," she said, feeling nausea rise.

"You'd better take something while you still can," Clara said worriedly.

"I'll do it right now."

She went quickly to her room, picked up the bottle that contained the capsules that she took for her headaches. She should have noticed that they weren't in the drawer where she'd put them. They were sitting on the table under the lamp. But she was hurting too badly to pay attention.

She shook one capsule out into her hand and popped it into her mouth, swallowing some water to get it down. The prescription was for two, but she hoped she'd taken it early enough to prevent the headache from developing.

While she sipped water from the plastic bottle on the same table as the pills, she glanced at the window curiously. The blinds were askew. She straightened them before she moved back to the bed and slid down onto it. Clara brought her a wet washcloth and put it over her eyes. "Just lie still, honey," she told the younger woman. "It will pass soon. Can I get you anything?"

"No, I'll . . . be fine. I just took one capsule. Maybe it will be enough. Turn off the light and close the curtains, will you?" she whispered.

"At once."

She did, and tiptoed out, closing the door behind her.

■ ■ ■ ■

The phone rang at the Kirk ranch. Mallory picked it up. "Hello?"

There was a hysterical barrage of words from Clara. As he listened, Mallory's face grew quickly somber.

"Yes, I'll tell him. Is Carson with you?"

He listened and nodded. "Did you call the EMTs? Okay. Fine. Yes, we'll be right there. Try not to worry."

"What's up?" the others asked, almost in unison.

"Merissa's in the hospital. Apparently she took a capsule for a migraine headache and had a violent reaction to it. We're going to pick Clara up on the way to the hospital."

Before he could even get the words out, Tank was headed out the back door.

Mallory called Darby on his cell phone. "You drive him, I don't care what he says," he told the foreman after he'd given him the bare bones of the conversation. "He'll kill himself trying to get there alone. Don't worry about Clara, we'll pick her up and take her to the hospital with us." There was a pause. "She said Carson was setting up some sort of devices out on the property. She hasn't seen him in a while. We'll worry about that later. Drive Tank to the hospital. Hurry!"

He hung up and looked at his family. "He'll head him off and drive him to town," he assured them.

"We should go, too," Cane replied.

"Yes. You stay here with the baby," Mallory told Morie, "and you should stay, too," he added, smiling at Bolinda. "I know, but it's really bad outside and you're delicate. Morie can't leave the baby and she needs someone with her," he lied.

Morie grinned. "Yes, she does."

"Okay, then, but give Merissa my love," Bodie agreed finally.

Cane gave Mallory a grateful look.

"Mine, too," Morie told her husband.

He nodded, kissed her gently and left Cane to say a brief, affectionate goodbye to his own wife. Then they drove over to pick up Clara and rushed to the hospital.

Tank was pacing the waiting room.

"How is she?" Mallory asked as he and Clara and Cane moved to Tank's side.

"Bad," Tank said unsteadily. "They won't tell me anything because I'm not a relative," he added angrily.

"It's all right," Clara said. She'd been crying, but suddenly she was more positive.

"I'll find out what's going on."

"You sent those capsules she was taking with the EMTs, didn't you?" Mallory asked.

She nodded. "Yes, I did. The first thing I thought was that it was an allergic reaction. She only took one, so maybe it isn't too bad. I made sure they took the bottle along with her. I'll see if I can find out anything." She went to the emergency room desk.

"They were doing tests, they told me," Tank said to his brothers. "Tests! They won't let me see her," he groaned.

"Take it easy," Cane said gently. "Just breathe. We'll know something soon. Okay?"

Tank calmed down. He nodded.

Mallory put his hand on his brother's shoulder. "First rule of medicine is 'do no harm,' " he reminded him. "If they treat her in the dark they could kill her. If you weren't so upset, you'd know that."

Tank looked up at him with the fear in his eyes that she wouldn't recover, that they wouldn't be in time . . .

The doctor, a small, dark-haired woman in a lab coat with a musical accent came to where they were standing in the waiting room, with a relieved Clara at her side. "It's all right. We know how to treat her now," she said, smiling. "The interesting thing is that, after we ran the toxicology screen on the capsules and a blood sample, we couldn't understand how she would ingest such a substance in a headache remedy. There was no trace of it on her mouth, her clothing . . ."

"What was it?" Tank asked.

"I could give you the technical name, but you probably know it as Malathion. It's used . . ."

"As a pesticide," Tank said for her. "Yes, we use it on the ranch. It's considered one of the safer methods . . ."

"The capsules were tampered with," she interrupted gently. "Someone substituted the Malathion for the prescription medicine. It was a very professional sort of job, although there was not enough in the one capsule her mother said she ingested to kill her, but there was enough to make her very sick. All the remaining capsules in the bottle were similarly replaced with the pesticide, with a very pure form of it. I've telephoned the authorities. It is my professional opinion that she was deliberately poisoned."

"Good God!" Tank burst out, agonized. His face tautened. "Will she live?"

"I think so," she said cautiously. "We'll keep her on cardiovascular support, administer antidotes, keep her sedated. You need to contact law enforcement, as well," she added. "This was an ugly business. For someone to do such a thing to a young woman . . . it's monstrous."

"Yes, it is," Tank agreed. "Can I see her?" he asked. "Please?"

"And me?" Clara pleaded.

The doctor was kind, but firm. "I would love to be able to do that, but we must work to save her life. If she had ingested more, or there had been a long delay in getting her to the hospital, she would certainly be dead."

"When can we see her?" Tank persisted.

"Come back in a few hours. We'll see," she promised. "Meanwhile, try not to worry. I think the prognosis will be good, since she was seen so quickly."

"Okay, then." He managed a smile. "Thanks."

She smiled back. "We'll take good care of her."

Tank didn't want to leave. He wanted to sit with her, comfort her, hold on to her. When he thought of the deliberate poisoning, the underhanded, low-down manner of it, he wanted to kill the man who had him targeted.

"We have to find this perp," Tank told his brothers on the way to Clara's house. "We have to find him now, before he kills her! Why her?" he added in anguish. "Why not just kill me?"

"He seems to be into torture," Cane said quietly. "He's playing with you. If he'd put enough Malathion in those capsules, she'd be dead already. He just wanted to make her sick, to scare you."

"Well, it worked," Tank said through his teeth.

They didn't comment. Mallory, who was driving, pulled up at the cabin. All three got out, along with Clara, who was sitting in the cramped second seat.

"Cody isn't here yet," Mallory noted, looking around, referring to the sheriff. "I called him before we left the hospital."

"Can we see her room?" Tank asked.

"Of course . . ."

"No," Mallory said, stopping him. "It's a crime scene now. Let Cody's investigator get to work."

"Crime scene," Tank said numbly.

"Attempted murder," Mallory replied tersely. "If we can catch him now, he'll go away for a very long time. We just have to prove it was him."

Carson came from around the side of the house. "I've got cameras on top of cameras . . ." He stopped, staring uncomprehending at the others. "What's happened?"

"You didn't hear the ambulance?" Tank asked, astonished.

Carson scowled. "What ambulance? No, I've been all over the property putting up sensors . . ." He stopped and stared at them. "Oh, my God. Merissa?"

"She'll be all right, the doctor thinks," Tank said worriedly. But he looked at Clara and she was nodding and smiling. He relaxed a little.

"I was only gone for thirty minutes," Carson groaned. "I didn't realize it would take so long. God, I'm sorry!" he told Clara.

"It's all right," she said. "She's going to be fine."

"The sheriff's on his way," Tank told Carson. "With his investigator. Don't touch anything."

Carson's eyes narrowed. "I'll go along with the investigator if there's a trail. I can track an ant." He moved closer to Tank. "You can slug me, if you like."

"You were trying to protect them," Tank said heavily. "I might have done the same thing. At least she didn't die."

"What happened to her?" Carson asked, still grim.

"She took what she thought was a pre-scription medicine for a headache," Clara said, "but someone had substituted Malathion for the drug in the capsules. It's a miracle it didn't kill her. She only took one capsule, thank God."

"I don't think that was his purpose at all," Mallory repeated. "I don't think he meant to kill her. He's toying with Tank."

Carson's eyes narrowed. "I knew a guy like that once, who worked in spec ops," he said, frowning curiously. "Eb knew him. He came along for a special job overseas. He was an independent contractor for the government, like us. His specialty was covert assassination, but not with military hardware. He was an expert at disguising poisons as medicine. He was assigned to take out a military strategist, but he did it over a period of days, using different everyday poisons to torment the man before he gave him the final dose. None of us liked the way he worked. He enjoyed killing."

The brothers looked at each other with sudden inspiration. "What did he look like?" Tank asked.

"Insignificant sort of man," he replied. "Medium height, nasal drawl. The only thing about him that stood out was his hair. It was a flaming orange color."

"I can see how that would help him camouflage himself," Cane said facetiously.

"I always thought he did it to draw attention away from his face," Carson replied. "His hair was concealed when he went out at night anyway, not much risk of anyone seeing it. He did wet work with knives, as well. He bragged about one job, but when he saw the reaction he was getting from us, he clammed up." His face hardened. "Anybody who enjoys killing needs help. I did it for ideological reasons, to help save innocents. He did it for fun."

"This man," Tank said slowly. "Did he have a nick on one ear?"

Carson blinked. "A what?"

"Did he have a cut on one ear, a scar?"

"I don't remember. I can't say I noticed." He smiled faintly. "I was too occupied with the sight of that flaming mop of hair."

Tank's cell phone rang. It was the hospital. In fact, it was the doctor herself, whom he'd given his phone number.

"She is awake," she told him, "and feeling somewhat better now."

"I'm on my way," Tank replied.

"Go," Mallory said when he hesitated, because they'd come in one ranch vehicle. "Here." He tossed him the keys. "We'll get Darby to take us back to the ranch."

"Okay. Thanks!" He ran for the truck.

"Don't speed!" Cane called after him.

"One tragedy a day is enough!"

"I'll keep it under a hundred!" Tank called back.

Cane groaned. He'd been in a terrible wreck before he and Bolinda had been married. He took speed very seriously.

"I feel bad that this happened on my watch," Carson said. "I was careless. I won't be again."

"We all slip from time to time," Mallory assured him.

Two vehicles approached the cabin as Tank drove rapidly away with a wave. It was Sheriff Banks and his investigator.

They greeted the men, asked questions of Clara and started investigating Merissa's room. It soon became apparent that her window was unlocked and someone had come through it quite recently. There was moisture from melted snow on the sill, and a partial footprint outside the window, among the leaves. A mold was taken of the print.

When the investigator had collected what evidence he could find, and another officer had been sent to the hospital to retrieve the bottle of capsules and enter them into the chain of evidence, Carson and the investigator started backtracking the faint trail through the woods.

Mallory and Cane returned to the ranch to update the wives on what was happening.

At the hospital, Tank sat beside Merissa in the intensive care unit, holding her hand.

"Scared me to death, baby," he said softly.

She managed a wan smile. "I feel awful."

"You're going to be all right," he said firmly. "Nobody's coming near you, or touching you again, no matter what I have to do to keep you safe."

"So sick," she groaned.

"I'm sure they're giving you something to make that better."

"Yes. They said so. How's Mama?" she asked suddenly. "She was so scared!"

"She's fine," he replied. "She came in with us to talk to the doctor."

"Do you know what happened to me?" she asked.

He turned her hand over and traced the palm. "Someone doctored the capsules you were given for migraine headaches," he said grimly. "We don't know how yet, but we're pretty sure who did it."

She drew in a shaky breath and fought down the nausea. "Wow. I only took one capsule," she whispered. "I remember Mama asked me when the ambulance came. I went out like a light pretty soon after that."

His hand tightened on hers. "Thank God you didn't take more."

"What did he put in it?"

"Malathion," he muttered. "It's dangerous. Very dangerous. We have to use precautions when we put it out on the ranch. Once we had a guy covered with it. We had to have him decontaminated and we had to call the EMTs. That was an accident. What happened to you wasn't. The sheriff's investigator will probably want to talk to you, too."

"I'll tell him anything I can." She looked up at Tank. "I remember that the blinds in my room were sort of crooked. I didn't think anything about it . . . I just straightened them before I lay down. My head was throbbing. Oh, and the pills weren't in my drawer. Why didn't I say something? I never leave them sitting out . . . and there was an odd odor to them, but I thought it was the headache making me smell things."

"Your head was hurting." He smiled gently. "You gave us a real scare."

She smiled. "Sorry."

His expression became grim. "We have to get this guy, before he does something worse."

"I totally agree. Unfortunately I won't be able to help you run him down and hog-tie him," she teased. "The way my doctor talks,

I'm going to be here for several days."

"You'll be safe here."

"Yes." She sighed. "But tomorrow's Christmas Eve," she moaned. "Mama will be all alone."

"Don't worry about Clara," he added before she could speak. "We've got people watching her."

"Okay."

"Carson offered to let me punch him," he then told her. "He felt bad that he was out of sight and sound when it happened."

"He was trying to keep us safe," she said. "Don't be mad at him."

He frowned. "Don't tell me he's working that magic on you, too?"

"Excuse me?"

He averted his eyes. He hadn't thought of Carson as a rival. Now, remembering the man's way with women, he was stunned. Merissa had been almost his until Carson came back with him. Now, she was backing away. Because of Carson?

He glanced at her. "You and Carson, you've been talking, haven't you?"

She nodded. "He isn't what he seems," she said softly. She smiled. "He's had a very hard life."

"He told you about it?"

"Yes. He isn't the sort of man who tells

anybody private things, I think. But he told me a lot. I felt really bad for him."

"I see."

"So don't blame him," she said softly. "I know he feels terrible, like he let me down. But it could have happened anytime. This man seems to know very well how to get to people," she added quietly. "He's like a snake. He can get in anywhere, without being noticed."

"We'll find him."

She turned her head on the pillow. "You have to be very careful," she said. "If you have medicines that you take, check them."

"I'm way ahead of you there," he assured her. "But there's no way anyone could get into my house without being noticed."

"Don't assume that," she said. "It's what we assumed, too. And here I am."

He grimaced. "You could have died."

"Yes. But he miscalculated," she said. "That will hurt his confidence. It will make him pause and rethink his methods. It will give you an opportunity to find out who he is." She squeezed his hand. "Dalton, he's done this before. Not exactly like this, but he's killed someone. Someone important. That's your key. That's what you have to look for . . ." She swallowed, hard. She let go of his hand. "Sorry. I'm so . . . sleepy."

"It's all right. You rest. I'll be back to see you tomorrow."

She nodded. "Thanks."

He smiled, when he'd never felt less like smiling. "Hey, what are friends for?" he asked her softly.

She opened her eyes and looked at him. Something flashed there, something odd. But she only smiled back and said, "That's right." Then she closed her eyes again.

He left her. His mind was working overtime. He wanted to throw Carson through a wall. The man was the devil himself. He remembered Carson charming the beautiful flight attendant, all smooth talk and smiles. It hadn't mattered about that woman, who was a stranger. But this was Merissa. And Merissa was his.

If only he hadn't botched it when he'd blurted out that proposal. He'd even had the rings in his pocket. He was going to press them into her hand and ask her right then. That wasn't really how he'd meant to do it. He wanted to do the whole courtship thing. Send her flowers, buy her presents; take her on moonlight rides. But he'd lost it when he had her so warm and soft in his arms.

She loved kissing him, he could tell that.

But she was backing away and just when he wanted to get closer, much closer.

So was it Carson pulling them apart? Was he a rival? And if he was, how could Dalton, who was no rounder, compete with him? The thought tormented him.

"What do you know about Carson?" he asked Rourke later, when they were going over new safety precautions for the ranch.

Rourke lifted both eyebrows. "Not a lot. Why?"

"He told Merissa things."

"Oh?" Rourke's one brown eye was twinkling. "What sort of things?"

"Hell, I don't know," he muttered. He ran a hand through his thick hair. "He's one smooth operator. He turns on the charm and women fall at his feet."

"Well, yes, they do. But he's a one-nighter, if that helps."

"What do you mean?" Tank asked.

"I mean, he doesn't date the same woman twice. He has no staying power. In fact, if you want my honest opinion," he added, "he hates women."

Tank gave him a disbelieving look.

"No, I'm not joking," Rourke continued. He finished connecting two wires on a monitor. "He even said something about it once, to the effect that women are no damned good. He said they'll crawl to a man who treats them like dirt, but turn their backs on one who'd die for them."

"The reverse of that is often true," Tank commented.

"I know."

"I've seen him in action, too," Rourke added. "I can't say I wasn't a bit envious. Never had that sort of luck with the ladies."

"And that's not what I've heard about you," Tank mused.

Rourke shrugged. "I'm like Carson. I like variety."

Tank pursed his lips. "I believe you helped Carson feed a man to a crocodile over a woman . . . ?"

Rourke's face hardened like steel. He averted his eye and didn't say another word.

"Sorry," Tank said.

Rourke didn't look at him. "There are things I never discuss. Tat's one of them." He turned his head, and his one good eye was blazing. "K.C. Kantor's another."

Tank held up both hands. "I didn't say a word."

Rourke shrugged. "Sorry." He tuned the device he was working on. "I used to have a higher boiling point."

"We all have weaknesses." Tank leaned

back. "Mine's lying in a hospital bed, mooning over your damned womanizing comrade."

Rourke's eyebrows almost blended into the blond hair at his forehead. "She's what?"

CHAPTER ELEVEN

Tank felt embarrassed. He shifted his posture. "He tells her things."

He chuckled softly. "She's that sort of woman. It doesn't mean she's got eyes for him," he pointed out.

"Well, I think . . ."

His cell phone rang. He pulled it off his belt and answered it. "Kirk."

"Can you bring Rourke and meet me in the parking lot of the Custom Kitchen?" Carson asked.

"What in hell for? Are you hungry?" Tank asked sarcastically.

"I'll tell you when you get here." He hung up.

Tank relayed the message.

"He's found something and he isn't willing to talk at the house," Rourke said grimly.

"Surely he didn't leave Clara at the house by herself?" Tank asked worriedly.

"I can almost assure you that he's got her

with him. He may be a womanizer, but there isn't anybody better at the job than he is."

"He wasn't there when Merissa was almost poisoned," Tank pointed out coldly.

"None of us would have expected the SOB to walk into the house and poison her meds," Rourke retorted. He stopped and frowned. "You said he left tracks?"

"Yes."

Rourke cocked his head. "Now, isn't that interesting? He's sneaky enough to poison prescription meds so that they're undetectable, and yet he leaves footprints?"

"We need answers." Tank moved ahead of him to a nearby ranch pickup.

"I think we're about to get them, too," Rourke predicted.

Clara was with Carson. He sent her inside, with a gentle smile, to have coffee while he talked over some things with his colleagues.

Tank was somber and cold. Carson either didn't notice or didn't care. He was intent on what he and the sheriff's investigator had uncovered.

"The tracks led to the highway about a mile behind the house," Carson told them, leaning casually back against the bed of the truck with his arms crossed. "They vanished. We assume a car or another vehicle was parked there. We found a partial tire track in the snow on the side of the road. We couldn't track any farther on foot, but the sheriff's department has dogs. They marked the spot with GPS and they're bringing out bloodhounds in the morning." He sighed. "But if you want my take on it, they'll track him to a deserted house or a parking lot, and another dead end." His black eyes narrowed. "He's just playing games. That's all."

"Games. He almost killed a woman!" Tank exploded.

"To him, it's just a game," Carson replied calmly. "Cat and mouse. He's playing you."

Tank looked menacing.

Carson's face softened just a little. "I know what she means to you," he said quietly. "I'm not downplaying how serious it could have been, if she'd taken more than one of those Malathion-laced capsules. I'm telling you how he feels about it."

"How do you know so much?" Tank asked.

"Men work in patterns," he said surprisingly. "I was a math whiz in college," he added. "Top of my class, in fact. I have a photographic memory, which came in handy when I majored in history as an undergraduate. History, as you may know, is mostly case law. I had in mind being another F. Lee

Bailey," he mused. "But I dropped out of law school just before graduation, due to . . . personal matters." He straightened. "What I'm saying is that people have habits that make them predicable, like equations. This man shows a few traits that may help us track him down."

"Such as?" Tank asked, mellowing.

"He's a master of disguise. We know that already. He's single-minded, methodical, careful, and he knows how to tamper with pharmaceuticals without being caught." He shook his head. "So how is it that this careful, methodical man leaves a trail a kindergarten child could follow?"

Rourke and Tank exchanged glances. "We were just discussing that," Rourke confessed.

"He's keeping you off your guard, unbalanced, by placing Merissa and Clara in danger," Carson continued.

"So?" Tank asked.

"He's afraid that you're going to remember something that will hurt him, point him out to the authorities. He'd like to kill you, but he can't get close enough. So he's keeping you focused on the women instead of the past."

"He may have a point," Rourke said.

"There's another thing," Carson continued. "Remember what I said about the man I worked with who was an expert at covert poisonings?"

"I do," Tank said.

"You met him once, too, I believe," Carson told Rourke. "The red-haired fellow who was always talking about sharks."

"Sharks!" Tank straightened.

"What?" Carson asked, diverted.

"Sharks." He paced, touching his forehead. "Sharks. Why can't I remember? Someone was talking about a man who mentioned sharks . . ."

"Carlie," Carson said quietly. "In Cash Grier's office."

"Yes!" Tank turned. "Remember, she said the rogue agent came into Cash's office and he was talking about sharks and how misunderstood they were. She said he told her he liked to swim with them in the Bahamas!"

"Sharks. Disguise. Poisons. The Bahamas." Carson's eyes narrowed. "I need to make a couple of phone calls."

"Why did you want us to meet you here?" Rourke asked as the other man pulled out his cell phone.

"The man we're looking for knew that Merissa kept her headache pills in her bedside table, and that she was starting to get a headache. How?"

The men looked at one another.

"I missed a bug. We missed a bug," Carson told Rourke.

"Impossible!" Rourke said angrily. "I ran the rooms four times, just to make sure!"

"You were out of sight yesterday," Tank said, "when Merissa took the medicine."

"Only for thirty minutes."

"About that time, I was driving Merissa home. Where was Clara?"

"I don't know, but we can ask," Rourke said, leading the way into the restaurant. "If she was out of the house at all, that gave him the opportunity to sneak in another bug."

"How about the capsules?" Tank asked. "That would have taken time. The doctor said it was an almost perfect job of tampering."

"He knows she has headaches. All he lacked was the opportunity to place the capsules."

"Why not when he was bugging the place?" Tank wondered.

"I imagine he makes it up as he goes," Rourke replied quietly. "He plans, but he plans as situations develop. He might have learned about her headaches for the first time after he placed the bugs. The tampering could have taken place over a period of days."

"Yes." Rourke paused. "And he might have counted on Merissa's father to take her out for him, along with her mother." He glanced at Tank's hard face. "The man is unbalanced. Brilliant, but unbalanced."

Clara saw them come in and motioned them to the booth where she was sitting. She smiled. "We could eat while we're here," she suggested. "Then, if I could impose on you to drive me by the hospital . . . ?"

Tank said as he slid into the booth, "I'll go, too."

"Clara," Rourke began after they'd ordered barbecue plates, "when Carson was out placing his surveillance units, did you leave the house at all?"

She blinked. "Why, yes, just to run by the drycleaners and leave a comforter. I wasn't gone five minutes. Why?"

Tank and Rourke exchanged glances. Tank nodded.

"Don't say anything in the house that you'd mind being overheard," Rourke told her. "You must be extraordinarily clever. I'm not going to remove the bug he's just placed. Let him think we're too dim to realize it's even there."

"Bug? I don't understand," she began.

Tank explained how they thought the bug was placed, and how the intruder knew where Merissa kept her headache medicine.

"Oh, goodness," Clara said heavily. "I opened my big mouth. Just like I did, telling them where Bill was, and I got him killed," she added sadly. "Then there's that other man. The one Merissa told us about, that she saw in her mind, a man who knew about this intruder and was going to tell on him . . ."

"You can't save the world," Rourke said heavily. He gave her a weary smile. "I know. I've been trying."

She smiled weakly. "I see your point. It's very hard, though, to know something and not be able to warn anyone."

"In that case," Tank told her, "you have to consider that some things just happen the way they're meant to. We can't see very far down the road. God can."

"Okay."

Carson came back in. He slid into the booth beside Clara. "I've put some things in motion," he said. "There's been a development back home."

"What?" Tank asked.

"It seems that Cash Grier managed to track down the man who attacked Carlie's father with a knife. He turned up in the morgue in San Antonio. He was poisoned."

"Good grief!" Tank exclaimed. "Merissa told him that there was a man who knew him and was thinking about going to the authorities. He said he knew who it was and he'd take care of him." He groaned. "It's going to hit her hard."

Rourke's one eye narrowed. "Don't tell her."

"The man had a rap sheet seven pages long," Carson added. "One of his arrests was for rape. He's no loss to the world."

"Did he talk to the authorities?" Tank asked. "Do you know?"

"He made a phone call before he died. It was to a police officer in San Antonio. They're trying to contact the officer to see if a conversation even took place. One more minor detail."

"Yes?" Tank asked.

"The man was taking a prescription medication for allergies. The capsules were tampered with. Like to take a guess at what sort of poison was in them?" Carson mused.

"Don't tell me," Rourke said. "Malathion."

"Exactly. He had access to it on the ranch, didn't he?" Carson asked Tank.

"He was in and out of the barn where we

keep it, but it's in a locked shed room," Tank replied.

"You keep your keys hanging just inside the back door in the house," Rourke recalled. "Does one of them fit that storeroom?"

Tank's eyes closed. "She warned me about those keys the first day she came to the house," he said. "She said, 'he'll find them there.' "

"She's very perceptive," Clara remarked gently.

"I wish I'd listened!" Tank groaned.

"He'd have found another way," Carson said. "Anything can be used to poison someone, even common household items."

"Like hand grenades?" Rourke said, tongue-in-cheek. "I believe El Ladrón's convoy was treated to a few of those . . . ?"

"The convoy of El Ladrón was accidentally blown up by a few equally accidentally tossed hand grenades." He looked perfectly innocent.

"Nice aim," Rourke said, grinning.

Carson grinned back. "I get in some practice from time to time."

Tank started to ask a question when the jukebox, a holdover from the past, started up. The sounds of rock music filled the restaurant.

"Try talking over that," Carson groaned.

The song was an old hard rock tune by Joan Jett, called "I Love Rock 'n' Roll." It had a hard, heavy beat and it had been a favorite of the Kirks' mother when she was still alive. It brought back memories for Tank. He smiled as he listened. And then, quite suddenly, he frowned.

"What's wrong?" Clara asked.

He caught his breath. "That song," he said.

"Yes, it's loud," Carson muttered.

"No! The man who was, or who was pretending to be, a DEA agent when I was ambushed," he said, feeling all over again the impact of the bullets. "I heard that song."

"The mind plays tricks in dangerous situations," Rourke began.

"It was that song. But it wasn't sung. It was . . . I don't know . . . like wind chimes," he faltered as he tried to recall it.

"Wind chimes?" Carson mused.

Rourke frowned. "My . . . employer," he said, hesitating before he gave the relationship, and not the real one at that, "has a very expensive Swiss watch that he customized with a tune he was fond of. It plays the opening bars of Beethoven's Ninth Symphony." He lifted his head. "It sounds like wind chimes. Or chapel chimes that used to come out of the steeples at churches."

Tank sat very still. He closed his eyes, trying, trying to remember the man. "It's no use," he groaned. "When I picture him, all I can see is that damned gaudy paisley shirt he was wearing." He opened his eyes. "But I know I heard chimes. It could have been a watch. I'm not sure he was wearing it. Judging by his suit, he couldn't have afforded an expensive Swiss watch with customized music," he added. "His suit was strictly off the rack."

Carson pulled out his cell phone and opened an internet browser.

"What?" Tank asked.

"It's a long shot," he said. "But I'm curious about that tune. It rings a bell somewhere in the back of my mind."

He tapped in a search string and waited. Then he thumbed through the results, which seemed to go on forever. Finally he paused, tapped the screen and his face grew even more grim.

"Several months ago," he said, looking up, "about the time Hayes Carson made his bust and you got ambushed, a district attorney was murdered in San Antonio."

"And?" Tank asked.

"They think it was a theft because of what

269

was stolen. His wife was wealthy. He was wearing a very expensive Swiss watch. They said it had a musical alarm, but not what the tune was. It was never found."

Tank's dark eyes twinkled. "A break. Maybe."

Carson nodded. He was still pulling up websites. He frowned. "There's a photograph of the prosecutor who was killed. I want you to look at this." He handed his iPhone to Tank, who took it and his face paled.

"What?" Rourke asked when he saw Tank's expression.

"The damned shirt. The damned paisley shirt." He drew in a long breath. "That looks like the shirt the so-called federal agent was wearing."

"Can you find out if the shirt went missing?" Rourke asked Carson.

"Let me find out for you. I know a homicide detective with San Antonio P.D.," Rourke said. He pulled out his own phone and put in a call to Lieutenant of Detectives Rick Marquez.

"Rourke," Rick Marquez stated when he heard the South African accent.

"That's me. How are things?"

"Busy," Rick replied, chuckling. "My wife

and I are expecting any day now."

"Congrats," Rourke replied.

"Thanks. We're pretty excited. Big changes coming."

"You're telling me. Listen, I'm working for a bloke up here in Wyoming. Tank, excuse me, Dalton Kirk . . ."

"Hayes Carson told me about that," Rick interrupted. "Any luck catching the culprit?"

"That's where we're hoping you could give us a hand, unofficially," Rourke replied. "A San Antonio district attorney was murdered some months ago, and some things were stolen from him, yes?"

"Yes," Rick said. "He was a good guy. Hardworking and honest and relentless. He left behind a wife and two small children. Damned bad luck. He was walking through the car park after hours when somebody jumped him, shot him to death and robbed him."

"You've never caught the perp, yes?"

"That's right. Why?"

"I understand that a watch was one of the stolen items . . . specifically an expensive Swiss watch."

"I don't remember exactly, but I think so."

Tank asked for the phone and held it to his ear. "Dalton Kirk here. Lieutenant Marquez. Was your murder victim also wearing a paisley shirt at the time, and was it missing?"

"Let me think. Oh, I remember now. It was one of the more puzzling aspects of the crime. Of course, criminals come in all colors and mental persuasions. The man's shirt was removed by whoever killed him. Left his suit coat, which was very expensive, lying on the ground. His wallet was taken, the watch and the shirt."

"Was he shot in the chest?"

"No. In the head. There was some blood, not a lot, on his suit coat. Although there was quite a bit on the pillar behind him . . ."

"The shirt, was it identified by anyone?"

"His wife said it was a couture paisley shirt she had a famous Paris design house create for him . . . What is it?" Rick asked when Tank drew in his breath.

"The man who shot me was wearing a shirt like that. Sheriff Hayes Carson remembers the agent who was with him at his drug bust also wearing one. I don't know if he saw the man's watch, but you might ask him."

"This is going in a strange direction," Rick said.

"Tell me about it! It looks like we may have your prosecutor's murderer up here in

Wyoming trying to kill me," Tank said. "I didn't know why. But I think it might have something to do with your unsolved murder down there in Texas."

"I think you may be right. Tell me everything you remember about the man," Rick said. "We have one witness who saw the killer running away. He passed right by the window of her bake shop. We pulled in all the usual suspects and did a lineup but she couldn't identify anybody. In fact, the description she gave us was, frankly, right up there with the ones we get from people on hallucinogenic drugs."

"How so?" Tank asked.

"She said he had flaming orange hair and that he was carrying a blow-up children's swimming pool toy."

"To draw attention away from his face," Tank said, remembering something he'd heard Carson say. "Or to make the witness sound foolish when giving a description of him. Probably he grabbed a child's toy from someone's yard when he fled the scene."

"Possibly, yes."

"Tell him about the man who stabbed Carlie Blair's father. That perp was poisoned," Carson prompted.

"Yes." He told Marquez about that, but Marquez already knew. He just hadn't connected the two cases. There might not be a connection, he added, but he'd check it out anyway.

"It might be nothing, but I have a feeling there are some connections here. I'll get people looking into it. Give me back to Rourke. Nice to meet you, by the way." Marquez chuckled.

"Same here." He handed the phone back to Rourke.

Rourke listened for a minute. "Yes. That's right. He tried to poison a young woman, a friend of Dalton's, and he's repeatedly put her in the line of fire. He's bugged the Kirk home and her home. We thought he was a nutter, but now I'm beginning to realize that he has a lot more at stake than we realized. Apparently he was afraid Dalton might remember what he just has, to connect him with that murder. Same for Hayes Carson. It also explains why he wanted the computer wiped at Hayes's office. He didn't want anybody to see that shirt he had on, possibly the watch as well, and make a connection."

"Which leads us to still another question, if he's some random killer, why is he so concerned that he might be linked with a particular murder?" Rick asked.

"He made it seem like a robbery, didn't

he?" Rourke said thoughtfully. "Maybe he didn't want it connected with a case your prosecutor might have been working on."

"Damn! Good detective work there, Rourke," Marquez said. "Why don't you give up feeding people to crocodiles and come to work for me? You can have free coffee and your own parking spot."

"Sorry," Rourke replied. "Feeding crocs is a bit more lucrative at the moment. Here's my cell number. I'll be with the Kirks, so if you need to reach Dalton, this is the best way. Their phones might not be safe. We'll have to recheck everything."

"Good idea."

Rourke gave him the number then they exchanged a few more words and hung up.

"Well!" Tank said heavily. "All this, over a murder in Texas!"

"It would seem to connect," Rourke replied. He shook his head. "But it doesn't make a lot of sense. He's gone to an incredible amount of trouble to cover his tracks, but since then, he's made himself a target with attempted murder here."

"He might be in on the hit they planned for Hayes Carson," Tank said solemnly.

"I wouldn't have agreed even two days ago," Carson interrupted. "But I believe you're on to something."

"I know he is," Clara, who had been sitting quietly, listening, said. "That was what Merissa saw. She said that you were being targeted because of something you didn't even remember. It makes sense now."

"It certainly does." Tank glanced at the other men. "We have to be more careful than ever. We can't assume that he hasn't placed more devices around the ranch. We have people coming in all the time, from USDA inspectors, to cowboys, to suppliers, even men who drive the cattle trucks and are sometimes temporary hires. It's a big ranch. Takes a lot of people to keep it operating. We do run background checks on the people who come most often, but we don't extend it to temporaries who work a day or two."

"I can run a check on everyone who comes through the gate with facial recognition software," Carson said quietly. "It will take time, but anyone who isn't a regular will stick out like a red flag."

"Good idea. I'll make sure everyone knows to keep conversation general and away from anything concerning the intruder," Tank told them. He looked at Clara. "That goes double for you, and for Merissa, when she gets home."

Clara nodded. "We'll be very careful this time."

"I'll get you a scrambler," Carson said with a smile. "It's not an obvious block, like jamming. It will just give you a little privacy by confusing the transmitters for anyone eavesdropping."

"Thanks," Clara said softly.

The waitress delivered trays of food, mostly turkey and dressing plates in honor of Christmas, and they fell silent while they ate.

After finishing at the diner, and saying goodbye to the two men, Tank took Clara with him to the hospital.

Rourke climbed into the car with Carson. He gave the other man an odd look.

"What?" Carson asked.

He shrugged. "Just curious about something."

The other man raised an eyebrow before he turned his attention back to the road.

"You've changed," Rourke remarked.

"Explain."

"All the time I've known you, there was nothing you hated more than women. Now, suddenly, you're Don Juan."

Carson looked out the windshield intently. "Variety is the spice of life."

"That wasn't you, even a year ago."

Carson laughed coldly. "It was. I have moods. Sometimes I think about things, and women go right down on the scale like a rock falling. I was Mr. Conservative for a while. Then I had a . . . personal tragedy," he said, glossing over the tragic death of his wife. "Afterward, I saw women in a different way. Well, most of the time. Hell, they want to play around like men, notch the bedpost at night, laugh at commitment — why shouldn't I avail myself of the opportunities that present themselves?" he mused. "I'm no monk."

"Neither am I," Rourke replied. He smiled. "But I'm not in your league." He shook his head. "Damn, you've got skills."

Carson chuckled. "I gather pretty bouquets. Some have long stems, some have short ones. But the more beautiful they are, the more I enjoy them. For a while."

"Women who aren't beautiful can have other traits just as worthy," Rourke pointed out.

"Not my thing. I don't like plain women with ancient attitudes."

Rourke glanced at him. That had been said with pure venom. "Known a few of those, have we?"

"One." Carson thought back to Carlie and

what he'd said to her. He closed his mind. "Life's too short not to appreciate beauty when it drapes itself over your arm and purrs like a kitten."

Rourke smiled. "Yeah. I guess you have a point." He looked out the window. His face was hard as nails. "Variety is less abrasive than trying to cope with just one woman."

"I totally agree," Carson said.

Rourke glanced at him. "You're putting Dalton's back up. Did you notice?"

Carson pursed his lips. "Jealousy," he said with a flash of white teeth. "And he should be jealous. If I were a little less scrupulous, I'd take her right out from under him. She's . . . special."

"Very special." Rourke hesitated. "Do you know about Tank?"

Carson glanced at him. "He's a rich rancher."

"He served in Iraq with a forward unit," Rourke said. "He waded in when a tank pinned down his unit, and blew it up. That's where he got the name."

"Impressive."

"He came home with hardly a scratch. He was at a loose end. His brothers were parlaying the ranch into an empire, but Dalton wanted more excitement. He liked the idea of a federal job, with those nice benefits. One of the officers he knew pulled a few strings and got him a job as a border patrol agent." His expression became somber. "One day, a DEA agent came into his office and asked for immediate assistance with a drug bust going down. Dalton had no reason not to believe the man. He went with him, walked into an ambush and was almost shot to pieces in the attack that ensued. He was in the hospital for weeks, undergoing surgery after surgery."

"Good God!" Carson said heavily.

"He's walking again, and he doesn't have any obvious marks on him. But I can tell you that it left scars he'll never lose, physical as well as mental. He had to leave the job, obviously. Mallory and Cane had bought this ranch several years earlier and the two of them had sweated blood to grow it while Tank was in Iraq, and later, working for the feds. They've made some amazing improvements here, turned the place into a totally green operation. It's skyrocketed in worth since they took it over." He shook his head. "Mallory's got a real knack for investments. Tank does the marketing and Cane shows the cattle. They're amazingly successful."

Carson was quiet. He was thinking about Dalton's injuries and especially about the ones that wouldn't show. That would make it hard for him, with a woman.

"He never spoke of how bad it was," Carson said.

"That's like him. He doesn't advertise his problems."

Carson was reminded of Carlie's shoulder, where he'd seen the odd fit of the fabric. He wondered if she, too, had scars that didn't show.

Rourke drew in a long breath. "God, I'm tired. I just hope Marquez can come up with some answers that will help us solve this case before anyone else is hurt or dies."

Carson's lips made a thin line. "That makes two of us."

Tank had stopped by the gift shop at the hospital while Clara went in to see her daughter. Merissa was just out of intensive care, into a room. Tank made his purchases and then made his way up to the floor where her room was.

He held his hand behind him as he entered after a light tap.

"Come in," Merissa said in a weak, but happy tone. Her eyes lit up at the sight of him. She smiled.

"Hi, kid," he greeted softly. "How's it going?"

Kid? Then she remembered. He'd said, "What are friends for?"

Her face fell.

He saw that, and his heart sank. He moved closer to the bed. "How are you feeling?" he asked gently.

"Better, thanks," she said huskily. "Sick. Tired. Scared," she added, glancing at Clara.

Clara pressed her hand. "I'm fine. I have plenty of protection."

"Okay," Merissa said, relaxing a little. She looked past her mother at Tank. "Something's come up. Hasn't it?"

He raised both eyebrows.

"Sorry," she said shyly. "Can't help it."

"I wasn't criticizing. But yes, something has come up. I just can't tell you about it." He was probably being paranoid, but he didn't even trust the hospital room not to be bugged. He must be spending too much time alone, he figured.

"Okay," she said. She was quick. He didn't want to talk in here. Maybe he thought the room was bugged. It wasn't beyond imagination. After all, that man had managed to get into her bedroom at the cabin and tamper with her headache pills.

"Brought you something," he said.

"You did?" Her face brightened when she

smiled. "Is it something nice to eat? Something besides gelatin and soup? Maybe?"

"It's a T-bone steak in a plain wrapper," he whispered in a conspiratorial tone.

"Wicked!" She laughed.

Her face lit up when she was happy. She was beautiful. He had to shake himself to stop from blurting it out.

He drew his hand from behind his back. "It's probably corny . . ."

She took the small ceramic sculpture from his hands. It was a hawk. No. It was two hawks, one male, one female, sitting together on a limb. The piece was carved from wood and hand-painted. It was beautiful.

Tears stung her eyes. "I'll treasure it forever," she choked out. She looked up at him. "Thanks!"

He smiled. He'd been uncertain, but that smile made his whole day. "I'm glad you like it. Merry Christmas."

"I didn't get you anything," she said miserably.

"Oh, that's not a Christmas present," he replied. "Just an impulse thing."

"Okay, then, I feel better. Thank you again. Did they say when I could go home?" she asked Clara.

Clara sighed. "Nobody tells me much. But I can go ask, if you like."

"Would you?"

Clara smiled. "Of course. Be right back."

She left the room and Tank dropped into the chair beside Merissa's bed. He took her small hand in his and held it tightly.

When she met his searching gaze, everything since their last meeting went right out of her head, and she thought her heart would beat her to death.

CHAPTER TWELVE

Tank looked into her eyes with aching longing. He wanted to tell her how jealous he was of Carson, how he wished he could take back the things he'd said, that he didn't want her for a friend. He wanted her for the rest of his life.

But how could he do that, now that he'd ruined everything?

"You're troubled," she said softly. "Can you talk about it?"

His lips made a thin line. He shrugged. "I wish I could," he said.

Her fingers closed around his. "Something to do with that man," she guessed.

He just nodded. He turned her hand over and winced. There was a big bruise on the back of it.

"It just looks bad, that's all," she said. "They couldn't hit a vein at first so they had to put the needle there, for the drip," she added. She smiled, indicating her other arm, where a drip was still running into a needle in the fold of her elbow. "They got it right this morning."

"I'm so sorry," he said heavily. "We all are."

"There's no need for that," she said gently. "This criminal is very good. He started when he was barely in his teens. Someone trained him, someone very expert in espionage." Her eyes were almost opaque. "Someone in a tropical place. Palm trees. Cruise ships." She flushed.

"Keep going," he said, encouraging her. "He likes sharks . . ."

She blinked. "Yes. He likes sharks. He acts the same. No emotion, no regret, just a predator who takes advantage of opportunities."

He wanted to ask her if she'd seen a watch in her visions, but he was paranoid about being overheard. Just in case the man had managed to bug her room, and why wouldn't he; it was stupid to say anything that might be overheard. Sharks excluded, he mused. If the man was listening, that information wouldn't set him off. After all, he was aware that people knew he'd mentioned sharks once.

"You look tired," she commented.

He managed a smile as he looked at her.

"I haven't been sleeping well."

"I can imagine," she replied. "All this worry about what he's going to do next . . ."

"No!" His fingers closed around hers. He shrugged and didn't meet her eyes. "I was worried . . . we were all worried . . . about you."

"Oh."

She sounded surprised. He met her searching eyes. "My brothers came to the hospital with me when you were admitted. Their wives wanted to come, too, but I didn't think it was wise to try to bring Harrison down here, or a very pregnant Bolinda."

She smiled. "How very nice of them!"

"They like you," he replied.

She flushed a little and laughed. "They don't think I'll curdle the milk?"

He shook his head. "We're modern in some of our attitudes. No pitchforks and torches. Stuff like that."

She did laugh then.

He drew in a breath. "At least you have a little more color today."

"I'm feeling much better. I don't know what they've been pumping into me, but it really has helped."

"Any visitors? Besides us, I mean."

"Just Carson." Her eyes softened. "He

came and sat with me for a few minutes."

His face grew cold. He let go of her hand. "I just saw Carson. He didn't mention he'd seen you."

"He felt guilty because he left us alone in the house," she replied, "and gave the man an opening to tamper with my meds."

"What did you tell him?"

"That it wasn't his fault, of course," she replied. "I know you don't like him," she added perceptively. "But he's not what you think. He's a good person."

He almost bit his tongue trying not to tell her some of the things he knew that Carson had done.

"How's Mama doing?" she asked to divert him. "She seems okay, but she was very worried. And she's still getting over Dad being shot."

He lost his jealousy all at once. "She's doing very well. That was an accident of fate. Your father was a cruel, vindictive man. We make our path in life, then we walk it. His ended as violently as he lived."

She sighed. "I suppose so. It's still hard." She looked up. "Are your parents still alive?"

He shook his head. "Our mother, died some years ago. So did our father. It's been just the three of us for a long time." He smiled sadly. "You know, there's nobody in the world who feels the same pride for you that a parent does, or the unconditional love you get. A parent will excuse things that the world won't. I suppose we're poorer for the lack of them."

"I always hoped for a father who'd be loving and kind," she replied sadly. "Mine was neither. I learned to stay out of his way almost as soon as I could walk. Mama took a lot of blows that were meant for me." She closed her eyes. "My childhood was a nightmare."

He smoothed his fingers over her soft hand. "I'm sorry for that."

"Me, too."

She wasn't resisting so he linked his fingers into hers. It gave him a thrill, like parachuting from a great height. "Any other visitors?" he asked.

She smiled. "Not really. Just the sheriff's deputy. He asked me a lot of questions for a report."

"I guess Cody sent him," he said.

"I guess."

He glanced at the hall. Hospital workers were moving trays off some sort of mobile rolling cart. He grimaced. "I suppose it's supper time and I have to leave," he said reluctantly.

"They really have very nice food here,"

she said. "Well, except for the gelatin." She whispered loudly, "Can't you please smuggle me in a steak?"

"I heard that," one of the volunteers called through the door with a chuckle.

"Sorry. Couldn't help it," Merissa replied.

The woman came in with a covered tray and placed it on the hospital table that looped over the bed. "You'll like this. It isn't steak. But it's good." She lifted the cover.

"Roast beef!" Merissa exclaimed. "And carrots! I love carrots!"

"Her first solid food, I gather?" Tank asked the woman.

She laughed. "However did you guess? Only someone on a liquid diet would go all googly-eyed over carrots." She rolled her eyes. "And there's this, too." She put fruit juice, milk and a small serving of vanilla ice cream on the tray.

"I've died and gone to heaven," Merissa whispered.

"Not quite, but you came close, I hear." The woman chuckled again. "Now you eat every bite, okay?"

"Okay," Merissa promised.

Tank smiled at her. Odd, he thought, the way her voice sounded. It was familiar. He wished he could place it. He almost asked if they'd met, but it would appear as a pickup line, and he wasn't doing that in front of Merissa.

The woman went out. Merissa enthused over the food. But when she tasted the roast beef, she made a face.

"How very strange," she murmured.

"What?"

"I'm just paranoid, I guess, but it tastes a little funny. It smells like someone got happy with the garlic. I guess it's just my taste buds," she added, and started to fork it into her mouth.

"No." Tank took the fork with the meat on it. He sniffed it. He frowned. He knew that smell all too well. He'd worked, very carefully, with a commercial grade of Malathion. First the capsules, now this . . . !

"You're not eating that." He opened his cell phone and called Cody Banks.

"Hi, Tank. How're things?" he replied.

"Did you send a deputy to the hospital to question Merissa today?" he asked.

The other man laughed. "Well, not yet," he said. "I mean, she's barely out of ICU . . ."

That was when Tank remembered the voice on the phone. He'd called the surveillance company and talked to a woman about installing the security cameras. That was the voice. The woman who brought in Merissa's tray. She wouldn't be working in a hospital if she was an accomplice for the assassin who was after Tank, and that was who she sounded like.

"Tank?" Cody asked when there was a long pause.

"You'll think I'm crazy. But can you send your investigator over here right now?"

"Why?"

"Don't hang up. I think the assassin has an accomplice working here, and part of Merissa's meal that the woman just delivered may have something in it. Something dangerous. It smells like commercial Malathion. We already know that was what was put in the capsule she ingested."

Cody knew Tank. He wasn't an alarmist. His word was good enough for the sheriff. "I'll not only send him, I'll come with him. Don't let them take that tray away until I get there."

"I won't."

He hung up. Merissa was listening, and she looked more nervous than ever.

"Cody didn't send a deputy over here to see you," he said. "Tell me everything you remember about the man."

She frowned. "He was medium height, wearing a uniform," she said. "He was wearing a bib cap. He seemed very nice. He asked about my mother, and remarked about how lucky I was to still be alive. He said the man probably hadn't meant to kill me at that point in time, or he would have put a bigger dose of poison in the capsules. He said that perhaps he was waiting for just the right moment to erase me, when it would have the most impact." She looked at Tank. "That's a strange thing to say, isn't it?"

Tank was really worried now. He wanted to go out into the hall and find that damned woman, tie her up, make her talk. He wanted the man, the rogue agent. He pulled out his phone again and called Rourke.

"You'd better come down here. Make sure my brothers are in the house with their wives and that Carson is with them."

"I'll do it right now," Rourke said without a single argument.

"Rourke?" Merissa questioned.

He smiled. "He once fed a man to a crocodile," he mused. "I'm hoping he hasn't lost his touch," he added, just in case that paisley-shirt-wearing snake was listening.

"Dalton!" she exclaimed. "Shame!"

He curled her fingers closer into his. "On second thought, maybe something more creative than a crocodile."

She was solemn. "He burns."

"Yes, he burns to kill me . . ."

She shook her head. "No, Dalton," she said softly. "He burns. Alive." She shivered. "I saw it. I couldn't see his features, but I know it was him in the vision. He burns. He screams . . ."

He nipped her thumb gently with his fingers. "Don't dwell on things like that," he said softly.

"That's what I see. That's the kind of thing I see, all the time. Death. Violence. Pain." She drew in a long breath. "All my life. I had a friend when I was in grammar school. I knew she was going to die, and how. I tried to warn her. She thought I was joking. I told her not to go swimming in the lake that day, that a man driving a boat, drinking, would run over her." She closed her eyes. "She just laughed. They went swimming. A man was driving a speedboat too fast, drinking. He didn't see her. He ran right over her and the propellers caught her." Her face was tragic. "After that, I didn't want to have any friends." She looked up at him. "People say this is a gift. It's not a gift, it's a curse. Nobody in his right mind would want to see the future if he knew what was lying in wait for him."

"I suppose I've never thought of it like that."

"I'd love to be just normal," she said sadly. "You know, have a regular job, do regular things, get married, have kids . . . live a happy life."

"Why can't you?" he asked softly.

"My children would suffer because of me," she replied. "They'd pay the price for my . . . gift."

"You shouldn't decide not to have children on such a basis," he said quietly. "Merissa, we all have things in our lives that make us stand out. It isn't necessarily a bad thing. Your children might have similar gifts. It isn't a curse. It really is a gift. I wouldn't be sitting here today if you didn't have it."

She knew that. She began to relax. She smiled. "I suppose I'm letting it all get to me." She looked at her tray. "I'm so hungry," she moaned.

"I'll have them bring you something else, but Cody's investigator's having a look at that," he added, indicating the tray.

The woman who'd brought the tray came in, smiling, to collect it. She stopped dead when she noticed that Merissa hadn't touched it.

"Well, you haven't eaten a thing," she exclaimed. "Now that won't do. You have to

eat that right now," she began. "All of it."
She moved to the bed. "Come on, Miss
Baker, don't be difficult. Here, I'll feed it to
you . . ."

"Like hell you will!" Tank exploded.

He got to his feet just as Cody Banks
walked in the door. "Grab her," he told
Cody, indicating the woman. "She's the assassin's accomplice!"

"I'm . . . what . . . Who . . . You're crazy!"
the woman exclaimed, red-faced. "I'm leaving!"

"You are not," Tank said, and covered the
doorway. "Cody, there's something wrong
with the food on that tray. It needs to be
tested. I recognize this woman's voice. She
worked for the so-called surveillance expert
who bugged my house."

The woman gaped at him. But she didn't
really protest when Cody cuffed her and
told his investigator to call for a deputy to
pick her up.

"You'll sit right there," he told the woman,
indicating a chair near the window.

"You'll never prove a thing," the woman
scoffed.

"Think so?" Tank asked, and his eyes were
ice-cold.

They ran a toxicology screen on the meal.

The roast beef was laced with Malathion, enough to kill anyone who ingested it. Far from the normal grade that was used on the ranch as an insecticide, this was a commercial grade of the pure chemical, which was greatly diluted when in use. Tank was willing to bet that when they compared the Malathion in this food, and that in Merissa's capsules, it would be a match for the product under lock and key on the Kirk ranch.

"Good God, he's insane," Tank exclaimed when the doctor gave them the results of the tests she'd ordered.

The doctor was grim. "I have never had such a case in all my career," she confessed. "What do we do, Sheriff?"

Cody drew in a breath. "For one thing, we put someone with Merissa around the clock."

"I can do that," Rourke said. He'd joined them earlier. "I have another man watching the ranch. Both of us have backgrounds in, shall we say, deadly endeavors." He smiled.

Cody gave him a wary look.

"I've done nothing illegal in this country," Rourke reassured him.

Cody pursed his lips. "All right. Your man Carson can sure track," he added.

"He can do a lot of things," Rourke said. "Tracking is one of them. He'll keep the family safe."

"Clara has to move in with us," Tank added. "I won't have her at the cabin alone."

"I'll take care of that," Rourke assured him. "I'd better get Merissa's computer and bring it along as well. Wouldn't want our anonymous friend messing with it."

"Good idea," Tank said. "And nobody says anything about what we're planning in Merissa's room. Chances are pretty good that it's bugged, since we know a man pretending to be your deputy," he told Cody, "came to interview her."

"He's in dead earnest this time," Rourke said quietly. "He wants to kill her."

"It's a link in the chain," Tank said. "He's putting pressure on me. If she died, I'd never spend a second thinking about the past, when I met him. What he doesn't know is that we've already made the connection he's so afraid of."

"What connection?" Cody asked.

"It's better if you don't know right now," Tank told him. He clapped the other man on the shoulder. "It doesn't concern this business, anyway. At least, not at the moment. Right now, our only concern has to be keeping Merissa alive."

"Carson will stay at the hospital until she's released," Rourke said.

"Thank goodness," Cody replied, oblivious to Tank's offended and angry expression. "I don't have the budget to do that."

"He does," Rourke said, jerking a thumb at Tank.

"My investigator will interview her while he's here. This guy is a nutcase," Cody said curtly.

"You can bet money on that," Rourke replied.

"Why does he want to kill such a kind young woman?" Cody asked. "I just don't get it."

"She sees things," Tank replied. "He's afraid she'll help me remember something he doesn't want to get out. I'll tell you the minute I can," he promised. "It's very complex."

"Something to do with that case in Texas maybe?" Cody asked dryly.

"Maybe."

"Uh-huh."

"It's even darker than that," Rourke added. "This is a piece of a puzzle. A deadly one."

"There are dozens of poisons that have no taste, or color," Cody puzzled. "Why didn't he use one of those?"

"He's cocky," Tank said coldly. "Arrogant. He thinks we're all fools. Probably he thought it would be amusing to kill her with a substance we use on the ranch, in lesser doses, every day during the growing season."

"Boy." Rourke chuckled. "Has he got a surprise coming!"

"Indeed he does," Tank added. He looked at Cody. "No chance you could suspend that woman you arrested on suspicion of murder over a lake or something by her thumbs to make her talk?" he teased.

He shook his head. "Sorry. Wrong century."

"It was just a thought." He glanced at Rourke. "Think she might sell him out for the right price?"

Rourke shook his head grimly. "I think she won't be alive this time tomorrow."

"Hey, I run a tight jail," Cody protested. "He'd never get in past my guys. Not in a million years!"

Rourke and Tank didn't answer. They knew enough already to be certain that if their killer wanted her dead, she would be.

Sure enough, later that very day Rourke phoned Tank, who was still at the hospital, with the news.

"The woman who tried to poison Merissa had a sudden coronary, right in her holding cell," he remarked.

"How convenient," Tank said. He wasn't overflowing with sympathy. Merissa could have been lying dead in her bed, thanks to that witch.

"Isn't it?" Rourke agreed.

"Did she have any visitors, do you know?"

"There was an old man with a cane who said he was her attorney and asked to see her. He was very convincing. The jailer let him use an interrogation room to talk to her. The old man came out, hobbling on the cane, thanked the jailer warmly, talked about the weather and left. They found the woman slumped over in her chair. EMTs responded, but all attempts at resuscitation failed. DOA at the hospital. He doesn't like loose ends apparently."

"So there goes our case," Tank said angrily.

"Something like that." Rourke drew in an audible breath. "Malathion. Good God, man, there are thousands of poisons that are undetectable by taste or smell. Why use Malathion?"

"Terror tactics," Tank replied, his voice very quiet. "Something for impact. We know he can be stealthy when he wants to. Either he's deliberately baiting us, or he's getting sloppy. If he gets sloppy enough, we can hang him out to dry."

"Lovely thought, and I just seasoned a brand-new rope," Rourke said with a lilt in his accent.

Tank laughed, but without any real humor. "Well, we'll see what happens. But I don't like having Carson here with her," he added involuntarily.

"You're barking up the wrong tree, mate," Rourke replied. "He likes loose associations. Your lovely Merissa is a forever sort of person. Not at all his type."

"I hope you're right."

Rourke chuckled. "You'll see. I'll go now. I've got things buttoned up tight here at the ranch. No worries."

"All right. I'll take your word for it that my family is safe."

"A word to the wise," Rourke added. "Don't taste anything you've left unattended. Tell her, too. Carson will be watching, but it never hurts to emphasize certain things. He was careless with one poison. He might not be with another, especially now that his plans have been thwarted." He hesitated. "I've seen men react under those conditions. A perfectly normal man, going by a set of mental plans, can go berserk when something unplanned happens. In this case, it could be fatal to a lot of people. Watch out."

"Good advice, and I'll take it. Thanks." He paused. "You've been a lifesaver, Rourke."

"You're welcome," the other man said as he hung up the phone.

Merissa was solemn. Carson was pensive. Neither of them spoke when Tank went back into the hospital room. He scowled.

Carson sighed. "He thinks we've been having a quick affair while the nurses' backs were turned," he mused, "somewhere between the checking-your-vitals and doctor rounds." He smiled at Tank, who was really glowering now. "Just for future reference, I never conduct affairs with women of faith," he pointed out, indicating Merissa. "They just aren't into group sex, for some reason I can't fathom."

Tank couldn't help it. He burst out laughing. So did Merissa, although she flushed a little at the explicit remark.

"No offense meant, if you're into it, of course," he told Tank dryly.

"Not me." Tank sat down in the only vacant chair and leaned back. He met Merissa's eyes evenly. "I'm a one-woman man."

She stared at him with wide, soft eyes. She wondered at the words and the expression on his face. It could be just a male thing, jealous of another man. On the other hand, he was looking at her with pure delight. Could he really have meant that he only wanted friendship from her? Had he said it because he wasn't sure of her?

"I feel decidedly like a third wheel," Carson remarked while they stared at each other. He got up. "I'm going down the hall for coffee. Can I bring you back a cup?" he asked Tank.

"Yes, please, cream only." Tank slid a hand into his pocket and presented him with a twenty-dollar bill. "Don't argue," he added. "Think of it as an expense account."

"In that case, I'll splurge and get a chocolate bar to go with it." Carson chuckled.

"I like mine with cream and sugar," Merissa told him.

Carson gave her a patient look. "The nurses would carry me into a back room and do God knows what to me if I gave you caffeine."

"Oh, you can paint a rose on that," a cute little red-headed nurse said as she came into the room and shot Carson a voluptuous glance. "Really terrible things. Unimaginable things." She gave him a mock growl.

"How many cups of coffee would you like, then?" he asked Merissa with a big grin.

Tank laughed. So did the nurse. Carson shot her a wink and a smile as he went out the door.

The nurse whistled and waved her hand as if fanning herself. "If I weren't happily married and a mother . . ." she mused, looking after Carson.

"He does have that effect on women," Tank joked.

"Most women," Merissa corrected. She looked at Tank in a way that conveyed she wasn't one of them.

Amazingly his face changed. He relaxed. He looked . . . happy. Content. He let the nurse do her job, then when she left, he moved close to the bed and leaned over Merissa.

"I lied."

"Excuse me?" she asked.

He bent his head and brushed his mouth tenderly over hers. "I don't want you for a friend."

"An enemy then?" she teased, but she was breathing as if she'd been running.

He nibbled her upper lip. "We can talk about it when you're out of the hospital and all this insanity ends."

She touched his cheek with cold fingertips and smiled while his mouth moved against hers very softly. "Okay."

He chuckled, because that didn't sound like a refusal.

She sighed as she looked up at his hard, gorgeous face. "You are so incredibly handsome," she murmured huskily.

He actually flushed. "Who? Me?"

"You." She smiled. "It's not only the way you look. It's the way you are."

"You don't really know me yet," he pointed out.

"I know you down to your bones," she said in an old, wise tone. "You'd lay down your life for your brothers, for their wives, for people who are close to you. In time of danger, you never run. You're honest and loyal and you don't even drink. Or smoke." She shook her head. "Your only real flaw, and it's a small one, is that temper."

He made a face at her. "It only peeks out from time to time in extreme circumstances."

"Like when you think Carson's trying to charm me." She laughed softly.

He sighed. It was impossible to deny it. "Yeah."

She touched his chiseled mouth. "He's very attractive. He seems like a rock sometimes, but he has a soft center. He doesn't want to get serious about anyone ever again, but there's a young woman somewhere who's driving him up the wall."

"She'll have to get in line," he teased, relieved to hear that Carson wasn't mooning over his girl.

"It's not like that," she replied. "She's very religious. She won't like some of the things she finds out about him." She searched over Tank's face. "I think it will shock him. He isn't used to women who don't think of intimacy as an itch you scratch whenever you feel the need."

"You're that sort of woman," he said softly.

"Yes," she replied. "I'm not judgmental. I don't want to make the world over into my own image of how things should be."

"I know what you mean. But there will always be people of faith, and women who don't follow the crowd over the cliff of . . . group sex," he added jokingly.

She laughed.

"And what's so funny about group sex?" Carson asked haughtily as he rejoined them. "Honest to God, you people!" He hesitated for effect. "Haven't you ever seen an anaconda mating ball on those National Geographic specials?"

They burst out laughing.

He handed Tank a cup of coffee and looked regretfully at Merissa as he dropped into a chair on the other side of the bed.

"Sorry, but they really would throw me out on my ear if I brought you a cup."

"I know. It's okay," she said, smiling at him.

Tank sat down in his own chair, but his eyes never left Merissa.

"Heard anything from the sheriff?" Carson asked.

Tank shook his head. "No, but he'll let us know if he finds anything. Shame about that woman," he added darkly. "I expect with a little incentive, she might have given something away."

"Or not," Carson added. "Men like that don't choose partners for their loose tongues." He crossed his long, muscular legs. "However, a little background check might turn up something."

"I was thinking the same thing." Tank smiled at Carson, because he knew what the man was doing. He suspected there was a bug in the hospital room. He was upping the ante, giving the shadowy assassin something more to worry about.

"Unless she was working for the government in deep cover, she isn't invisible. Someone will have known her. Your friend the sheriff will run her through the NCIC database and see what shows. I'm betting she's got a rap sheet. Not too long, maybe.

But there'll be something there."

"Enough, I hope," Tank added deliberately, "to give our shadowy friend a lot of worries. I wish him as many as he's given me lately."

"I expect when he hears what the Texas authorities are researching, he'll need to change his underwear," Carson said deliberately, and stared at Tank, to warn him not to speak.

"You think so?" was all Tank asked. He sipped coffee. "This isn't bad, for coffee out of a machine."

"Philistine," Carson scoffed. "This is real, honest-to-goodness coffee from a real coffeemaker."

"How did you get that?" Tank asked, surprised.

Carson leaned toward him. "There's this really pretty nurse. I just smiled and mentioned how much I hated coffee out of those damned machines." He held up his cup and grinned from ear to ear.

Tank couldn't resist laughing, too. Merissa just shook her head.

CHAPTER THIRTEEN

Tank had to go back to the ranch to shower and shave and check in with Cody Banks. He didn't want to talk to the sheriff in Merissa's hospital room, in case, as he suspected, the room was bugged.

He leaned over her and kissed her tenderly. "I don't care if he brings you a steak and a bouquet of flowers, he's off-limits. Got it?" he teased, nodding toward Carson.

She grinned back. "Got it."

He chuckled. He kissed her again and glanced at Carson. "You got it, too?"

"Absolutely," Carson mused. "She's safe with me."

"I'll be back in the morning, first thing, to wish you a Merry Christmas," he told her. "Have a good night."

"You, too," she replied huskily.

He left, but reluctantly.

Carson followed him just outside the room.

"Why did you say that about Texas?" Tank asked Carson. "It's a fair bet he heard you."

"He's pulling our chains, I'm pulling his chain," Carson replied coldly. "He's had a plan go wrong. Now he knows we're looking in another direction for something about him. His girlfriend is dead. He's got to be feeling the pressure. If he makes a mistake, we'll get him."

Tank relaxed a little. "You know, you're sort of diabolical."

Carson assumed a surprised expression. "Who, me? I have wings. You can't see them, but they're there."

"Angelic, you ain't," Tank said.

Carson made a face. "I know. But as far as she's concerned —" he jerked his head toward the hospital bed inside the room "— I am. You're one lucky man."

Tank flushed. "I know it."

"I'll keep her safe. Nobody's getting past me this time," he added.

"If you need help, call."

Carson nodded. "Tell Rourke what I said in the room. He'll take it from there."

"I'm telling Cody, too."

"The more the merrier." He smiled enigmatically. "Isn't it fun, putting a burr under the saddle of a murderer like this guy?"

"You know, it actually is. I just hope we

can catch him before he comes after her again," he voiced his fear. "He meant her to die this time. And there are poisons we couldn't detect."

"I am now your new food taster," Carson said. "I'd prefer to test steaks, but I'll do gelatin in a pinch. She'll be fine."

"Watch your own back, too," Tank said.

"Always."

He called Cody and met him in a grocery store parking lot.

"I don't even trust my own damned phone anymore," Tank said. "I think everything's bugged."

"It might be. No cause to apologize for being careful. What's up?"

"Carson mentioned in the hospital room that we were looking toward Texas for answers in this case. His idea is that the man's plan to kill Merissa flubbed, so that's put him off his stride. Now, he knows we suspect a Texas connection, although he can't know just how much we've already found out. That's going to panic him."

Cody nodded. "Not a bad strategy, so long as everyone's properly guarded. It could go down hard, if he loses himself in revenge."

"I know," Tank said heavily. "I don't want her hurt. I don't want anybody hurt."

"Neither do I." Cody was pensive. "What if it turns his attention back to Texas and he leaves town, though? It does lessen our hopes of capturing him."

"It also lessens Merissa Baker's chances of meeting a sudden and terrible death," Tank added grimly.

Cody relented. "Yes. It does. My idea would be to alert the authorities in Texas and mention this to them."

"That's a very good idea. I'll do it as soon as I get home."

"If I can help, in any way . . ."

"You're already helping, as a lawman and a friend," Tank said, clapping the other man on the shoulder. "Thanks."

"Hey, you're my buddy," he teased.

"And I'm yours. You can have anything on the place except Diamond Bob."

Diamond Bob was the famous herd sire who had his own air-conditioned, heated barn.

"Aww, darn," Cody said, snapping his fingers. "And I do love a good steak . . ."

"You bite your tongue," Tank retorted.

"Just kidding." Cody laughed. "Drive safely."

"I always do. See you later."

Tank called Hayes Carson in Texas and told

him what was going on. Hayes approved.

"It just might do the trick," he told Tank. "If this is the same guy who tried to have both of us hit, and who put your woman friend in the hospital, panicking him in this direction would be mostly fatal for him. We know what to look for this time."

"I just hope we can catch him," Tank said heavily. "It wears on the nerves, especially when a woman's involved."

"I know that feeling. If we can do anything on our end, let me know. I'll fill Rick Marquez in on what's happening. He told me about the direction the case is taking and the connections. He's still chasing down leads on the prosecutor's murder, now that you've given him a new angle to look at. He said he loves the chance to solve that case. He knew the guy from when he was a public defender. Damned shame."

"Yes. Too many people have been hurt already. Thanks for the help."

"I haven't done much, but you're welcome. Keep us in the loop."

"I'll do that."

They'd put as many safety precautions into effect as they could. Clara still insisted on staying at the cabin, and they couldn't move her. But Tank did have a cowboy stay in the spare bedroom, with a gun, just in case.

Merissa got better very quickly. She and Tank had a nice meal together in the hospital for Christmas, complete with turkey and dressing and cranberry sauce. Clara joined them for it. Two days later, the doctor agreed to release her, and Tank and Carson drove her home.

She and Clara had a tearful reunion. "Oh, it's so good to be home!" Merissa almost wept as she hugged her mother.

"So good to have you here, my darling," Clara enthused.

"I wish I hadn't messed up Christmas for us," Merissa said miserably.

"We'll have a late one. I haven't even taken the tree down." Clara laughed.

"I guess I can go home now?" the cowboy, Rance, asked.

"No!" several voices echoed.

Rance put up both hands and laughed. "No problem! I like it here. She —" he pointed at Clara "— can cook!"

"So can Merissa," Tank said with a smile. "She's in a class of her own."

"I'll prove that to you in a day or two, when I get stronger," she promised him.

He grinned and bent to kiss her warmly. "Don't get off your guard. We have to talk."

She nodded, her eyes full of wonder. "As

soon as you like."

"Just a few loose ends to tie up first," he said. He motioned to Carson to go with him. "I'll see you first thing in the morning. If you need me . . ."

"I'll call," she promised.

He stared at her with such passion that she blushed. He walked back, scooped her up gently and kissed her. "See you in the morning."

She laughed. "Okay!"

One thing he was certain of as he walked out the door. That woman was his. And she knew it.

He phoned Rourke as soon as he finished telling the family about how things stood at the cabin now that Merissa was back home.

"I was going to call Marquez myself, but we've had a lot going on, with Merissa being released from the hospital. I did tell Hayes Carson, but Marquez should be briefed on everything, too. Since you know him," he asked, "do you think you could give him a call for me?"

Rourke chuckled. "I'll call him right now," he added.

"Let's hope there's some good news."

"Let's hope."

■ ■ ■ ■

Rourke called back a few hours later, from near the Baker house. The cowboy who'd been watching Clara had returned to the ranch. Rourke had released him, and he was anxious to get back to his regular chores, despite Clara's wonderful cooking. Carson was working around the Kirk ranch, keeping an eye on the family.

"Sorry it took so long. Marquez was in court," Rourke said.

"I figured he wasn't available or I'd have heard from you sooner. Are Clara and Merissa okay?"

"They're fine. They were having lunch just before I left to check the surveillance units Carson put up. If I get back in time, I'll get homemade chicken salad." He laughed. "Okay, here's what Marquez was able to find out . . ."

"Is that line secure?"

"Is it ever," Rourke said grimly. "I'm halfway up a tree talking on a throwaway phone. Yours is a prepaid. No way he's got access to these. And just in case he does, I'm running a scrambler on the line."

"Devious."

"I work in covert ops," Rourke reminded

him. "This is what Marquez told me. That watch was made by a Swiss manufacturer. It's a custom one-of-a-kind watch. It was a birthday present to the assistant D.A. from his very wealthy wife."

"So the guy couldn't fence it," Tank guessed.

"Very good. It could have been disassembled, jewels removed, gold melted down, but the watch was unique. My guess, and Marquez's, is that the killer liked the prestige of wearing a watch that was worth more than the price of a new custom Jaguar XK. Same thing for the shirt, which was couture, hand-painted and cost a mint. So he likes the shirt and the watch and starts wearing them. It's stupid, but brilliant people do stupid things. He wears them to Hayes Carson's drug bust and is photographed wearing them. Later, he wears them to your ambush and you saw him wearing them. Somebody, probably his employer, goes nuts when he realizes his man has been advertising a killing that could put them both in the slammer for life and there's a photograph to prove it. So the repentant employee goes after Hayes, tries to have him killed, but hires the wrong man and the gunman misses. Thus the kidnapping, which would certainly have led to

Hayes's murder except for some great escape work by Hayes's fiancée, whom he just married."

"The photograph would have been on the computer that was in Hayes's office that was erased by a cohort of the would-be killer," Tank finished for him.

"Most likely the woman accomplice was the one who worked for the so-called surveillance tech who bugged the houses up here," Rourke guessed. "Then when they realized the photograph could be recovered, they took the computer and killed the techie who was trying to do the recovery."

"Sloppy, messy job all around," Tank muttered.

"Isn't it, though?" Rourke mused. "To continue, then he realizes that you got a great look at him and you're another loose end he can't afford to ignore. Our guy is a pro. He's great at disguises, knows his poisons . . . knows his way around the underworld. But I've worked with some guys like that who were skilled at covert ops but lousy at strategy and tactics. Maybe in the past he's had someone else telling him what to do and how to do it, and he was great at it. Now, maybe he's on his own and finding that he's not covering all his bases like he used to. Or maybe he has a drug habit and it's getting out of control, so he's sloppy all of a sudden."

"He didn't try to hit the two federal agents or Cash Grier's secretary," Tank pointed out.

"They may have been further down the list. Take out the biggest risk first — Hayes Carson and his computer. Then you, because you could actually connect him with Charro Mendez and lead you back to his boss if you talked to the right people."

"Lot of maybes there," Tank pointed out.

"True."

"What else did Marquez tell you?"

"They've tentatively traced our would-be assassin to a sleazy politician with purported ties to a drug cartel. He's a state senator. But he's running for a high political office. The elderly senior U.S. senator from Texas has died suddenly of what they assumed were natural causes. That's being reinvestigated as we speak. There's also a serious rival for the unexpired term who just landed himself in the hospital with an undiagnosed illness."

"Did they look for poison in his bloodstream?" Tank drawled.

"They hadn't, but thanks to Marquez, they're going to."

"You think there's a tie to this politician?"

Tank asked.

"Now, there's the really interesting thing. Among the cases the prosecutor was investigating was one involving this sleazy politician. Bribery, misuse of funds, drug distribution connections, that sort of thing."

"Did he have evidence?"

"I think he might have. But the data in his computer was destroyed. And I mean destroyed. The hard drive was shattered. All the paperwork on the case disappeared. Seems the prosecutor had hired a temp to sub for his sick secretary just before he was killed and all the records went missing."

"There would have been police reports, investigator's notes," Tank began.

"I'm coming to that. All vanished. It's just the word of the police officers and detectives. Know what that's worth in court without a paper trail?"

"Damn!"

"Marquez's language was much more colorful," he said. "Anyway, there's nothing that can connect the politician to any of this. Except . . ."

"Except?"

"It seems he has an enforcer with expensive tastes. The enforcer, a man named Richard Martin, was seen wearing a paisley shirt just like the one the prosecutor's wife gave him."

"Don't tell me — he was also wearing a watch that plays Joan Jett."

"Bingo."

"Now what's the bad news?"

"Same as before. No paper trail. Nobody who saw him could identify him except maybe you and Hayes Carson and the feds. He'd have to be nuts to go after the feds, by the way. Or maybe he thought about importing some overseas talent for those. Oh, and Cash Grier's cute little secretary with the photographic memory — she saw him. They're still trying to tie in her father's attempted murder with the poisoned would-be assassin."

"Somebody had better be watching her back, just in case," Tank said grimly.

"I know things about her father that I can't tell you," Rourke said.

"The minister?" Tank asked.

"He wasn't always a minister. Leave it at that. Besides, she works for Cash Grier. I know career criminals who'd think three times before they even considered tangling with him. He may be a small-town police chief now, but those old skills aren't rusty. He also has a network of, shall we say, off-the-radar friends and associates. Some of them are reputedly wanted by a number of world governments."

"Very interesting."

"Isn't it, though?" Rourke's voice became serious. "Marquez said that the sleazy politician's enforcer has a reputation for extreme violence, especially in tight corners. We can't let our guards down for a moment."

"Clara and Merissa have to come over to the house and stay with us," Tank said firmly.

"I told them that. Merissa was willing at first. Now, she's not. She thinks they'll be all right at the cabin. Clara says if Merissa wants to stay, so will she."

"Don't even let them argue with you about it. Pick them up and carry them out to the car if you have to."

"It's a truck, but I take your meaning."

"Get Merissa's computer and any sentimental items you can carry, as well. Just in case he has any ideas about making a bad situation worse."

"I'll do it right now."

"Watch yourself."

"I always do. Take your own advice. Talk to you later." He cut the connection.

Tank took his brothers into the kitchen, turned on the mixer in spite of Mavie's exasperation, shooed her out of the room and told them what had happened.

"Things are getting very dangerous," Cane remarked.

"Yes, they are," Mallory agreed. "Carson set up his system to do facial recognition, and we pinpointed a man today with a criminal record who ran when we tried to question him."

Tank felt the danger. "I wouldn't have put you two in the middle of this, or the wives, or your son," he told Mallory, "for any-thing."

"It's worth the danger if we can keep you alive," Cane said tightly.

"It's Merissa I'm most worried about," Tank confessed.

"She's safe for now, though," Mallory told him. "Rourke won't let anything happen to her or her mother."

"That's not all." Tank shoved his hands into his jean pockets. "Something's got me worried."

"What?"

"The trail he left in the snow, the one that led to the highway."

"Old hunter's trick is to double back on a trail," Mallory mentioned.

"If he was laying a false trail deliberately, he'd make sure we saw it. So where do you think he's been hiding?"

Mallory's face was hard as rock. "In the cabin itself."

Tank felt his breath catch in his throat. "Merissa and Clara!" he exclaimed, fear in his expression.

He opened his cell phone and called Rourke. The phone rang and rang. But Rourke didn't answer.

"Something's wrong," Tank said. "I'm going over there."

"So are we," Cane and Mallory said together.

"No," Tank replied emphatically. "You stay here. I'll call all the cowboys to stand around the house with loaded weapons. Carson's going with me."

"Be careful," Mallory said tautly.

"You're the only little brother we've got," Cane added and tried to smile.

"I'll be fine."

Tank started out the door. He had Darby Hanes on the line before he reached it, slinging out orders as he headed to his truck.

"Carson!" he called to the dark-haired man on the porch.

Carson looked up from his laptop.

"Let's go. Right now!"

Carson put the laptop down and ran to the truck. "What is it?"

"You can eavesdrop." He phoned Cody Banks. "I've lost communication with my man who's guarding Merissa and Clara. How soon can you get there with a couple of deputies?"

"I'll meet you at the front porch," Cody said, and hung up.

"We think he laid a deliberate trail away from where he was," Tank said through his teeth. "He's in the damned cabin! Probably in the attic. We never even checked it!"

Carson groaned. "What a damned lack of foresight!"

"I just pray we're in time," Tank said, and stood down on the accelerator.

When they got to the cabin, the sheriff's car, a state police car, an ambulance and a fire truck were sitting on the road that led to it, sirens and lights just dying down.

"What happened?" Tank asked, trying to fight down terror as he joined Cody Banks at his squad car.

"He's got the women," Cody said in a hunted tone. "He won't negotiate. He says he's through trying to do it covertly. Now he's just going to kill them."

"They aren't dead?" Tank asked.

"Not yet," Cody replied.

Tank let out the breath he'd been holding. "Then what do we do?"

"I don't have a hostage negotiator," Cody told them. "The police department in Catelow has one, but he's back East on a long Christmas holiday with his folks. The state police sent us a man who did it for Houston P.D. a few years back." He indicated the man, who nodded. "Right now we're waiting for the utility companies."

"Utility companies?" Tank burst out. "What in hell for?"

"We turn off everything we can turn off," the state trooper said gently. "Then we negotiate for power, water, electricity . . ."

"He'll kill them before you get that far." Tank drew in a ragged breath. "It's me he wants. I'll trade with them."

"You will not," Cody said firmly. "Then we'll have three victims instead of two."

While they were talking, Carson was stripping off his jacket. He tossed it into the front seat of the ranch pickup.

"And what would you be doing then?" Cody asked.

"What I've made a living at for the past several years," Carson said. "Who's got a sniper kit I can borrow?" he asked grimly.

The men stared at him.

He stuck his hands on his hips. "Are we going to stand here and make judgments or let me save the women?" he asked curtly.

"Sorry," Cody said. "Wasn't thinking. Frank," he called to one of his deputies, "break out that new rifle with the scope."

"New. Damned things never shoot right until they're used," Carson muttered.

"It's what we've got," Cody told him.

"You'll never get close enough." Tank tried to reason with him. He was sick with fear. "He'll see you coming."

Carson lifted an eyebrow. "Remind me to tell you a story or two when this is all over." He glanced toward the deputy, who was carrying a heavy metal gun box. He sat it on the lowered tailgate of the ranch pickup and opened it.

"Sweet," Carson said as he fingered the light wood of the stock.

"Ya, isn't it?" the deputy asked with a sigh. "I've just used it on targets, but it's accurate to a hair."

"Shoots true?"

"You bet."

Carson took it out of the box with a faint reverence and looked down the scope toward the house. "Nice optics," he said. He concentrated. He could see movement at one of the windows. It fluttered, and a woman's frightened face looked out. It was Clara. She was talking to someone behind her, scared and crying.

Carson's jaw set. "He sent Clara to look out the window, to see what's going on out here." He took the rifle and slung the strap over his shoulder. "I need a diversion," he told Cody Banks. "I'm not going to tell you where I'll be. But when you hear a shot, move in quick."

"Don't miss," Cody said firmly.

"It would be the first time," Carson replied solemnly. "But I won't."

He turned and went off toward the end of the driveway.

"He's going in the wrong direction," the deputy muttered.

"Think so?" Tank asked. He knew Carson. He turned back to Cody. "If those utility trucks showed up right now, it would be a great help."

Cody pressed the mike on his radio. "I'll see if I can hurry them up. Dispatch," he began, talking into the unit, "I need an ETA on the power company."

"This is dispatch, Sheriff. He's two minutes away."

"Tell him to turn on his yellow lights and come in fast," Cody said.

"Sir?"

"Just do it, okay?"

There was a smile in the voice that answered. "Okay."

Cody turned to his deputy. "There's a sudden emergency you have to handle. Turn on the lights and sirens full blast and make a big production of turning around in the driveway. Go closer to the house when you do it, but not too close."

The deputy nodded. "Yes, sir!"

He jumped into his car, turned on the lights and sirens and went careening a little way toward the house before he cut the wheel sharply and tore off down the road.

"There," Cody said. "Maybe that will give him time to get in place. And here's another diversion."

The power truck pulled up next to the squad car. "I had some really strange directions . . ." the driver began.

"No time to talk, I'm afraid," the sheriff told him with a weary smile. "We have a hostage situation. We need you to cut power to the cabin, as quickly as you can."

"I'll get right on it." He turned off the engine, got out, pulled on his tool belt and climbed into the cherry picker. He lifted himself up to the connections. A few twists and turns with his tools and the cabin went dark.

"Nice work," Cody said when he came down again.

"Now what?" the man asked.

"Can you stay with us for a few minutes?"

"Unless we get an urgent call about something," the lineman agreed.

"Thanks."

Cody turned to the state trooper. "I'll try to get him to answer the phone, if it's still working." Some phones wouldn't work without power.

The trooper nodded.

Cody dialed Clara's number and waited. The phone rang once, twice, three times. It rang again. And again. Just when Cody was about to give up, there was a click.

"Yeah. What do you want?" a man with an Australian accent asked.

"Your hostages," Cody said.

There was a cold laugh. "No way, mate. Messed up all me plans, they did. Now they have to pay for it."

Cody handed the phone to the state trooper.

"Can you let me verify that both women are still alive?" the trooper asked in a gentle tone.

"You'll just have to take my word for it," the man replied.

"What do you want?"

"For starters, turn the power back on."

"Can't do that, I'm afraid. Not yet, anyway. Talk to me. What do you want?"

"You'll find out, very soon."

He hung up. The trooper relayed the message.

Tank groaned. He should have married Merissa weeks ago. He should have carted her off to a minister the night they had Chinese food. Why had he hesitated? He knew how he felt. He knew how she felt. Now it might never happen. That murderer in the cabin was going to kill her, kill her mother, and it was all his fault.

A telephone truck came down the road, followed by a county water truck. They pulled into the driveway.

"What do you want us to do?" they asked Cody Banks.

"Wait." He turned to his deputy, who was just driving up. "Rev that thing up, hit the lights and sirens, hard, and head toward town!"

"Yes, sir!"

The deputy went through the same routine he'd used earlier, and cut out onto the highway. Just as he vanished into the distance, a shot rang out.

Heart in his mouth, hammering, Tank

disobeyed a direct order from Cody Banks and ran toward the cabin just as fast as his legs would carry him. Who'd fired the shot? Carson had said to come running if they heard one, but what if it was the man in the cabin firing and they cost the women their lives by running in on him?

He couldn't stop. He already was imagining seeing Merissa lying dead on the floor, blood in her mouth. He'd never live if she didn't. He couldn't go through the process of losing her, not again, not when she'd almost died of poison just days ago.

His chest was bursting as he followed the other men up on the porch. Cody reached for the door handle and there was an explosion.

The concussion from the explosion knocked the men backward onto the ground. Tank, flat on his back, breathless, saw the fireball go up into the air, like an orange balloon that just kept growing. The sound of the explosion followed seconds later.

"Get them out of there!" Tank yelled.

The firemen were already on the way. They pulled the tanker up next to the steps, jumped out and started stretching hoses.

Tank tried to go onto the porch, but Cody tackled him and brought him down again.

"No!" Tank raged. "God, no! I have . . . to get . . . in there!" he pleaded with his friend.

Cody wouldn't let go. "If you go in there, you'll die with her."

"I don't . . . care!" Tank choked out. "I can't live without her! I won't!"

Cody ground his teeth together. He'd never heard so much raw emotion in a man's voice. He was dying for his friend. But he wouldn't let go, either.

The water jetted into the cabin, the pressure of it breaking the rest of the glass that the explosion hadn't.

Tank watched in horror as a flaming human body came diving out the door, screaming. It was too tall, too big, to be a woman.

The man, because it had to be the killer, went running toward the driveway. A fireman in full gear tackled him and brought him down while another fireman aimed a fire extinguisher at him. His clothing was burned half off; his body under it was black already. The foam covered him. Still he screamed and screamed. But very quickly he lay still, shivered and died.

Merissa and Clara. Had they already burned to death? Tank looked into the cabin with dead eyes. His life had burned up in there. What would he do now? He had no life left. His Merissa was gone. Gone, like the cabin that was slowly being consumed in the bright yellow flames, in the thick black smoke that rose up into the sky.

He sank to his knees and just sat there, watching the structure burn.

He closed his eyes and said a silent prayer for their souls. He felt a wetness in his eyes, rolling onto his cheeks.

"Merissa!" he groaned. His voice echoed the anguish in his heart.

Somewhere, in the back of his mind, he could hear Merissa's sweet, clear voice calling his name. It would haunt him forever.

"Dalton!"

He smiled. It was like an angel singing.

"Dalton!"

How odd, it seemed so real.

"Tank! Dammit!"

Tank. Dammit?

He got to his feet and turned around. There, black with soot but still very much alive was Merissa, in Carson's arms. Clara was standing to one side, grimy, too, but smiling.

"Oh, dear God," Tank whispered, and it was like a prayer. He went to her, took her gently from Carson's arms and kissed her. And kissed her. And kissed her!

"I thought you'd died in there!" he whispered as he rained kisses on her face and hair. She smelled like smoke, and to him it was the sweetest perfume on earth. She was alive and breathing and cursing him. He loved it.

"We thought we were going to die," she said wearily. "He'd already opened the valve on one of the gas canisters." She coughed. "The fumes were choking us. We didn't know why he did that, although we knew he had them wired to some sort of timer. He was looking out the window when the sirens started up. He'd just cut off some cord from a roll we had. He was going to tie us to the chairs. The gas was making us dizzy, and we knew what he planned. I motioned to Mama, and we covered our mouths and ran to the back door. We figured we were going to die anyway and being shot was easier than burning up."

"My poor, brave girl," he groaned. "Come on." He picked her up and carried her to the paramedics, who were giving Clara oxygen. She'd inhaled more of the gas than Merissa had, because the shooter had made her stand at the window to watch the law enforcement people.

"Better now?" Tank asked when she'd had a few whiffs of oxygen and the EMTs had examined her and her mother.

"Yes," she whispered. "Thanks," she told

the EMTs with a smile.

"What happened when you got to the door?" Tank asked.

"Well, I managed to unlock it. He was yelling at us to stop or he'd just shoot us. We panicked. I threw open the door. Carson was just a few yards away. He threw up the rifle and fired once. The man behind us in the house cried out. I heard him fall over a chair or something, I didn't stop to look. Carson yelled for us to run and he'd cover us. We did, we ran like mad toward him. I think the man's pistol went off, because there was a second shot behind us. Just seconds later, when we were barely away from the porch, the house blew up." She drew in a shaky breath. Dalton folded her close.

"Sorry." She laughed. "I'm still shaky."

"You're alive, honey, that's all that matters to me. Go on . . ."

"Rourke had gone to check something out. We were eating chicken salad in the kitchen when we heard bumping on the back porch. I thought it was Rourke so we didn't really pay attention. We went to watch the news on television. Just a little later, the man came into the living room with a pistol and told us to go into the kitchen and not make a move or he'd shoot us dead."

337

She shivered. He held her closer.

"There were propane tanks just inside the back door. He'd set them up with some sort of fuses. He made us sit at the table while he opened the valve on one of them. He said he'd kill Mama first if I tried anything." Her eyes closed. "We were scared to death. He was furious, cursing, raging because he couldn't kill you and that sheriff in Texas. And he'd just found out that the death of a man he hired to kill a woman in Texas was being investigated. He said he'd poisoned the man because he botched the job. He said there was another killing, one that happened before all that, but we'd never have time to learn about that one, because he was going to kill us and then make sure his tracks were covered. He said his boss thought he was addicted, but he wasn't, he could quit anytime he liked. He was yelling and waving his arms around. . . ." She shook her head. "I thought he'd lost his mind."

"It sounds like it," he replied grimly. He smoothed over her soft hair.

"He said he was going to blow us up and leave in the commotion that followed. He said you'd never have another moment's peace and he'd never be discovered. He was going to Texas afterward to finish up the business down there. He said he'd found

338

someone reliable to kill the woman in Texas who saw him. No more loose ends, he said." She leaned against him. "I was so happy to see Carson. But I was even happier to see you."

"I thought you were gone," he whispered huskily. "When the house went up."

She smiled and kissed him. She buried her soft face in his throat. "We were just going out the back door when one of the propane tanks went off. I don't know what caused it, but it must have set the others off." She looked at Carson, who was still holding the rifle and listening to their conversation. "Thank you for my life."

"You're quite welcome," he said, and smiled back.

Tank added his thanks. But he was too busy kissing Merissa to say much more.

CHAPTER FOURTEEN

"I don't understand about the propane tanks," Tank said a little later, while the women were being treated for the gas inhalation at the local emergency room. He and Cody Banks had superficial burns, but those had already been dealt with.

"From what Merissa said, he'd set them on timers," Carson explained. "The first one detonated and triggered the others."

"Yes, but how did the first one detonate?" he asked. "I saw a show once about propane tanks exploding. They shot a bullet into one. It just went straight through. No explosion."

Carson's face was grim. "It's the vapor you have to worry about, when the gas is released and concentrated in a room. If it's thick enough to hamper breathing, any spark will make it explode, even turning on a light switch."

"Is that what you think happened?"

"Merissa said he'd opened the valve on

one of the tanks, that they were having trouble breathing. He'd set the timer to go off and was probably counting on the fumes to cause the explosion, to cover his exit and kill the women. I assume he planned to tie them up first, but he didn't foresee someone getting close enough to shoot him before he could follow through. Nice diversion, by the way."

"Thank Cody, it was his idea."

"Anyway, I couldn't get a clear shot from the position I was in, so I moved closer to the cabin. All at once the back door opened and the women tried to come out. The would-be assassin was after them. I aimed past them, hit him in the shoulder, and motioned to them to run. He was stunned long enough for us to get clear of the cabin. I smelled gas before I even got as far as the porch. The women were coughing from contact with it. He fired after us, just before the explosion."

"You think the shot ignited the gas?"

"Yes," Carson replied. "When he shot at us, the spark from his pistol must have ignited the gas." Carson shook his head. "He burned to death. Even for an evil man, that's a hell of a way to die."

"Merissa said that's how he'd go," Tank replied heavily. "She knew."

"You take care of her," Carson said firmly. "If you don't, I'll take her away from you and marry her myself." He grinned.

Tank chuckled. He clapped him on the shoulder. "Thanks for saving my life."

"I didn't," he replied, puzzled.

"You saved her. Without her, I wouldn't have had a life."

"Got it," Carson told him, with an understanding look. "You're welcome."

Cody Banks joined them in the waiting room. "Well, we've got a dead body and no way to identify it," he said heavily. "Coroner's working on him down in the autopsy room, but there isn't much left to go on, unless his DNA is in a database somewhere."

"Did he have anything on him like a cell phone?"

"He did. It's pretty much toast. We'll send it to the state crime lab and hope for a miracle. Just between us, I doubt we'll get lucky."

"We need to call Sheriff Hayes Carson in Texas," Tank said grimly. "The shooter told Merissa that he'd hired someone reliable to take out some woman who'd seen him and had a photographic memory."

Carson's eyes narrowed. "I can only think of one woman who fits that description.

You'd better make that call fast."

"I will," Tank said.

"The man was a certified lunatic," Cody said angrily.

"What about his watch?"

Cody blinked. "What watch?"

"The one he was wearing . . ."

Cody was shaking his head. "He didn't have a watch on his wrist," he replied. "Nor a wallet. Go figure."

"He must have stayed someplace while he was hunting me," Tank said curtly.

"We thought he might have been staying in the attic of the cabin," Carson added.

Cody sighed. "Well, we'll give it a look, but the fire did catastrophic damage to most of it."

Tank winced. "Merissa's computer was in there. All her work."

"No, it wasn't," Rourke said, joining them. He was grinning. "Forgotten already? I moved out her computer and most of their little personal keepsakes earlier in the day, and was going to bring them to stay at your ranch."

"Great foresight." Tank chuckled.

"I am known far and wide for my foresight, which is exceeded only by my striking good looks," Rourke pointed out.

Carson rolled his eyes.

"We'll need to contact the Red Cross," Cody said.

"Why?" Tank asked.

"The women are going to be temporarily homeless . . ."

"They have a home," Tank said, smiling. "We have three spare bedrooms."

"Is that an invitation?" Rourke asked, big-eyed. "Because I've been sharing a room in the bunkhouse with him, and he snores," he grumbled, glaring at Carson.

"I do not snore!" the other man said indignantly.

"Then you're using a chain saw at night and you don't remember," Rourke countered.

"It wasn't an invitation," Tank told him. "You have to go home now. This case is closed. The would-be assassin is no longer a problem. Although I'm very grateful, to both of you, and your checks will reflect how grateful."

"I didn't do this for pay," Rourke pointed out. "So don't insult me."

"Same here," Carson added. He smiled, too. "Even famous attorneys do pro bono cases from time to time."

"Some lawyer," Rourke muttered. "Do your summations with a sniper kit, do you?"

Carson raised both eyebrows.

"If you ever get tired of working for Cy Parks, you can come and work for me," Tank told Carson. "I'll even build you a house of your own."

"Tempting," Carson said. "But Cy Parks would grieve for me."

"He did an Irish jig when you said you were coming up here," Rourke mused, "and he's not even Irish."

"Lies," Carson said easily.

"I only lie when I'm asked to," Rourke said haughtily.

Merissa and Clara came through a door, along with Dr. Harrison, who was grinning as he talked to Clara.

"Long time, no see," Tank said and shook his hand.

"What an extraordinary coincidence," the doctor said. "I brought a young man in with me who needed stitching up after a fight, and ran into these two."

"He knows the resident on duty," Clara said.

"I should, I taught him everything he knows." He grinned. The smile faded. "I was sorry to hear about your cabin. If you need a place to stay . . ."

"Very nice of you, but the wives have the guest bedrooms all ready for them at the ranch," Tank said. "And we'd better go. It's been a long day for all of us."

"I'd like to phone you later, if I may," the doctor told Clara. "To see how you're doing."

"That would be very kind of you," she replied. "Thanks."

"It would be my pleasure." He nodded to the others, smiled at the women and walked on to the desk.

"Ready to go?" Tank asked.

Merissa nodded. "I'm so tired. We both are."

"It's been an ordeal," Tank replied. "But with a happy ending. Come on. You can ride with me."

"You're sure we won't be imposing?" Merissa asked worriedly.

"How can you impose?" Tank asked with a smile. "You're family, aren't you?"

She looked up at him with her heart in her eyes. "Oh, yes. Definitely family."

He drew her under his arm and smiled.

The women settled in as easily as if they'd been born at the Kirk ranch. Merissa, who had a hard time interacting with most people, fit right in with Morie and Bolinda.

"It's like I've known them all my life," she told Tank when they were alone in his truck, driving back to the cabin to check out what was left of their personal possessions after the fire department and the crime scene investigators had done their jobs.

Clara had thought about joining them, but she knew Merissa wanted a little time alone with Tank, so she pretended to be too tired. Merissa had just grinned at her, because she knew better.

"I told you it wouldn't be an ordeal." Tank chuckled. He had her hand in his. He didn't want to let go. He'd come so close to losing her, twice now.

"Your family is very nice."

"So is yours."

"Thanks."

He pulled up just a little distance from the front porch. The kitchen was mostly scattered timber now. Half the cabin was almost intact, but there was a good bit of fire damage.

"Two deaths in so short a time," Merissa said softly. "My father and now this horrible man." She shook her head.

"But you and Clara are alive," he pointed out.

She smiled up at him. "So we are."

He got out and helped her from the vehicle. They walked up onto the porch and around to the back of the house. The ground was wet from the fire hoses. There were pieces of sharp metal lying around, and shattered glass.

"Careful," he told her. "Don't step on anything sharp."

"I won't . . . !"

He swung her up in his arms, laughing. "I'll make sure of it." He stared into her eyes with soft hunger. "I still can't believe you're here with me, all in one piece. I've never been so afraid in my whole life."

She linked her arms around his neck. "You asked me to marry you." She flushed. "I thought it was just because you wanted to, well, you know. And then you looked embarrassed and I said I didn't want to get married . . ."

She stopped because he was kissing her. He did it very carefully, very tenderly, because she was still fragile from her brushes with death. "I want to get married," he whispered, "more than I can even tell you. I wanted it then, but I got flustered and messed it up."

She smoothed her hand over his hard cheek. "I lied. I want to marry you very much," she whispered.

He carefully put her on her feet.

"Here." He put a box in her hand, a jeweler's box.

She opened it. There was a matching wedding set, rubies and diamonds. She caught her breath.

"I had that in my pocket the day I blurted out that we needed to get married. Ruined the whole thing."

"No, you didn't." She took out the engagement ring. "Will you put it on, please?"

He smiled as he slid it onto her ring finger. "Will you marry me?"

"Of course," she breathed, beaming up at him with tears threatening.

His lips nibbled softly at hers. "How soon?" he murmured.

"Yesterday."

He smiled against her mouth. "Day before yesterday."

"Last week."

"Last month."

"Last . . . year."

The kiss grew longer and deeper and harder, and she moaned. That was when he stopped, because he could feel how weak she still was.

He lifted his head and cleared his throat. "We can get married. But we'll wait until you're feeling better before we do intimate things."

She laughed shyly. "Okay. I mean, I want to do intimate things. But I'm still a little rocky."

"I know. It's all right." He searched her eyes. "I want you. That's part of it, for a man. But the reason I want to marry you is because I'm in love with you."

"You are?"

"Oh, yes." He brushed his mouth over hers. "When I saw that explosion and thought you were in the house . . ." He drew her close and hugged her, hard. "The world went dark. I thought I was hearing voices when you called my name."

"I cussed."

He laughed. "Yes, you did. I was thinking of ways and means to get to you, even if it meant finding my way across that dark line into death." He lifted his head and sobered as he looked into her eyes. "I have no life without you. I have no future. No world. No home. You are everything in the world to me. And I will love you until I die. Even longer."

Tears stung her eyes. "I will love you that way, too. Forever."

He kissed the tears from her eyes. "Forever."

They were married at the ranch, by the minister of the local Methodist church. Merissa was still fragile, but she wore a beautiful couture gown with silk embroidery over white satin, with Brussels lace and a fingertip veil. She carried a bouquet of poinsettia, because even though Christmas was over, it was still sort of a Christmas wedding, and they stood in the same room with the enormous, beautiful Christmas tree blazing with light.

Rourke and Carson had been persuaded to stay for the ceremony, after which they were en route to Texas.

The assassin was dead, but there was a faint trail leading back to Hayes Carson and even Carlie. The death of the district attorney in San Antonio was the key. But if the dead assassin had already hired someone to take care of Carlie and her photographic memory, time was of the essence. It went without saying that he could hardly call off the hit now that he was dead.

Carson didn't say much, but Tank noticed that he bristled when anyone mentioned the fact that Carlie could be on the hit list. For a man who hated her, he did seem conflicted.

"Did you call Hayes Carson?" a drowsy Merissa asked on the first night of their honeymoon in Montego Bay, Jamaica.

Tank drew her closer, smiling. "I did indeed. He and the feds and Rick Marquez are working on leads."

He drew the sheet away from her small, perfect breasts and bent to draw his lips over them.

"I hope they can save the woman in Texas," she said in a shivery whisper, arching her back.

"Me, too," he whispered back.

She pressed close against his warm, muscular bare chest. The thick hair on it tickled. It felt wonderful, just the same. She looped her arms around his neck. "And I was scared to do this," she added, fascinated.

"I noticed."

It had been a little difficult at first. Merissa, naturally shy even with her clothing on, had to be coaxed out of it with a nice glass of wine and a dark room. He smoothed his hands over her soft body with the same sensuous delicacy he used when playing the piano, teasing her into relaxing, accepting, participating in a feast of the senses that far surpassed anything he'd ever known in his life.

At last, when she was sobbing and digging her nails into his long back, he arched down against her hips and quickly overcame the small barrier that was barely noticeable except for a tiny flash of pain.

His movements, urgent and hard and

deep, lifted her off the bed in a shivering ecstasy of satisfaction even the first time.

"You said that it usually took a little time for people to get used to each other like this and enjoy it, especially for women," she reminded him as he laid her back on the pillows.

"Well, yes," he said, grinning. "But I neglected to mention that I was speaking about men who are far less skillful and patient than I am." He chuckled.

"Skillful. Patient." She gasped. "Sometimes a little too patient . . . !"

"Oh, am I?" He pushed down, hard. "Better?"

"More!" she gasped.

"Like this?" He caught her thigh and pulled her up to him, riveted her body to his and took her in a blind, pulsing fever that drowned them both in hot, sweet relief from a tension that had almost been pain.

She cried out, shuddering and shuddering as the pleasure went beyond anything she'd even dreamed.

"Yes," he groaned at her throat. "Oh, God, baby, never like this . . . never!"

"I . . . know!"

They paused just for a few seconds. But the fever was burning too high, too bright, and they no sooner stopped than they started all over again.

"I shouldn't do this," he groaned. "You're still weak . . ."

"Weak? I'll show you . . . weak!" She wrapped her legs around his hips and arched up at him, her eyes wide-open, watching him as the endless pleasure wrapped her up in fire and fury. He dimmed in her vision as the final explosion came, so raw and sensual that her teeth sank into his shoulder as he shivered above her in one last exquisite movement.

He drew her against him. Moonlight streamed in through the sheer curtains on their balcony window overlooking Montego Bay.

"I should have married you the night you came to the back door and said someone was trying to kill me," he said. "Think of all the wasted time!"

"That's okay," she murmured with a contented sigh. "We'll make up for it."

He smoothed back her damp hair. "Tell me about the future."

She smiled. "Long and sweet."

"Honest?"

"Honest."

He sighed. "I was pretty sure of that. But it's nice to have it confirmed."

She brushed her hand over his hair-roughened chest. "It's nice of you to have the cabin rebuilt for Mama. Now that it's safe for her to live there, that is."

"It was the least we could do. She loves the place."

"I do, too."

"You can't go live with her," he pointed out. "I'd be lonely."

"I'd only go if you went with me," she agreed.

His eyes were briefly troubled. "Merissa, there isn't going to be anyone else coming after me, or you or Clara?"

"No," she said. She was still. "But that young woman in Texas . . . There was already an attempt. She doesn't even know . . . !"

"It's all right," he promised. "I'll phone Hayes Carson first thing in the morning and tell him."

"He'll think I'm nuts."

"Not at all. He's a nice guy. I'll take you to Texas to meet him and his wife one day."

"That would be nice."

"As long as we go together," he told her, very seriously. "I'm never leaving you again."

"You can bet money on that," she agreed. "I won't let you."

He pulled the covers up with a sigh. "How about a tour of the historic places tomorrow?"

"Oh, yes, and I want to try ginger beer. I've been reading about it."

"You can have a whole keg if you like." He drew her closer and looked into her eyes in the moonlight. "In fact, you can have anything you like. Anything at all."

She reached up and pulled his mouth down to hers. "I just want you."

He kissed her back, tenderly. "You'd have to chase me away with a tank," he mused. "And even then I'd come back."

She nuzzled her cheek against his. "Life is sweet," she whispered.

He sighed. "Yes, my darling. Life is sweet."

Back in Texas, a furious politician was having a closed-door meeting with a shady character of his acquaintance.

"How the hell did he let himself get killed by some local yokel in Montana?" Matt Helm raged.

"Beats me, boss, but he was burned alive."

"Did he leave a trail that leads to me?" the politician demanded angrily.

"Not that we can find. I got one of my brother's friends who's a detective to check it out for me. He says everything's cool."

"Well, at least he got rid of the loose ends. His colleague, that stupid woman who got herself arrested at the hospital, is dead. The computer images of him wearing the damned watch are erased, we have the computer . . ." He stopped and shook his head. "Damned shame that man he sent after Cash Grier's secretary missed!"

"They think he was just some religious lunatic after her father," the man soothed. "No worries there. Martin said he hired another man to do it, someone reliable."

"Can we trust him, you think?" he asked sarcastically.

"Maybe. We don't know who he hired. He was hooked on meth and it was frying his brain," he said irritably. "He got nuts near the end, took crazy chances. He was delusional. He never used to make mistakes like that."

"People who use drugs are crazy," the politician agreed. "That's why we just supply them."

"Damned right."

"You go up to Wyoming yourself and make sure the trail's clean," Helm told his henchman. "And see if you can find that damned watch. If you do, destroy it."

"Gosh, boss, it's worth a king's ransom . . . !"

"It's worth life in prison for both of us! Got that?" he demanded furiously.

"Okay, okay. If I can locate it, I'll break it into small pieces and bury it somewhere."

"He must have had pieces of clothing with him, at least," Helm continued. "In a suitcase, in his car maybe. You find it!"

"I'll do my best, boss. But my contacts say they never found even a wallet, and his cell phone was too damaged to get any information."

"I just want this off my mind," Helm told him. "The governor's going to appoint a successor to the late lamented Senator Todd. I hope it's going to be me, but even if it isn't, I've got power and money behind me in the special election this spring. I don't want any chance discoveries messing up my future. You tell Charro Mendez the same thing. He'd better be watching my back, if he wants any special favors for his cartel when I get in office."

"I'll tell him, boss."

"I can't be seen with him again." He ran a hand through his hair nervously. "What a mess! What a damned mess! I can't believe Rick Martin messed things up this badly. He was the best in the business — infiltrated the DEA, fed us information to keep our drug shipments safe, took out the opposition. And here he's almost ruined everything because he couldn't keep away from drugs!"

"At least nobody's likely to connect the watch with us now," the henchman said comfortingly. "The photo's gone. Even if that girl can remember it, her testimony's worth nothing. They can't prove a thing."

"Even if they could, we could swear that Martin acted on his own," Helm said, nodding. "You're right. Our hands are clean. It's going to be fine." He turned. "But you get up to Wyoming and tie up the loose ends."

"What about the girl?"

Helm hesitated. She worked for Cash Grier. He knew Grier. It was dangerous to provoke the man. But they'd camouflaged their attempt on Carlie's life once before by having their assassin seemingly target her minister father.

"Her father seems to draw lunatics, doesn't he?" Helm said, staring at the other man. "I mean, it happened once . . . and we aren't involved. Hell, we don't even know who Martin hired, right?"

"That's true, boss. No way to connect us to it. If he paid a guy to kill her, let him earn his money, I say."

"So do I. Fewer complications. Find that watch and that shirt."

"You can count on me, boss."

Helm didn't reply. That was what Rick Martin had told him just before he went to Wyoming to take out Dalton Kirk. That hadn't ended well. In fact, his stupidity after the murder of the district attorney digging into Helm's business had been the first sign of a breakdown. Imagine stealing a dead man's watch and clothes and then actually wearing them to a drug bust where he was photographed? The utter stupidity of the act amazed him.

And then to alert Kirk about his presence and get himself killed . . . Where was that watch? He had to hope that his new enforcer could find it. He had a brilliant future ahead, replete with wealth and power. He wasn't losing it because of a damned watch!

Cash Grier came out of his office wearing a thoughtful expression. He glanced at Carlie. "Got that letter ready for me to mail?"

"Yes, sir. All it needs is a signature." She handed him a neatly typed letter, on department letterhead, with an addressed, stamped envelope.

He read over it.

"If you're looking for spelling mistakes, you won't find a single one, and I do not

360

use spell-checker," she said with a smug grin.

He laughed. "I'll take your word for it. Nice work."

"Thanks, boss."

He signed it, folded it and put it in the envelope.

"Oh, you had a call from that rancher in Wyoming. Dalton Kirk?"

He frowned. "Did he say what he wanted?"

"Something about that man who was killed. He said his wife had a premonition. He wouldn't tell me what it was. But he wanted you to call him."

"I'll do it when I get back from lunch."

"Yes, sir."

She watched him go out the door before she pulled out a sandwich and a soft drink from her lunch box. It was her habit to eat at her desk. The chief never complained. He probably knew she couldn't afford to eat out, except once in a great while.

She wondered what the Kirk man's wife had told him? She hoped it wasn't anything bad. Just lately, there had been quite a few unpleasant happenings around Jacobsville, Texas, including that wild man's attack on her father. She shivered, remembering how that had ended.

The phone rang. She picked it up, wiping away peanut butter on her lips before she answered, "Chief Grier's office."

There was a brief pause. "Tell your father he's next."

Before she could say a word, the caller hung up. Carlie stared at the receiver with her heart racing. It was not going to be a good day.

ABOUT THE AUTHOR

The prolific author of over 150 books, **Diana Palmer** got her start as a newspaper reporter. A multi-*New York Times* bestselling author and one of the top ten romance writers in America, she has a gift for telling the most sensual tales with charm and humor. Diana lives with her family in Cornelia, Georgia.